Two Lives

One Adventure

Two Lives
One Adventure

By Mill Woods

The characters of this book are fiction. Any similarities to real persons is coincidental and not intended by the author. Most area names used in the book are nonfiction — however, the scenarios and events within these areas are from the imagination of the author.

ISBN: 978-87-971819-1-1
Print version 4

Prologue

"...what we can do here is not magic, as you might think, but simply ancient knowledge forgotten by the modern world. Neither are we religious as how the modern world believes. We believe that God is the souls of our ancestors. They love us as we loved them, protect us as we protected them, and are always amongst us as we are with them. They are us as we are them. God is all of us. You might not understand now, but time will explain. One day you will understand."

-A monk named Sumit.

chapter one
ARRIVAL

- Flight -

Iris

"Final call for miss Iris Bjarnadóttir, please make your way to gate number nine immediately."

Come on, why does this always happen to me? Where is that gate? I'm running as fast as I can! Why am I this unlucky? Okay, it's kinda my own fault. I should be smart enough not to fall asleep while waiting for the gate number to appear on the dull flight schedule screen. But it's not like I have magical powers keeping me awake forever, right? I can't blame myself for being tired after those two boring plane rides since I took off from Reykjavik.

Oh, there is the gate. Please, tell me I made it in time.

"Miss Iris?" the grumpy woman at the gate asks as I reach her, sweat raining from my forehead.

"Yeah, that's me. I'm so sorry…" I mumble, trying to catch my breath.

The woman cuts me off by shushing at me. At first, her reaction catches me off guard, almost making me furious. However, the smile that appears as she lowers her finger from her shushing mouth removes all worries for a second. She is not rude. She is just speaking my language. How did she know that such a shush wouldn't trigger me? Well, maybe my messy hair, the loose baggy pants and my favorite "make peas n' loaf" vibrant shirt gave me away. People often judge me by my appearance after all. Luckily for them, and me, I don't give a crap.

"Can I see your passport and boarding card, please?" the smiling woman asks.

Putting my hand in my pocket, I realize that my documents aren't there. Come on, where did I put those documents?

William

Everything is so cramped in this airplane. I can both *hear* and *feel* the noisy flight engines, though the plane has not even taken off yet. The cabin light is cold and blinding, but at the same time, it is dark in here. I *hate* flying! Why is it not possible to simply teleport around the world yet? How hard can it be to create those wormholes that all these brainy scientists are talking about? It does not even help to try and focus on nerdy stuff. I can not take it anymore!

Okay, big breath. Calm down, William. You are just nervous. You survived three flights already without problems. This is the last one, and then you are there: Kathmandu in Nepal. Nepal with all the beautiful mountains from the online photos and videos.

I remember a particular photo of a golden temple, shining bright from the reflection of the warm sunlight, with an amazing mountain view in the background. Two elderly monks were pouring up some kind of purple wine to a happy tourist-looking couple. It was most likely a tourist attraction, but it appeared magical and made me wonder if there is anything genuine like that nowadays, without it being made for tourism. Anyways, I assume the photo was edited and appeared more magical than it probably was.

"Ow, seem like we have many space today," the Nepalese-looking man, two seats next to me says, pointing at the empty middle seat between us.

"Ah yes, we are lucky. Maybe somebody missed the flight," I respond with a forced smile on my face that most likely makes me look like a goose.

I doubt that he understood what I just said, but he returns

a few quick nods and a big grin. I glance out the window and watch the workers who check the flight for the non-existing damages that might crash the plane and kill me. I am indeed happy that I paid the extremely overpriced fee to get the window seat. The last time I flew, and actually the only time I have ever flown before, was when I was five. My parents took me to see the Vietnamese part of my family: my father's family in Vietnam.

"Don't you look out the window, son," my father told me with the Vietnamese accent he had back then.

He thought I would get scared if I looked out the window, so I never got to see the view. He was wrong. Looking out the window is, weirdly enough, the easiest way for me to forget that I sit in a bunch of plastic, way up in the sky.

A sudden noise from the front of the plane makes me look up. A young hippie girl is rushing down the cabin. Is she the reason why we have not taken off yet? That is just typical! I realize again that the chair beside me is empty, and I find that it is most likely her seat. My heartbeat accelerates as she stops right in front of my row.

Iris

Great, there's my middle seat. I don't even manage to point at it before the Nepalese man in front of me raises to let me in.

"Thanks," I say, throwing him a smile.

The young guy in the window seat nods at me. He is obviously not happy about flying. Within the billions of times I've been on a plane, I've somehow developed the skill to sort these flight-anxious people out quite easily. It's sad but also kinda cute. I throw my small rucksack under the seat in front, and as I do so, I notice the flag sewed on the guy's bag in front of his legs. American. Well, why not.

My eyes set off their usual stalker-scan, starting from his big, brown hiking boots and up. An attempt to try and stop this awkward inspection-journey would include a suicide. I'm just too curious. I'm too much of a person-analyzer, I guess.

Before my eyes' stalker-adventure really sets off, they automatically jump to meet the guy's dark eyes, as I realize he's looking at me. He flips his head and looks out the window. A shy hiker. Cute. I'm suddenly wondering from where his skin glow and the color of his short, black hair and dark eyes originates. However, I will need to control my curiosity this time.

"Welcome on board…" the planes' speaker begins.

The usual safety procedure. As if we'll ever need to use that knowledge. Silly. I grab my good, old mp3-player from my pocket and plug my ears. Bob Marley time.

William

Oh boy, here we go. The plane is accelerating so fast! I am never getting used to this. Even though I researched the statistics back at home, I am still a nerve wreck. When I know that the risk of a plane crash is only like one in ten million, I should not be scared. Yet here I am: *scared*. Do we seriously need that life-vest demonstration? Are they secretly expecting us to crash, so we actually have to put on life-vests or air masks? No, calm down, William!

As the plane leaves the ground, my panic makes me grab both armrests on each of my sides, and my fingers accidentally touch the hippie girl's arm. She opens her eyes and gives me a confused stare until she realizes that my panicking hands are cramping to the armrests.

"Are you okay?" she asks, nearly laughing.

"Not too fond of flying," I respond, not quite in the mood for small-talking.

However, in the brief moment I dared to look her in the eyes, I saw something out-of-this-world. I have never seen eyes so saturated blue, almost glowing like some sort of magical pearls. What witchcraft is that? Could it be because of the light in here? Maybe she wears some of those colored contact lenses? Well, perhaps I just see things because my brain fills with hallucinating chemistry from the panic or whatever.

"Calm down. If the plane is broken, I got parachutes for both of us," the girl assures me while putting her head back to resting position and closing her eyes.

With the headphones in her ears, I am not sure if she will notice a response, so I decide to let it go. Does she honestly believe that joking like that will help me? Who even says things like that out loud in a plane? She still has a smile on her face. A pretty smile. I notice that she has quite interesting hair too. Long and blond. It does not look like she does anything to control it, which makes her appear somewhat wild. A happy, wild hippie girl with strange, blue eyes.

I have to focus on something else. This is not helping. I pull up the air-company magazine from the pocket in the seat in front of me and start reading.

Iris

Great. No more battery on my mp3-player. My old-fashioned phone shows me that only an hour has passed, which means that there are still three hours left until landing in Kathmandu. All this flying better be worth it. I'll make sure it's worth it. After all, I have nothing to lose. Also, I will eventually lose everything anyway.

I glance at the scared, cute hiker. He's sleeping with a flight magazin on his lap, most likely dreaming about being on safe ground with his mom feeding him chocolate chip cookies. No, just kidding. Sleeping is good for him. A great way to skip bad situations. I realize that the Nepalese man is having a fight with a bag of peanuts.

"Do you need any help with that?" I ask him.

"Yes yes, you try?" he says, handing me the bag.

Within seconds, I find that this bag of peanuts is just plain stupid. After trying to rip it open for a few seconds, I give up. Luckily I have tons of safety pins on my rucksack. Safety pins are great for almost anything, so I grab one and poke a few holes in the bag. Now the ripping goes as smoothly as would be logical to begin with, and I hand the peanut bag back to the man.

"Ow, thank you," he says. "You like some?"

"Yeah, why not. Thanks!" I reply and get a small handful of peanuts.

After eating my thank-you-for-opening-my-peanut-bag gift, I'm in the mood for some chatting. I'll go with one of the classic flight-icebreakers;

"So where have you been?" I ask him.

This question initiates a flood of talking from the Nepalese man. He tells me stories from his two weeks of working in London. He tells stories about his life in Kathmandu, and how tourism has destroyed his old family home, but also how it helps the economy in Nepal. He's also giving me tips on how to behave in the Himalayan mountains and warnings about dangers like avalanches, earthquakes and sudden adverse changes in weather. After what feels like an hour of listening, he asks what my plans are in Nepal.

"Well. I'm surely going to take a hike in the Himalayas." I tell him. "However, I don't know where, when, and how yet. I just ordered tickets right after I…"

I stop myself from saying any more. I almost said too much there. I don't want anybody to know about my… *secret*. My newly found *secret*, which I guess is the main reason for this particular adventure.

"Let's just say that I've been traveling a lot the last few years, and hiking in the Himalayas is a thing, I've wanted to do for a long time. So now it's time for me to do it," I tell him.

"Ow, so happy for you. Beautiful up there," the friendly, Nepalese man says, seeming tired from all the English speaking.

He excuses and gets up from his chair before heading for the lavatory. I could use a little walk as well. A trip to the toilet sounds like a good plan for me also.

William

What the hell is happening?!
What the hell is all this shaking?!

I pull off my eye mask and take a look around to see reactions from other passengers. Yep, I am surely not the only one feeling this. Even the happy hippie girl, who just returned from the restroom, looks somehow frightened in her seat. A bell chimes and I notice that the seat-belt light turned on.

Oh god! This is not happening!

A blinding light flashes from outside the window. Are we in a thunderstorm? Pilots are supposed to avoid storms, so what the hell?

Shit! We are going to die!

I can feel it! The plane is dropping fast. Within a second, thousands of bright, glowing sparkles, in all colors of the rainbow, appear everywhere in the plane, hovering freely in the air. The amount of sparkles this time make my heart jump to my throat. This can not be happening! A baby starts crying somewhere behind me, which triggers my panic and makes me grab hold of both armrests again.

I keep holding the armrests tight, and realize that what I am grabbing is the hippie girl's hand, which is also planted firmly on the armrest. Embarrassed, I pull my hand back while the plane stops dropping. Deep breaths, William. What felt like an eternity was probably just a few seconds in an air pocket or something. I read a lot about this. It is not dangerous. But it is impossible to relax with all this turbulence. We would literally be human projectiles if we did not have seat belts.

Another drop! No, no, no!

This drop just keeps going. *Please make it stop!*
The baby is crying even louder now. I am sure that I heard somebody scream too. The colored sparkles accelerate in speed, bouncing chaotically around the cabin. I feel my hands pressing against my shaking thighs. Closing my eyes, I try to accept that I am going to die within a few minutes. I want to tell my family that I love them, like in the movies, though I do not want my final words to be a lie. They probably would not even notice that I am dead.

I can not believe that I am about to die!

The drop is not stopping! I cannot feel my legs! Oh shit, I cannot breathe! Hyperventilating!
Suddenly I feel something warm in my hand. I look down to see that another hand has taken a grip on mine. The hippie girl. She is holding my hand tight. I give her hand a squeeze back and look up into her sparkling eyes. They are so calm, yet I see a hint of unpleasantness in them. I hope it is the death-situation and not me who is causing that. As I somehow keep my gaze on her eyes, my panic turns into something else, yet I am not sure exactly what. Her vibrant blue eyes mesmerize me, slowly making the thousand of colored sparkles around us dissolve and disappear. She offers

me a little smile. What a smile.

What is it with this girl? I suddenly do not care about dying. All that exists now is this moment. Then death and nothingness. And it is completely alright. Even if the crash is going to be the most painful experience in my life, this is a fine way to die.

Without a word, the hippie girl learns back to her relaxed position and closes her eyes again, keeping the smile on her face. I did not even realize that the drop stopped. The last colored sparkle disappears from my vision. I find that the turbulence and the seat-belt lights are gone as well. How long have even passed since she took my hand, which she continues to hold?

A story about a pilot

Another day on the job. A little sudden weather change and a bit of turbulence, but besides that: perfect weather, perfect job, perfect day. And what a magnificent celebration of my 20th anniversary. The gift from my colleagues is too much to handle: a week-long cruise. Must have been darn expensive. What great colleagues.

Twenty years as a pilot and I have loved every minute. People often ask me about safety and if I'm ever afraid of going down with one of the aircrafts, and I usually inform them of how much security there is involved in aviation. I tell them about how every pilot is tested every six months, and how we are trained to handle every situation that could emerge. I tell them about statistics, like the one stating that you need to fly every day for twelve thousand years before you might encounter a crash, and that 25% of the victims still survive. You are more likely to be killed by tripping over your own two feet. I mention that the flight they board is one of more than 100.000 daily problem-free flights. Today's aircraft have tons of technical gear to make every journey safe. I was once told that almost half of our passengers have encountered some fear of flying, which is silly when I have never experienced any problems in my twenty years, nor have I ever talked with a pilot or a crew member who has. But I can't blame people. Those statistics are hard to find logic in. Fears are not easy to overcome with numbers. Still, this is a daily job for pilots like me and my great colleagues, and I would never trade it for anything in the world.

Iris

Okay, I need a moment before I'm ready to open my eyes. I have experienced turbulence before, but nothing like this. I guess I can cross that off my list then. I hope the anxious hiker guy is okay, and I hope that he's okay with me grabbing his hand. It just seemed so logical to try to calm him down. Well, maybe I needed it just a tiny bit myself. It was somewhat a dramatic event. And yep, I don't see any reason why I shouldn't keep calming him down by continuing holding hands. And yep, it does feel kinda good. I like those big, warm hands. A little too sweaty maybe, but who can blame him for being nervous. I mean, of course I'm giving him sweaty palms. Okay, not funny, Iris.

"This is your captain speaking..." the loudspeakers interrupt.

Ah, the usual *"sorry about the turbulence. We're ready to start landing..."* babbling. I open my eyes to see if I can get a view out the window, but no, two glowing, dark eyes are in the way. Both of us respond by pulling our hands apart and looking away. Weird. I never reacted this way before. It's funny. I open my mouth to say something to get rid of the awkwardness, but seeing him staring the other direction makes me empty of words. Nevermind, he doesn't seem to be in a social mood anyway. I'll let this pass.

William

Why can I not just say something to her? We have not exchanged a word since we left the plane and entered this strangely minimalistic airport hall. Now standing in line to get our Nepalese visas, I see her right there, only a dusin people away from me, speaking with a group of other passengers from the plane. There is a lot of laughter coming from her, somehow making me believe that she is, in general, a very happy girl. It makes me eager to speak with her, but she has not looked back to check up on me. Man, I am putting too much into this. She is obviously one of those free-spirited hippie-backpacking types, who grab random peoples' hands all the time.

A few colored sparkles emerge for a second. It has been a while since so many appeared at once. I have had this problem with glowing sparkles, which are actually quite beautiful, ever since I was born. When I was little, the doctors assumed that it was some kind of reaction from stressful situations, yet the sparkles seem to appear randomly. I have not spoken to anybody about it since. I do not want to be seen as a crazy person. Sure they are annoying, and I would like to get rid of them, yet, on the other hand, they aid me in my dreams. Often, when I have nightmares, the sparkles appear and help me out by being absorbed into my body and giving me abilities like flying or becoming invisible. It feels like they belong to my body, and when they find their way back, everything turns out fine. They make me feel complete. When they appear in reality, I often wish for them to absorb into my body, just like in the dreams. I always get the feeling that they belong to me in reality as well, though my dreams most likely cause that feeling.

Someone behind pokes me on my shoulder. It is an elderly man, probably in his 60's. He is quite fit considering being up in age, looking like a man with a lot of life experience.

"Excuse me. Are you planning on going to Thamel?" he asks.

I read about Thamel back at home. It is the 'rich' area where most of the hiking tourists stay before leaving for the mountains.

"Yes, I am staying at the Heritage Hotel," I reply.

"Are you taking the bus or should we do each other the favor of splitting a taxi there?" he asks with a discreet old-man wink.

"Oh, I have to wait here for my friends, sorry," I admit.

Actually, I am looking forward to meeting the two French guys that I am supposed to hike with. When I read that it can be dangerous to hike around in the mountains alone, I found these two guys on an online traveling forum. We have been writing together for a few months and have a lot of things in common.

"Ah, no worries. When will your friends come?" the man asks.

I look at my watch: 6 pm.

"Their flight should be arriving here in three hours," I inform him kindly.

Iris

I love these guys. They are a great standing-in-line company. It's a group of four Belgian friends on an annual trip to climb mountains somewhere in the world. Two boys and two girls. Two of them recently became a couple.

For the fun of it, this time the group randomly pointed on a map. The finger landed on Nepal, and they were like *"hey, why not?"* and started planning. When they told me the story, I couldn't stop laughing. *"Why not"* is *my* thing. I use the expression every day. After I lost my parents, I found this incredible sentence quite helpful. It inspired me to do things that made me forget about my loss. I never really saw it as an actual question but more of a "don't think, just do it" kinda sentence. I love inspiring sentences.

"So Iris, what are your plans?" one of the guys in the group asks me.

They did tell me their names just before, but I have already forgotten all of them. Names are not that important to me, so my brain kinda shoots them right out of my head as soon as I hear them. It's only essential people in my life that I will actually remember the names of. Unfortunately, I have trouble keeping people in my life, so at the moment, I only have few names to remember.

"Not sure about my plans. Just doing one thing at a time. Getting to Kathmandu is done now, so I guess my next move will be to find somewhere to crash for the night," I reply, realizing that I haven't given that one single thought yet.

The worst thing that could happen would probably be me sleeping on the street for a night. And that I've done before.

"You should come *crash* at our hotel," the other guy in

the group says, using air quotes when pronouncing the word *'crash,'* like he never heard the expression before.

"Yeah, we booked a room for six persons, so we have a lot of space for you to crash," one of the girls continues, giving the other guy a quick glance when saying crash.

This girl clearly heard the word being used this way before. The guy shrugs his shoulders, looking a combination of confused and apologetic. It's quite apparent that she's the one wearing the pants in that relationship. It's cute.

"That would be awesome! Count me in!" I tell them, excited that I have friendly people to stay with for the night.

Whoops, it's my turn to get my visa.

"How long is your stay?" the tired woman at the counter asks.

"Ehm, I dunno. A month, I guess. No wait, make it two months," I reply.

I haven't given this any thoughts either. Not a fan of planning. To be honest, I'm not even sure if my secret will give me any problems along the way. Ah, my annoying secret. I'm still content that I'll keep it a secret to everyone. For now, that seems to work perfectly.

After feeding the woman with money, she hands me my visa and begins servicing the Belgian group. I take a few steps to the side to wait for them, and I take a look down the line of people waiting for their turn. I notice the cute hiker guy there. He speaks with some older man. I guess he's more open for conversation when not being a trapped nerve wreck in a plane. Should I go talk to him? Ask if he's okay? Maybe introduce myself and not be the silly hand-holding girl he most likely thinks me as. Wait, perhaps that's just *my* way of titling people: no first names that I will not remember anyway, but instead making up weird names based on how I know people or how I see them. Yeah, I will let this be as it is. I will store him in my memory as *cute-hiker-guy*.

"Ready to go get a taxi?" the last girl in the group asks, pulling me out of my thoughts.

They all got their visas and have formed a small circle with me. Everybody in the group nods.

"Let's go then!" she continues after realizing that nobody else wants to take the first step.

Low giggling comes from each of us while we head for the door to the baggage claiming area. Before leaving the area, something makes me turn my head to glance back at the line. I immediately catch eye-contact with cute-hiker-guy. He stopped the conversation with the man, now watching us leave. I smile at him. He gives me a smile back. What a cute smile.

- Kathmandu -

William

So.. TIRED!

Why did the French guys want to get up this early? I am nearly falling asleep again. Sitting on my bed in a dark, cramped hotel room, waiting for the last guy to finish his morning-toilet routine, is not the ideal situation for me right now.

I need coffee!

I can not imagine a day without my morning coffee. I always go full zombie-mode until I get my caffeine fix. Luckily Noah and Tom feel the same way. None of us have said a word since the alarm clock on our phones rang. All three of us sat up simultaneously. We all yawned and made a small morning stretch simultaneously. And we put on clothes simultaneously. We are probably going to laugh about this later, but right now none of us have the energy. It is strange to see these two guys like this. When I met them at the airport yesterday, they were so funny and energized, making jokes about everything. I have not laughed so much in years. When I told them about me being scared of flying, and about this hippie girl who grabbed my hand, Noah almost died from laughter. Well, I guess that it *is* quite a strange story and I *did* tell it with a joking tone. I must admit that I joined the chuckling myself, after telling the story. However, what happened in that plane was on my mind all night.

Oh, finally, Tom is out of the bathroom.

"Guys, are we ready for some breakfast?" he asks, running a hand through his wet, orange hair.

A story about two French friends

Tom and Noah. Best friends since kindergarten. They both grew up in Marseille, in the southern part of France. They both had average grades in school. And they are now both unemployed after the store they both worked in closed down.

Tom. In his mid 20th. Has a pregnant girlfriend. Expects to be a combination of a great father and a best friend for his upcoming child. He grew up with an average, loving family: father, mother, sister and dog. He likes to play football and video games. Favorite dish is pizza.

Noah. In his mid 20th. Does not have a girlfriend. Grew up as an only child with his loving adoptive parents. He is originally from Rwanda in Central Africa, but came to France as a refugee, fleeing from the Rwanda Civil War, when he was two years old. His biological parents did not make it. Got adopted right away. Does not remember anything from that time, though. He likes to play basketball and video games. Favorite dish is everything with cheese on it.

Tom and Noah. Two boys who winged it their whole lives. None of them ever had real problems. None of them ever cared about important stuff. None of them ever had a day together without laughing and making jokes. Life is about having fun. Nothing else.

William

This fruit pancake is fantastic! The distinctive look, the fresh smell, and the delicious sweet and salty taste. It is just perfect. Sitting here on this small, plant-filled rooftop restaurant balcony, feeling the fresh morning air, is just fantastic. The coffee is already working, especially for Noah. His joking and exaggerated happy mood spread to other people around us like bees from a broken hive. His deep, loud laughter makes people at the few tables around us chuckle.

"Dude, do you know, that in Asia, they don't remove bugs from the fruit in pancakes? You're eating a lot of protein there!" Noah jokes with his hilarious French accent.

I almost spit out my coffee. Not that the joke was particularly funny, but because I certainly did not expect the sudden change of subject. Two seconds ago, we were talking about how Noah was adopted but had no problems with it.

"Oh, I know. I need the protein to pump up my legs before our mountain trekking, you know," I reply.

Yet again, Noah bursts out into huge laughter which wakes up Tom, who has been reading a guidebook while the adoption talk was going.

"Guys, I've made us a plan for the day!" Tom says all excited, clapping his hands together

"Okay, boss. What do you have for us?" Noah asks.

"Listen up! We're going to spend the day at the monkey temple. Then we're having some beers and some dinner. Tonight we'll go out celebrating our upcoming adventure: the adventure which will fulfill all of our dreams!" Tom informs.

He might be exaggerating a little there. The fulfill-our-dreams part is probably based on me telling them about my reasons for making this trip: that I somehow need to find inspiration to do something new with my life. My parents wanted me to become a lawyer, like themselves, and I have been studying for that all of my life. At first, I was okay with a goal like that, but as the years progressed, I began having doubts. I have always secretly wanted to be a sailor. I never told it to anybody, though, other than my best friend. I just did what my parents expected me to do: hunting the American dream. When my best friend moved to Europe, I suddenly felt all alone, so I did a lot of thinking and came to the conclusion that I needed new inspiration and a new beginning. That is my main reason for this trip. Noah and Tom, on the other hand, they are just here for the fun of it.

"Well, sounds good, boss!" I yell, giving him a soldier's salute.

It has been quite a while since I was in a mood like this. I feel a lot more open than I usually am. Almost ready to try anything. Almost…

"Oh, Tom, did you bring the… box?" Noah suddenly bursts out.

"Yes, yes, yes!" Tom replies while pulling up something from under the table.

Weird. I did not see Tom bringing that.

"William, this is for you, from Noah and I. But you cannot open it until we're drunk tonight, okay?" he says, handing me a small wooden box with a red string wrapped around it.

"Wait! Why? What is it?" I chuckle in surprise.

"You will see, my boy," Tom replies. "You will see."

Iris

These streets are just like I imagined: narrow streets with millions of colorful signs on the shop facades. Fortunately, it's still early enough to experience the streets without them being too crowded. On top of that, I still feel the fresh morning air on my face. It makes me wonder if the Belgian group is awake yet. I couldn't sleep anymore, so I just took off for a little sightseeing and left them a note.

"Good morning," a Nepalese man in a doorway says as I pass him.

It seems like the shops are opening. I peek through the shop-window next to the man. Apparently, it's a small outdoor shop, and I start wondering if there's some kind of gear that I haven't thought of or that I don't know about, so I greet the man and enter his shop. It's a small, cramped place filled with everything from backpacks to technical clothing. The Belgians told me about these outdoor shops as we passed by a lot of them yesterday evening on our way to the hotel. They informed me that most things are fake, yet they are of excellent quality. I am not quite sure what to look for, but one container in the store does catch my attention. I find my way over there and pull up a woolen hat. I've always wanted one of these. I remember having one as a child, and how I loved it. I haven't managed to find one that I like ever since, and this one is just perfect. A typical Nepalese, woolen beanie-hat with protection for the ears and strings hanging from the ear protection flaps. This one has an incredible texture. A combination of light and dark, brownish colors. I need this!

"How much?" I ask the man.

"You get good price. 1000 rupees," he replies.

I have no idea if that price is good or bad. I know that I'm supposed to haggle with these sellers, but not how much. I mean, a thousand rupees is not a lot of money. I wouldn't even be able to get a meal back in Iceland for that. Well, I'm just gonna give this a try.

"1000 rupees? Too much. I can give you 500!" I tell him, maybe giving away that I think this is done for the fun of it, more than actually wanting to save money.

"No, no, no. 1000 rupee is good price," he claims.

Okay, so this is not the usual meet-on-the-halfway situation. This dude is an excellent salesman.

"Okay okay. 700 rupees is my last offer," I try.

"I can go 900 rupee! Not more. I have family," he replies.

Oh, I see, he's using dirty sales techniques now. But it is kinda working. For me, that amount of money is not much to save. For him, those few hundred rupees have more meaning. Should I just accept this offer? Nah, I'm trying one last time!

"800 rupees and a big smile! Last offer!" I tell him.

I see on his face that he didn't expect that ending on the haggle. He bursts out in colossal laughter, and I can't stop joining him. He agrees to my strange little offer, and we make the deal. I find the money from my wallet, but secretly add 200 rupees and hand the man his full starting price with a big smile on my face. I'm so happy with my new purchase. I say goodbye to the man and leave the store with my new Nepalese beanie hat on my head.

William

"Where you wanna go?" the taxi-bike driver asks us as we find our seats in his small taxi-bike.

"Take us to Swamya... swayamn... sham..." Tom tries.

"Could you take us to the Monkey Temple, please?" I kindly interrupt.

"Ah! Swayambhunath! Okay," the driver replies and immediately begins the ride.

Swayambhunath is the real name of the Monkey Temple. None of us, besides Tom apparently, have the nerves trying to remember and pronounce that. I have a few guesses why it is called Monkey Temple, but I will see if I am correct soon. Even though I usually research everything beforehand, I forgot to look up tourist attractions in Kathmandu. All I have thought about was how the mountain trekking would be.

"He sure knows how to maneuver this bike," Noah says, sounding all amazed.

I agree. The way this man can get through the crowd of people without having to use the breaks is impressive. Even though I am aware that we pay for the trip, I have a strange feeling in my stomach, thinking about how we are lazy enough to pay another person to transport us on a bike. It must be a hard job. Well, it is only a few kilometers, so I hope it is okay.

Watching the people we pass, somehow embarrasses me. I feel that they study us and think: "Look at those rich bastards. Too lazy to walk on their own feet." But I guess...

Hey! Is that...

I stop breathing for a moment and look back at the girl that we just passed. She is wearing a strange beanie with strings hanging down her chins.

It is! The hippie girl!

She is looking back at our taxi-bike, so I send her a silly hand-wave. She does not react. She just turns her head and continues sauntering. Maybe she did not recognize me. Perhaps she never saw a taxi-bike before and just wanted to take a fresh look at it. Or could it be that she did indeed see me but had no absolute interest in me?

"Dude, what are you waving at?" Noah asks.

Iris

Those things are so much fun. Cycle-taxis. Good for the environment and a great way to stay in shape on the job. The passengers also seemed quite happy, sitting there and waving to everybody. Should I try one? No, not alone. That wouldn't be fun.

"Nice hat!" someone almost yells at me with an elegant British accent.

A young woman, probably her mid 30's, smiles at me. She's wearing a similar Nepalese hat. Her blond dreadlocks fall out beneath it, all the way down her back. I return a huge grin.

"Ah, same to you!" I reply. "We look like sisters with these."

"Ow, what is that accent, dear?" she asks me, unexpectedly.

Weirdly enough, I find myself blushing from the question.

"I guess you're referring to my Icelandic accent? Icelandic girl here," I reply.

"Ow, I see. It has been a while since I visited Iceland. Dear, have you got plans or would you like to join me in the park?" she asks.

I like these types of people. She seems to be a well-traveled woman with a lot to tell, so of course, I would like to go to some park with this stranger. Special people and random meetings like these make life exciting.

"Yeah, I would very much like that," I tell her.

We begin moving towards this particular park that she knows, which she says is a ten-minute walk from here. While walking, we talk a lot about Iceland. She has been visiting three times, and has even been living there for a few months, volunteering and helping out building hiking trails. She talks about how hard she found it at first to be a vegan there. A problem that I know all about myself: we have to import most vegetables, so it's a costly diet until you learn what vegan dishes to cook in Iceland, and what is an expensive no-go that might be cheap and normal in other countries.

"This is the park, dear," she says as we reach a short, spiky fence.

There's a counter at the entrance, and apparently, it costs money to enter the park. The sign shows that it's only foreigners who have to pay, which makes sense. Nepal needs all the help they can get, especially after the devastating earthquake they encountered some years back.

I pay the man at the counter and follow my new friend inside. Beautiful, small bushes are everywhere, and the smell is just amazing. The park is filled with a perfect combination of fresh grass and a sweet scent from the colorful flowers growing all around. The sun has risen just enough so that I can feel it heat my skin at an ideal temperature. We walk around the park for a while until we sit down at a big grassy spot. A lot of other foreigners sit here, so it's obviously the place to hang out and relax.

"I'm Diana by the way," she tells me, reaching her hand out for a handshake.

"Nice to meet you, Diana. I'm Iris," I reply while completing the handshake.

I forgot to ask her name when we met. But again, I never ask names, and I don't remember them anyway. She's most likely the same way, now just being polite.

"So what are you doing here?" I ask her, leaning back, resting on my elbows.

"Ow, I live here, dear. Been here for five years now. I often go hiking in the mountains, and when not, I'm just working with my husband in a small store right beside Thamel," she says.

"That's cool!" I say. "You must really like those mountains then. How is it like up there?"

I can see on her face how she lights up when I mention the mountains. That must be the reason why she decided to move here.

"The mountains are the most magical places on Earth," she says. "I've hiked most of the Himalayan mountain range, and have even lived up there with the monks. They can do unimaginable things. They are incredible people. Unfortunately, my husband couldn't handle the… air pressure, let's say. We had to return and settle in Kathmandu. We usually don't talk much about it, though, as not a lot of people know about the existence of these monks. They wouldn't want to be a tourist attraction."

"That sounds so exciting! You have experienced a lot, haven't you?" I ask, not able to control my excitement, wanting to hear more.

"More than the majority, yes. Still, there's a lot of experience to be gained. Anyway, are you going to trek, dear?" she asks.

"Definitely," I reply. "I don't know where and when yet, but I will! No doubt about that. I need this to be my best adventure ever. Like it's my last adventure on this planet. I have this… secret. I want to find a way to… end it… in a good way."

I might have said too much again. I should stop mentioning my secret. It's stupid. Diana looks at me with eyes that appear both calm and concerned. She opens her mouth to say something, but closes it again, loudly exhaling through her nose. A sweet smile appears on her face.

"Promise me that you'll take care up there, Iris. You are a good person, never forget that," she says.

William

"Hey, give me that back!" Noah shouts at the monkey who just stole his cereal bar from his hand.

Tom and I can not stop ourselves from being loudly amused by the situation. Noah is doing his best to catch up with the monkey, but it is not a fair fight. The monkey climbs up on a big stone sculpture and starts chewing the cereal bar, while staring evilly at Noah. The monkey even has the nerves to throw the cereal bar away after taking a few quick bites. Monkeys clearly have enough food up here to be picky.

After a lot of angry mumbling, Noah gives up and turns around to watch us laugh and applaud. When he finally understands the silliness of the situation, he bursts into laughter with us. As I expected, the Monkey Temple name comes from the many monkeys running freely around up here. It is not just one single temple, but a significantly big area on a hilltop, with golden and stony monuments, naked trees, buildings, artistic shops, and those colorful Nepalese flags, hanging all around on strings. And of course the monkeys.

"So Noah, what key opens up bananas?" Tom asks Noah as he approaches us.

Noah starts thinking, looking confused about not knowing the answer to this joke. His eyes flicker for a moment, but before he finds the solution, something catches his attention.

"Hey, look at that!" he shouts, pointing at a man sitting on the ground near one of the monuments.

A few people stand around the man, watching him roll wooden balls on the ground. He is wearing a layered, blood-red robe. Is he a monk? We find our way over there to try and figure out what is happening. A small, golden bowl, with some rupee-notes in it, lies next to him. I figure that this is a Nepalese street artist, monk version. With hands flat, he keeps rolling the three small balls on the ground. I notice the blinding reflection from golden ornaments on the balls. They must have cost a fortune. I move my gaze to the monk and realize that his eyes are closed. What is this? Some ritual?

Suddenly the monk hammers his hands down the ground, next to the wooden balls, resulting in an unbelievable loud clasp sound. The balls begin hovering in the air.

"Woah..." Noah silently expresses.

I did not expect to see that, either. It is a magician, and he is good at his job. The balls create a formation as a triangle and start spinning. Faster and faster. How is he doing this? I have never seen anything like this before. It is obviously some fake-magic balls, but the technology behind it, I can not figure out. The balls keep spinning faster. Man, it will hurt if they lose connection and become projectiles. They are just accelerating, continuing spinning faster and faster.

The magician suddenly lifts his hands, and the balls hammer down the ground, almost creating an explosion of sound. Some kind of metallic dust spreads from the ground below the wooden balls. How did he do that? I am just as impressed as the people who are now applauding him.

All of a sudden, he opens his eyes and stares at me, looking me deep in the eyes. The expression on his face is something between anger and sadness. It scares me. His eyes penetrate mine. I almost feel my eyes bleed from the penetration, yet I can not stop holding my gaze at him. What is this? I feel like screaming. I want to run away. Escape. Were the balls just for hypnotizing purposes? Now he makes me faint and steals my belongings? This can not be happening!

In an instant, he removes his eyes from mine, looks down to the ground, and restarts rolling the balls with hands flat. People have stopped clapping and are dropping money into his golden bowl. I am speechless. I am no expert in magic tricks, but this was something new. Noah and Tom move to the bowl and throw in some money. I grab my wallet and pull out a few rupee notes and carefully put them in the bowl as well, while keeping my eyes on the magician. He scares me, though, I am probably just exaggerating. This was just a simple magic trick, and the eye-staring is just a natural, psychological reaction from that, which the magician knows. I guess. Impressive.

"So guys... Let's find a taxi-bike and return to the city for some food and beer?" Tom proposes. "Oh and by the way, the answer to my riddle earlier was a monKEY."

Iris

Oh, I hope that the Belgians aren't mad at me. I have been gone all day without saying a word, with only the small note stating that I was going for a short walk giving them some clue. Diana made me forget all about time. I could definitely use more time with her. The five hours in the park wasn't enough, but she has work to do. Well, here's my hotel room.

There's nobody in the room. However, a new note lies on the small counter in the corner:

—

Hey Iris!
We are at the monkey temple.
If you wish - find us there.

We are going to some "Hiker's Party" tonight.
You should come!
If we don't see you before that,
we will be back at the hotel this evening
to pick you up!

See you!
-The Belgian homies

—

Sounds good! It's afternoon already, so I'll stay here reading until they come for me. A nap would be helpful as well if we're going to a party later. I still find napping a bit strange. I've never napped before in my life, not until recently. My body has been telling me to get the extra sleep in the last few months. It's annoying. But I can live with it. Anyway, now to bed!

William

This restaurant is great. We are sitting on cushions on the floor, in the corner of a small and cozy place. Everything is illuminated by warm, orange-tinted lamps and for now, we are the only ones in here. The food is super cheap. We ordered two meals each because we thought the portions would be tiny at that price. To our surprise, each one is a full, complete meal. We all ordered something called *momos* for starters, which the guys told me is a Nepalese specialty. It is some sort of green pasta-clam with filling inside. Back in New York, I would call these ravioli, but I guess it must be the filling which makes it unique.

"Cheers, guys!" Tom says, raising his beer. "Ready for our last night in Kathmandu. Let's make it unforgettable."

We cheer with him and take our sips, emptying our bottles. Time to try the momos. They are quite soft and a bit sticky, but they taste like heaven! A taste explosion of tomato, potato and spinach filling.

"Masala, William! That's the secret," Tom informs me, after clearly seeing my surprised face. "My favorite spice!"

Masala? Wauw! I am very much aware that things taste better when traveling, like if I tasted these momos at home, in my boring everyday-life, it would probably not taste as good. Still, this taste is fantastic. I place another momo in my mouth, close my eyes and chew like a lazy sloth, enjoying every second of chewing. I do not even realize that our second meal is already here: burgers for all of us.

"Can we have three more beers?" Noah asks the waiter.

The waiter nods and leaves for our beers after placing our burgers on the ground in front of us. It is a fine detail that the plates are made of wood. It makes the burgers look exotic, though they are similar to the ones back in the states. I suddenly remember the wooden box that I got from the guys in the morning. As I pick it up from my small daypack, Noah slams his hands together.

"Ah, yes! Open it!" he demands, all excited.

I pull off the red string that holds the box together. I would never expect a gift like this from these guys. A gift from them would more likely be a book with silly jokes wrapped in tin foil. I should probably not jump to conclusions before I see what is actually inside.

Opening the wooden box, I see a round silver object. I take the object out from the box and open up the silver lid. It's a compass. A lovely, old compass.

"Guys..." I let out in surprise.

The compass works flawlessly. It must have cost a fortune. The silver compass has small carvings of suns and moons between the N-E-S-W letters. Just amazing.

"To help you find a new direction in life," Tom says.

I am speechless. Tom and Noah nailed this gift. They are certainly much more than the shallow, joking-about-everything friends that they appear to be at first.

"Thank you! I do not know what to say. This is the nicest gift I have ever had," I tell them.

And I mean it. My parents give me presents from time to time. Even expensive ones when I have achieved something that they think is a great achievement. But the presents were never personal. It was only stuff like a new TV, a new cellphone or envelopes with cash. My two new friends here, on the other hand, they bought me something based on the very few pieces of information they have about me.

"Aw. Now, don't be a wimp. Drink your beer, lad!" Tom says with a horrible Scottish-like French accent, trying to stop the awkward situation that I am about to make.

We all laugh, cheer and drink. I offer the guys to buy dessert and the next round of beers, and they agree to the deal.

"So after dessert and a few more beers, we are heading out for a bar?" I ask, starting to feel the effect of the previous two beers.

"That's the plan, lad," Tom replies.

What a horrible accent.

Iris

"The bar with the Hiker's Party should be just around the corner," the Belgian wearing-the-pants girl informs.

They brought a pack of beers back to the hotel, when they picked me up, just in case they were too early and had to wait for me. We drank the beers anyway while having some quite informative conversations. They gave me very detailed information about their plans. I'm a bit embarrassed by not asking them about their plans before that, but as I'm not much of a planner, I guess I just forgot. They will meet up with a guide and take an airplane tomorrow morning, flying to the starting point of the Mount Everest Base Camp trail. They asked me if I wanted to come with them, but I had to decline, unfortunately. I have no correct gear for that, and to be honest, that trek sounds a little too difficult for me. We did exchange phone numbers though, just in case we'll not see each other again here in Nepal. It's convenient to have contacts from around the world.

"Here it is!" the same girl informs us and makes an enormous pointing-maneuverer.

Not really what I expected from the word party, but I like it. It's a cozy outdoor area with basic tables and chairs. There's a small bar in the corner and a DJ next to it, playing some electronic chill music. Above everything, there are colored flags and string lights in various colors hanging all around the place. Even though we're in the middle of the city, the air somehow smells fresh.

The place seems full, but we manage to find an empty table right in front of us.

"Let me get the first round," I say, before sitting down

on my chair.

"No way! This one is on us!" the not-wearing-the-pants guy demands, pulling me down onto the chair.

"I can't let you do that," I reply. "You guys have been so nice to me, letting me crash with you for free and having me hanging out with you. I really appreciate that. Buying some beers is the least I can do."

"Seems fair," the wearing-the-pants girl concludes with a happy smirk, looking like she dislikes that "Let me. No, let me…" game just as much as I do.

I get up and find my way to the bar. The bartender suggests that we drink Nepal Ice, which is his own favorite Nepalese beer. As I have no clue what is good beer and what is not, I just accept, and the bartender hands me five half-liter bottles of beers. As I turn around, I notice three guys laughing at a table filled with empty bottles. Hey, that's the cute hiker guy! What a coincidence. I'll go greet him in a minute. Let's see if he remembers me at all. Oh well, I have this beer delivery first.

I find my way down to my Belgian gang and hand out the bottles. They have an intense, Belgian conversation going on, so I think this is my time to do my greeting.

"Here you go, guys. I'll be right back," I tell them kindly, keeping my own beer in my hand.

As I walk up to the guys' table, I realize that they are playing a drinking game. A perfect way to break the ice.

"Hello there, can I join your game?" I ask them, pointing my bottle at the table.

They all simultaneously look up. It takes a few seconds before the hiker guy recognizes me, and an incredibly cheerful expression appears on his face. I smile back at him.

"Of course you can! Sit down and take a question card!" one of the other guys says.

William

I can not believe it. The airplane-girl is sitting right there! She is so beautiful. Wait, how much are the beers influencing my feelings now? I have no clue how much we have been drinking, but I am drunk as hell. Well, I have to talk to her. Please do not sound drunk, William. Do *NOT* sound drunk!

"You the girl from the plane! The… is so good to meet yo again," I say, hopefully sounding as a sober gentleman only drinking beer for the taste, and not for effect.

She smiles at me. Such a beautiful smile.

"That's true! And you're the guy calming me down with some old-fashioned hand-holding," she replies happily.

She remembers me! She talks about our hand-holding. I am gonna marry this girl.

"Oh, you're that girl! We heard the story," Tom shouts out, a little too loud.

I am glad that I am not the only drunk one here, though.

"Did you really?" she says, smirking at me. "That was a good moment, I agree. Now… What are your names and what are we playing?" she asks.

I have got this, guys.

"My name is William. Those two are Thom an Noeh.. from France," I inform her, still sounding sober, I hope. "We ae playing Ever Have I Never. Take a question card from the stack. If you have don what the question asks, you drink. If we'h want it, you have to tell then story."

She nods.

"Sounds perfect. Good to meet you guys. I'm Iris by the way," she says.

Iris. What a wonderful name. And what is that incredible

accent?

"Take a card, Iris," Noah commands.

The hippie girl… Iris… takes a card and reads it out loudly:

"Never have I ever been in a fight."

We all look at each other. None of us drink. Do I have to be honest about this in front of this gorgeous girl? Will she despise me if I tell about my old temper? And what about the guys?

"Really, William?!" Noah shouts surprised.

I realize that I just sipped my beer while considering sipping the beer. So drunk. Man, there is no way out of this now.

"Tell the story!" Iris commands.

I lock my eyes on my beer bottle. Okay, here we go.

"Having had a… old temper problem. Been fighting a lot in school. Not exactly proud about it, though. But I have changed since, no worry," I admit, not feeling like going deeper into the subject right now.

I dare to take a quick glance around. Iris sends me a big grin. I hope she liked the honesty. The guys look drunk and probably just want to pick a new card so they can drink themselves.

"My turn," I say and take a card.

"Never have I ever seen the Northern Lights," I read out loud.

Again we all stare at each other, waiting to see if anybody drinks. Iris sips her beer as the only one, and I find myself sending her a curious stare.

"Hey, I'm from Iceland! Of course I have seen the Northern Lights," she informs us.

Iceland. That explains the accent. She is the first Icelandic girl I have ever met. I wonder if all Icelanders are just as pretty.

"Never have I ever been making out with someone of my own gender," Tom says, making me realize that the game is already continuing.

Time for another inspection of each other. I doubt that we are supposed to consider this much before drinking. Iris finally takes a sip. The rest of us turn our heads to watch her drink. Noah chuckles and takes a sip with her. He pushes Tom with his elbow, resulting in giggling and sipping from Tom as well. Okay then, I admit and drink as well.

"So I guess we've all been young, drunk and on to anything," Tom giggles.

He cheers, and we drink yet again. Man, I have to slow down. I am not feeling well now. Everything is so blurry. Actually... I... need... fresh air...

A story about a chemistry professor

Look at all these drunk people. Most of them will soon go hiking in the mountains and might experience the time of their lives. Still, they feel the urge to drink like that. My colleague and I came to this bar to taste some different beers, but not to get drunk. I wonder if these people would drink this much if they knew what the alcohol actually does to their bodies. I admit that I didn't think much about it myself before I started my studies as a chemistry teacher. I did drink a lot in the past. Maybe I'm just getting tired of it. Maybe I don't need it to enjoy myself. Maybe I just don't like the chemistry behind it. Maybe I do miss it a little.

I usually don't overthink this, but my latest lecture was about alcohol, and I still have the beginning of it memorized;

-

"Oh, that men should put an enemy in their mouths to steal away their brains! That we should, with joy, pleasance revel and applause, transform ourselves into beasts!"
-William Shakespeare; The tragedy of Othello, Act 2, scene 3.

Alcohol is known for opening up people, silencing people, making people happy, making people sad, giving energy, and tiring people. Alcohol has many different effects - some good - some bad. Some people use alcohol as medicine - others, like Shakespeare, see it as 'an enemy.' Alcohol is widely used around the world. Alcohol comes in many different forms. But what is alcohol exactly? Is it a gateway to who you truly are - or is it a way to escape your own personality?

Iris

I wonder if William is alright. It's been more than fifteen minutes since he left for the toilet, and he did seem quite drunk.

"Iris, what are your plans in Nepal?" Tom asks me.

While chatting for the last 10 minutes, Tom and Noah referred to each other with their names in almost every sentence, so I've actually been able to memories the names now. They are hilarious people.

"To be honest, I'm not sure what to do. The plan is to trek in the mountains, but I haven't done any research yet. I'm not much of a planner. Just call me lazy," I reply.

They glance at each other. I'm not sure what's happening exactly, but Tom and Noah clearly have some kind of secret conversation going on through their eyes. What a friendship.

Noah turns his head and looks at me.

"You could come with us to Pokhara tomorrow. We're taking the morning bus to that town, to stay there for a day, and then start climbing the Annapurna mountain," he says. "You can group up with us or go alone, whatever you feel like."

Annapurna. I remember that my newly gained hippie friend, Diana, told me about that mountain when we sat in the park earlier. She said that the mountain would be perfect for me if I wished to go alone. I'm still not sure if I want to group up with anybody or hike by myself, but at least these guys can help me get there. To be honest, I also have a slight urge to get to know these guys better. Especially the cute hiker guy, William.

"That sounds great!" I announce. "Where and when do I meet you tomorrow?"

"You can meet us at the bus station at 11 in the morning," Tom replies.

The relationship couple from the Belgian group suddenly stands at our table.

"I think that your friend needs to get home," they tell Noah and Tom. "He's sitting totally wasted outside the bar."

Noah laughs. That guy is indeed a happy one.

"Okay, I guess it's time for us to get home then," he says and gives Tom a clap on the back. "Thank you guys," he tells the Belgian couple.

"I'll be right with you," I tell the couple as they start walking away.

Tom and Noah get up and put on their jackets.

"Well. We'll see you tomorrow at the bus stations, Iris," Tom says.

I get up to give them a goodbye-hug.

"See you tomorrow. Say goodnight to William for me," I order.

"Will do," Tom replies.

They leave the bar, and I return to the Belgian group.

"So Iris, are you ready for a great last night together?" the wearing-the-pants girl asks as I sit down.

"I am! Let's make this night unforgettable!" I command.

William

I can not wait to be on the bus. So tired. The walk to the bus station feels like an eternity.

I have to thank the guys for getting me out of bed this morning. It was not the best feeling waking up extremely hungover. However, the painkillers did its magic. I am a bit ashamed for having the guys carrying me all the way to our hotel room last night. I do not remember much of that night, but I do remember meeting Iris. Man, I hope I did not embarrass myself too much. Anyway, I am probably not gonna see her again ever, so why should it even matter.

The guys told me that they have a surprise for me at the bus station, but to be honest, I am not really in the mood for surprises. I just want to get on the bus and sleep the rest of my hangover away. Back at home, I would sleep all day, only to be woken from time to time by my parents telling me to get up and make something of the day. I hated that. Give me a break for just one day! It does not kill me with a day off from progressing in life. Hangover-drowsing is also a way to grow and learn, is it not?

"Here we are," Tom announces.

Finally, there is the big white bus. Wait, who is that besides it? Is that?

"Iris!" Tom shouts as we approach.

"Hi, guys! Good to see you!" she replies when she recognizes us.

She is standing with a dreadlocked woman. Was that the surprise? What a great and weird one.

"This is Diana," Iris informs after we greet her. "I met her yesterday. One of her friends in Pokhara got sick this night, so she is joining us on the bus."

Iris looks at me with a massive smirk on her face.

"Are you alright?" she asks.

Oh man, I must have made a big fool of myself yesterday after all. And for sure I look like trash right now.

"I have felt better. Whatever I did and said yesterday night, I probably meant it," I joke with a silly hangover giggling, which accidentally ends in coughing.

"Oh, don't worry. You did great in the ten minutes I got to hang out with you," she replies laughingly.

The bus driver commands us to drop our backpacks in the back of the bus and get in. Tom and Noah find seats together, and so do Iris and the dreadlocked Diana. Perfect for me. I am going to sleep the whole way to Pokhara anyway. I see that there are two seats free in the back of the bus.

"Please pull me out of the bus when we arrive," I tell the guys and go to my seats.

The bus starts driving. Ready for some sleep.

- Pokhara -

Iris

Here we are. On a bus station in Pokhara on a sunny afternoon, with the air feeling fresh and clean. In a minute, Diana will have to grab a taxi to get to her friend's house, and I'm not happy to say goodbye to her again. There have been too many goodbyes today already. Saying goodbye to the Belgians this morning was hard enough. I'm *not* good at goodbyes. I hope that the group will be alright in the Everest mountain. Maybe I will see them again one day, just like I got to see and talk with Diana again, totally unexpected. I'm mentally storing all of the stories that she told me on the bus. She's a very spiritual woman for sure. She believes that there's more to earth than we can see. That humans still don't fully understand what is around us. She said that she had experienced things that scientists would never accept to be true. At some point, she convinced me. There's still so much stuff which scientists admit that they have no clue of how it functions, and there are so many theories with no actual proof. So why shouldn't there be some sort of energy-ish stuff around us? Why limit our beliefs to what scientists say? Diana is so inspiring, and I love to talk about these spiritual things.

Nevertheless, I have to say goodbye to her now. I hate it. I've had too many goodbyes throughout my short life. Though, nothing compares to the nightmare of having to say goodbye to my parents when they… left me. It haunts me every time I say goodbye to someone. I miss my mom and dad. I would give anything to have them back in my life. Diana told me that their energy is always around me. I

51

cried. I love the idea, and I'm gonna stick with it. My parents will always be with me. They will watch me and protect me. One day I will become energy like that as well, and be with them again. "Someday in a distant future," Diana said. She then shortly mentioned something that reminded me of my secret. I felt that this woman knew exactly what the secret is. She told me that everything will be okay. It's sweet of her, but in the end, I guess everything will not be okay, and there's not a lot I can do about it. I'll just have to not think about it, at least until things get real. Well, time for another goodbye.

"It was so nice to see you again, Diana," I tell her while going in for a hug.

She hugs me back tight. I haven't felt this safe since I hugged my mother as a child. I'll miss this woman so much, even though I've only known her for a couple of days.

"Don't you worry, dear. I'm sure that we'll somehow meet again eventually. Please don't see these situations as sad farewells. Remember that all of our energies are connected, and if fate wants it, we'll meet one day again," she whispers, keeping the hug going.

A tear escapes my eye. Even though I don't truly believe in what she just said, it still comforts me.

"Well. I hope that fate wants us to meet again soon then," I tell her with a smile.

William

Aw, Iris surely does not want to separate from that woman. The hug has been going on for several minutes now. I wonder if Iris will ever hug me goodbye like that.

That reminds me of my dream on the bus. How was it? I had to leave Earth for another planet or something like that. I was not really told to leave, I just wanted to go for some reason. A strange dream. Some combination of an adventure and a nightmare.

Leaving everything that you know behind, and going to a completely unknown planet, was scary. I was frightened. But I felt some kind of excitement in the dream as well. Not because Earth was a horrible place, but because I was curious about what is out there, I guess. I felt selfish and unthankful, but I felt *alive*. When I arrived on the unknown planet, I was all alone in this strange orange-tinted dessert. Again I got filled with fears and doubts if I chose the wrong or right decision when leaving Earth, and I had no idea if I could ever return.

As I started roaming the desert, tiny orbs of purple light ignited all around me, and I felt excited again. It was so beautiful, yet nothing like the pulsing sparkles I usually see. I felt the freedom of being in this unknown place with these new orbs of light. I felt that everything could happen. Literally everything. Then a flock of bright, glowing birds appeared in the distance. The dessert contained life after all, and I somehow knew, that if I followed those birds, I would find something that I have been missing all of my life. I wandered for what felt like an eternity. A pleasant eternity, that is. I saw a bright light in the distance. Something was idling in the light, but I was blinded by the brightness and could not see what it was. I started sprinting towards it, but all of a sudden, something grabbed my leg and pulled me back. I did not realize what it was before I woke up to Noah's laughing head in my face. I had been sleeping through the whole bus ride, and we arrived.

Usually, I am not much of a dream analytic, and I do not normally dream such adventurous dreams, but I guess that being out of my comfort zone can change ways of dreaming. It annoys me that I did not manage to see what was hiding in the blinding light, and what grabbed my leg and pulled me back. Also, I am curious what dreamish feeling or superpower those purple orbs would give me when absorbing them. It is like one of those dreams that are somehow scary, but you do not want to end.

Never mind. The hug between Iris and the dreaded woman has ended, and the woman left. I guess it is time to find our way to our hotel now.

A story from a spiritual being

Long nap passed quickly. Unique being emerged into another reality. Some conclude this reality of being visions of the future. Others presume it to be memories of the past. Some interpret entering another realm. Another world. Another universe. The limbo between life and death. A world of spirits. A world of thoughts. A world of chemistry. Biological needs. Science. Knowledge. Ignorance. Forgotten truths.

Dreams are what they appear to be. What they have always been. Dreams never changed. Humanity did. Humanity forgot. The truth that lies right in front. A blinded human in search of knowledge that was once obvious. A truth that is present. A truth that is surrounding. A truth that sounds like magic. The forgotten truth. Humanity. Wake up!

Iris

"Let us get to the hotel by foot. It is only a thirty-minute walk from here," William says as I rejoin the boys after finishing my goodbye hug with Diana.

We all agree, pick up our backpacks and start moving. I've found that William is the one with the plans in this group. He has booked and researched the whole trip in advance. Or at least what is possible to plan. That's good for me, I guess. He hasn't said much to me today, nor even dared to have eye contact with me. I'm not sure if that's good or bad. I'll find out later.

Leaving the bus station, I notice that this town doesn't look as crowded and busy as Kathmandu, and there's not a ton of sellers on the streets. It appears more like we're back in the western world, but of course with a Nepalese touch. Well, this walk might be an excellent opportunity to get to know these guys better and to hear about their plans.

"Guys, now that I'm somehow a part of the group, can I get an update on the plans?" I ask them.

William is surprisingly the one opening his mouth to give me information.

"Of course. So, the plan is to stay here in Pokhara for the night. Tomorrow morning we will take a taxi to our starting point at the Annapurna mountain, and we will hike from there," he informs me.

"Do you know what the mountain is like?" I ask. "I mean, is there anything I need to know about safety, for instance?"

I'm not truly curious about safety. I just want William to continue talking to me.

He finally looks at me, giving us a moment of eye contact.

I'm not sure what that expression is, but it seems like an *'are you kidding me'* one. However, he ends it with a cute smile before replying.

"To be honest, I have not done much research on exactly how it is in the mountain," he replies. "Safety, though, yes: the weather up there can be tricky sometimes, but besides that, it is a peaceful mountain. So it is safe enough that we can go without a guide and without people to carry our backpacks."

"What? People to carry our packs?" I ask.

"Yes. A lot of tourists hire 'porters' to carry their stuff for them when climbing the mountain," William says.

Noah lets out a low chuckling.

"Lazy, rich tourists," he says in a joking, but serious tone.

"Hey, not everybody has your super strength!" Tom jokes back, giving him a light punch on the shoulder.

"OUCH! Stop killing me!" Noah shouts in response.

A timid smile appears on my face. I take a peek at William. There's no reaction from the joke, and it seems like he's thinking of something. Then he suddenly looks at me, with his eyes sparkling from the reflection of the sun.

"So are you going to stick with us in the mountain?" he asks.

"I'm not good at making decisions about the future," I tell him. "I will at least start out with you guys. You are always welcome to kick me from the group if you ever get tired of me. No hard feelings."

"Oh, no no, sorry. It was not meant like that," William assures me. "I was just curious."

He gives me a big, warm smile, which I return to him right away. There is something about that boy. Some kind of attraction that I can't quite put my finger on. When I look into his eyes, it feels like he's somewhat attracted to me too, but I might be wrong. I have been wrong about that before. Plus the fact that my openness often hurt people. Somehow people see my 'open and friendly mind', as my friends call it, as flirting, even when it never was the intention. Honestly, I'm terrible at reading people myself. I have a hard time seeing if people are attracted to me or not, and so I have a hard time telling people to stop hoping for romance, or whatever, or to see if I should make a move myself. Hopeless is what I am with attraction and love. I often wish that I was better at these things. I want to be better at keeping friends too. But it doesn't matter now. Even though I always state that things are never too late, that soon doesn't work for me anymore.

Anyway, I need to stay positive.

"You guys wanna play some more Never have I Ever, while we walk?" I ask. "It's a great way to get to know each other a little better."

They all agree.

William

I can not believe that Iris never had an official boyfriend. She sipped from her water bottle when the Never have I Ever question came, and she did not consider much before sipping, just playing the game correctly, I guess. She did not want to talk about it, though. It was almost like she became shy when talking about that subject, which only made me curious if she has a reason for never being in that kind of relationship.

Oh, there is the hotel. It does not look like anything fancy. Just a gray concrete building. Well, it was the cheapest hotel I could find.

There is a man in the entrance, greeting us as we approach him.

"Hello there. Welcome welcome. You must be William, Noah and Tom," he says, clearly not expecting anybody else but us today.

"That is right," I reply while giving him a handshake.

"And who is this fine lady?" the man asks as he greets Iris.

"I'm Iris. Nice to meet you. I hope you have some space for me in there too," she says.

The room I booked was a four-person room, so it should be no problem having her staying with us.

"Of course, of course, my friend. Name is Ram. Let me show you to your room, and we can have a cup of tea after," he says and waves us inside.

We take the stairs to the second floor, where Ram stops outside a small, white door, and hands me the key to the room.

"Please come down for some tea when you're ready," he

says before heading back down the stairway.

I unlock the door and push it open. The room is quite small, with horribly yellow walls, a drawer and two king-size beds. Man, I forgot about the beds. Tom and Noah agreed to share a bed when I booked the room, but I am not sure how Iris feels about this. You know, having to share a bed with a total stranger. That is creepy, is it not? I might just tell her that I can sleep on the floor somehow.

Just as I open my mouth, a loud noise sounds from the open window. Another building is being built just across the street. Not the most perfect view, but I guess we can live with that for this one night. Again, this was a cheap room.

"I call dibs for this one!" Tom shouts and jumps onto the bed on the right side of the room. "Noah, we're going to have a great time here!" he jokes.

Noah immediately jumps onto the bed as well.

"Oh, don't worry. I will cuddle you to death!" Noah jokes back and grabs Tom in a big bear hug.

Tom ends up in what looks like a weird panic attack, and I realize that Noah is tickling him.

"Okay, I got the point," Tom shouts in a tickle-giggling.

Iris and I chuckle from the silliness within these guys. I stare at her, not quite knowing how to bring up the subject of sharing the other bed. Luckily for me, Iris does not feel the same way.

"So I guess we'll share that bed?" she asks me, nodding at the empty bed.

"I guess. Or… I mean… I can get the floor if it…" I start replying.

Iris stops me.

"Don't be silly! We'll share this. Just don't be as psychical as that one," she says, pointing at Noah.

Noah turns his attention to us, like a dog hearing its name. A moment of silence appears, right before a pillow smashes into his head, and a childish pillow fight starts between the two friends.

"Yeah okay. I will try my best not to," I reply, relieved that this bed problem was settled this easily.

We drop our backpacks on each side of the bed and together remove the bedspread. The sleeping blankets on the mattress are disgusting. I am definitely not going to sleep with that, so I pull out my sleeping bag from my backpack and unzip it all the way, so it becomes a thick, clean blanket. Iris curiously watches me.

"You know what. That is actually a good idea. I'll do the same," she says after some consideration.

I am not sure if she really means that or if she just wants me to not feel wrong about being a freak about cleanness. Nevertheless, she does find her sleeping bag as well. I gaze at Tom and Noah, only to see that they stopped their fight and are doing the exact same thing. Maybe I am not that extreme then.

"We should go have that tea with Ram," Iris says after dropping her sleeping bag on the bed.

"Tea! Why doesn't he offer us a beer, like a real man? What is this nonsense?" Tom says. "Well, let's have this tea then. Maybe it's magic tea. We might see funny things and buy all kinds of crap after drinking it."

Tom is in a happy mood today, which is refreshing. With him in the lead, we leave our room and walk down the stairs to see Ram greeting us, just as excited as when we arrived.

"Please sit down," he says and points at a table in the

corner of the small lobby. "I will bring some delicious Masala tea," he continues and leaves for a small kitchen.

Just as we find our seats at the table, Ram arrives with a big silver tray which he places on the table. He takes the silver teapot from the tray and pours tea into five ornamented silver cups. The tea does not look like what I expected. It is not transparent and thin, but a more solid beige color and a bit thick. After pouring up tea and handing a cup to each of us, he sits down on the chair at the end of the table.

"So, so. Welcome to my humble hotel. I hope you like the Masala tea. A Nepalese specialty, I believe," he says.

We all take our cups and stare at the strange content. It does not look appealing, though it smells good, like a mild mixture of fresh herbs and sweet spices. I take a sip from the cup and feel happiness appear on my face. This is really good! I hear a little sound of enjoyment coming from Tom. He appears happy, and so does Noah. Iris, on the other hand, suspiciously studies the content of her cup. It seems like she is unsure if she should drink it or not. In the end, she *does* take a small sip but puts the cup down on the table again. I await to see if she gestures for us to put down our cups as well, but she does not, so I guess she just does not like it. Ram drinks it as well, so it can not hurt. It is so delicious and sweet!

"So what can I help you with? What are your plans in Nepal?" Ram asks us.

He is surely taking good care of his customers. Perhaps he does not get a lot, which I hope is not the case. He seems like a great man.

"Can you tell us anything about the Annapurna mountain?" Iris asks.

Ram leans back in a relaxed position, probably getting

ready for hours of talking.

"Oh yes, I know much about Annapurna. Amazing mountain, stunning views and well-marked trails," he replies. "But you have to be very careful about the weather. Mountain weather can change in an instance. My brother and his group got caught up in a lightning storm a few years back. It came suddenly out of the blue. Nobody saw it coming. I lost my brother up there that day…"

He cuts himself off. His expression went from excited to sad within these few seconds of talking.

"Oh sorry. Stupid, stupid Ram. No bad moods here. Just be careful up there, alright? Everything can happen on that mountain. Bad, but mostly good exciting things, that's for sure," he says, all happy again. "So what trek are you going to do?"

"The plan is to do the Annapurna Base Camp trek," I tell him. "We talked about doing it slowly, and maybe use about two weeks to walk both up and down."

"Ah, ABC trek. Good choice. Done it three times already," Ram informs.

The telephone on the lobby counter suddenly rings. Ram excuses and leaves the table to pick it up. At the exact same time, Tom and Noah open their mouths and begin talking about being hungry and wanting to find dinner. Neither of them stops talking to let the other one finish his sentence. They just keep on completing their own set of words, expecting the other one to stop. It is weird. They have done it a few times before. One would think that they should have learned by now. Maybe that is what happens when you become too good friends. Or perhaps it is a French thing? Maybe it is just a Tom and Noah thing. Who knows. In the end, we all agree that it is time to find some food soon.

Ram reappears at the table.

"I'm sorry friends. I will have to pick up my son a short drive out of the city. The bus broke down," he says. "I will be back soon. Are there anything I can do for you before I leave?"

Noah is quick on deciding the last favor.

"Is there any good restaurants nearby?" he asks Ram.

Iris

I watch the flames from the candlelight on the restaurant table. This place is not fancy enough for cozy candlelights, but the food should be good, Ram said. I move my gaze to the guys. How can I tell them without sounding important? I've feared this moment. I hate telling people about this. I hate all the comments, and I hate being stereotyped, but I better come clean now. There's no chance that they don't want an answer for why I asked not to put cheese on my veggie pizza, and why I ordered a veggie pizza in the first place, which should be quite clear on its own. People just tend to need the words from my mouth.

"Come on, tell us!" Noah laughs, leaning back in the restaurant chair.

"Well, okay, as you clearly see on me, I don't like telling people, but I am a so-called vegan and have been for the last ten years or so," I admit.

"Vegan? So that means that you don't eat... what? Meats? And...?" William asks.

"Yeah, no meats, no eggs, no dairy products. Simply just everything that comes from animals is a no-go," I inform. "But please don't see me differently. It's just food. And please don't bring up meat jokes. I've heard them all, and it's getting a little too repetitive for me, sorry."

I smile at the guys. They are obviously not sure what to say about this and all three just stare at the candlelight on the restaurant table. Okay, maybe I was too harsh on them. They didn't do anything wrong yet.

"Noah, you can have *one* meat joke, and that's it," I say.

He lightens up and opens his mouth, but closes it again.

"Nah, I'll keep that joke for later use," he says.

William looks at me.

"So that's why you didn't drink the Masala tea at the hotel? It was based on milk?" he asks.

"That's right. I just didn't want to bring up the subject before I had to," I reply.

"I totally get why," William says. "I could imagine people being offended by such a choice of living."

That's so cute. William gets the reason why I hate bringing up the subject. I don't feel like I'm better than anyone else, I just made a choice not to support the horrible industry behind it all. Treating animals like products is not my thing. But I don't judge others for what they eat and wear, or what they don't. I'm not telling people to stop eating meat. I would love it if they did, but I would never ask them to. It is *my* choice, and their choices are *theirs*. Simple as that.

"I'm glad you understand. People have so many prejudices about veganism and vegans," I say. "But no more veggie talk now. You guys can hear more about it when you get to know me better. I don't want you to think of me as that vegan girl, if you know what I mean."

"Hey, no problem. No prejudices or bad feelings here. I would even suggest that we all have a vegan day once on this trip, to show our support," Tom proposes.

"Sounds great!" I respond.

"I agree!" William says.

We all watch Noah, who keeps quiet.

"Well... I guess I'll have to go with the idea as well then," he says, looking a little insulted.

We're all surprised by Noah's lack of team spirit in this. It's not often that he doesn't smile or chuckle when speaking.

The mood gets all low and quiet for a moment around the table.

"I'm messing with you! Of course we should have a vegan day," he says, now exploding in peals of laughter.

Suddenly the mood is back to normal. Noah surely has a significant impact on the spirit of the group, which is quite fascinating.

Here comes the food: pizzas for all of us. It smells delicious. Who would have guessed that they make this fresh pizza in Nepal? Wait, what is that? Oh no! They put cheese on my pizza anyway. That's another thing I hate about my food choice: when having served things I didn't order. I hate food waste, so bringing the pizza back and having what I asked for is no good. I have eaten dairy products before to not be rude if somebody made a dish with it by mistake, but I always feel so sick afterward. What to do?

"I will need more pizza than this one, that is for sure," William says and looks at the two other guys.

"Yeah, me too. These look very good!" Tom joins in.

"Definitely! And I'm gonna need it quick," Noah says. "Iris, it's not to be greedy, but I think you should hand us your pizza and order a new one."

I feel my sad face morphing into a surprised one.

"Wait. What? Are you sure?" I ask them.

"That is an order!" William says, pointing at the pizza. "Give us that pizza!"

How incredible are these guys? They must have seen my disappointed face when I got the pizza and noticed the bunch of cheese on it. What a perfect way to get me out of the situation.

"Thank you! You are the best!" I tell them and hand over

my pizza.

I wave over the waiter and order a new one, making sure that the chef will remember the no-cheese part this time. I'm so hungry, topped with being extremely tired. It's quite late, so I guess we'll head to bed after eating, to make sure that we will have a good mountain start tomorrow morning. I really look forward to that.

William

I can not sleep! The construction noise from outside our hotel room is still ongoing, and I believe the bus-nap was a bit too long for me to be sleepy now. And lying here in bed right next to an attractive girl does not entirely help. A single ray of moonshine escapes the curtains and illuminates a piece of her face. I have taken a few glances at her from time to time. Only quick ones. I do not want her to catch me staring at her like some creep, but I just can not stop examining her. She seems to be at sleep, all calm and peaceful. Not a snorer. Not a sleep-talker. Just all sweet and quiet.

Nope, I am never going to fall asleep like this, so I silently pull off my unzipped sleeping bag and find my clothes. Trying not to wake anybody up, I blindly put on my flip flops and unlock the door. Light from the hallway finds its way into the room, so I quickly close the door. A little too quickly. The door slams with what sounds like an explosion in all of the silence. I almost want to open the door again, to check and make sure that I have not woken up the whole room, but I decide to let it go. That is probably the smartest choice, not to accidentally slam the door again. Anyway, I am ready to get some air and hopefully become sleepy after a short exploration.

I get out on the street and inspect the surroundings. There are no streetlights, but the moonshine lights up the surroundings enough for me to clearly see everything. When I booked the hotel room, I saw on the map that there should be a big lake ten minutes by foot from here. That might not be a bad place to go, so I take a deep breath in and start walking.

Who would ever believe this? Here I am, wandering

around, all alone, in the middle of the night in a foreign country. That is so out of my comfort zone. But something has awoken in me. Like newfound energy and excitement. I am so curious about what is to come in the future. What will happen on the mountain? What will happen tomorrow when we get to the foot of it? And will I get control of my attraction to that Icelandic girl there? Even though I barely know her, it feels like she has been a big part of my trip already. It has been a while since my ex and I broke up, actually already three years, and I have only been dating one girl since, and only for a few weeks. I might just be desperate and affected by the whole traveling situation, but I think I somehow like her genuinely.

As I walk around the corner, I hear something dropping behind me, sounding like a plastic bottle. Looking back, I see someone picking up what does indeed appear like a plastic bottle from the ground a few blocks away. The person looks up and starts striding towards me. I immediately move down the corner, now with good speed. I am not up for meeting strangers at this time of night. I walk further down the street and get to another corner, which should lead to the lake. I glance back again, only to see the person coming even closer to me, and coming closer fast. Okay, maybe this exploration was a bad idea. I am totally defenseless. I got nothing of value on me. What will happen then? When this person finds out that he did not get what he hoped for? Will he beat me up? Or even kill me?

I turn at the corner, half walking, half running, down the narrow street to the lake. I glance back. No one is there. I am keeping the fast pace though. However, a shout comes from the person who is obviously following me now. What to do? Is it even possible to escape this? The lake is right there in front of me. Should I try to swim away? No, he will drown me easily. I watch my left and see a footpath with closed restaurants on one side and rocks and water on the other. Looking to my right, I see the path, also with closed restaurants on the land side, but with sand on the lakeside. Before I manage to make my decision on which direction to go, I feel a hand on my shoulder.

No! I am not ready to die!

"William, relax, it's just me," the person informs me.

Iris

"I'm so sorry. I didn't mean to scare you," I tell William.

The panic in his eyes, as he turned around when I grabbed his shoulder, was hilarious, but he is still shocked by the whole me-chasing-him situation. I really didn't mean to scare him.

"I didn't know how to make you stop. Sorry," I continue.

William inhales and looks at me.

"I understand. I just did not expect you here," he says in an exhale, almost sounding normal again. "And I could not recognize you with that hat on."

Of course. I'm wearing my newly-bought Nepalese hat. I haven't worn that around William yet.

"Sorry about the headwear disguise," I say. "I couldn't sleep either. When I saw you leave the room, I just felt like joining. It's okay if you need alone time, though. I need that myself from time to time."

He smiles and runs a hand through his soft, dark hair. His hair looks fancy in the moonshine.

"No, please join me," he says. "I was just about to decide if I should go left or right on this path when I tried fleeing from you."

I study our two possibilities. There's absolutely no doubt where to go.

"Let's go to the right then. I like sand," I decide for us.

We amble down the path to the right. There's a lot of closed restaurants on our right side. This might have been a chill place to be when they were open. The view on our left hand is impressive, though: the great lake with the hills and mountains around it; the small orange lights from homes on the hills; and the moon's reflection on the water surface. There are only a few clouds in the sky, but else it's full of stars. Why not also mention the handsome guy next to me? In this light, I can clearly see his well-carved cheekbones. It appears like he's thinking, staring at the ground as we walk. I know I shouldn't, but my curiosity is too big.

"What are you thinking about?" I ask him.

It seems like I awoke him from his own thoughts. He gives me a confused look.

"Ehm… Oh, nothing really," he replies after a while

I know it's an annoying question for many people. It's hard to answer. Why did I even ask? I hate being asked that myself, but I like making up silly answers for what I was thinking, when I don't want to be honest.

"Actually," he suddenly continues. "I was thinking about what it is like to live in Iceland? It seems so different from my life in New York."

"Iceland is amazing," I tell him. "But for me, it is sometimes a little boring somehow. I mean, I have been around Icelandic nature for all of my life, and I'm maybe just too used to it."

William looks up at the stars. His eyes remind me of two black mirrors in which thousands of tiny, bright dots are being reflected.

"I do not get it. Icelandic nature is so amazing in photos," he replies. "How can you ever get tired of that? I would kill to have grown up around such nature. New York City is hideous compared to that."

"Hideous? I would rather call it impressive. All that life and buildings. I haven't been in the states yet, but from what I've heard, in New York, everything can happen…" I reply.

William kindly interrupts me.

"What, no. Everything can happen in Iceland!" he exclaims. "You have all that uncontrolled nature. Volcanoes, geysers, boiling lakes, mountains, permafrost, polar lights... I can go on forever. You never know what nature brings there!"

"That's true, I guess. But we don't have as many different cultures in Reykjavik or any other town, as you have in New York City," I reply. "What I probably meant is that everything is possible socially. Like events and human-made stuff."

Something flies right past my face. Like a quick spark, yet there's no fire or anything nearby.

"Hey, look!" William shouts.

He points down at the lakeshore. Hundreds of tiny sparks are wiggling around just above the water. Fireflies! I have wanted to see fireflies ever since I was a little girl, after reading my favorite picture book for the first time. And here they are! It's an impressive sight. A mild, fresh wind comes from the lake and gently pushes the fireflies around, giving me goosebumps all over my body. This is incredible.

"Have you ever seen anything like that?" I ask William.

"No. Never," he replies all amazed.

We stand there in silence for a moment, just enjoying the situation. It somehow triggers my adventurous side. I want to do weird things. I got an idea!

"Hey, you wanna play the Odds Game with me?" I ask William.

"Odds Game? Never heard about it," he confesses curiously.

Time for some explanation. I want to play this.

"Okay, rules are simple. Here's an example: I can ask you a question like:

'*What are the odds that you run through that swarm of fire-flies?*'…" I begin explaining.

"…then you can answer your odds. For example:

'*The odds are 1 in 10*' or '*The odds are 1 in 50*' or whatever number you feel like…" I continue.

I look at William to see if he's with me so far. Seems like he is. Perfect.

"…then I'll count to three, and we'll both have to shout a random number between 1 and 10, or between 1 and 50, or whatever the number is you chose. We have to shout it at the same time, and if we hit the same number, you have to do what the question asked you too. No cheating. You understand?" I ask.

He appears confused now.

"Yeah, but then I would probably always just choose a high number, so I would not have to do it? So that the chance of us shouting the same number is low. I do not really get the point, sorry," he says.

"I see. Here's where the twist comes in. If we *don't* shout the same number, it's the asker's turn to have the same question with the same odds. So we will count again, and if we hit the same number this time, I, the asker, have to do what the question asked," I inform him. "That way the asker will always only make dares that he or she somehow dares to do themselves, and the one being dared wants to lower their odds-number enough so that the asker will have a high risk too."

"Ah, I see. That sounds like fun," William says. "And a little scary. But let us try it."

I usually wouldn't find questions for this game on demand, but just when randomly stumbling upon something that might be fun. Anyway, let's see. What can I dare him? Ah!

"Let's start out mildly. So, William, what are the odds that you will wear this hat, in reverse, for the next hour?" I ask him, pointing at my Nepalese hat.

He laughs.

"Really?" he says. "That *is* a mild dare, yes. Okay, the odds are 1 in 5."

"Great, are you ready?" I say. "Here we go. One… Two… Three…"

"FOUR!" William shouts.

"FOUR!" I shout at the same time.

I can't believe it, haha. He is losing his first dare. What an unlucky way into the game.

"So! What?! I lost?" he asks excitedly.

"Yep!" I tell him, handing him my hat. "Put this on for the next hour, with its back on your front."

He takes the hat, rotates it 180 degrees and puts it on. Aw, he looks cute with that hat.

"Does it suit me?" he asks.

"It does! It fits you perfectly. Even when wearing it the wrong way," I admit.

"It feels great wearing it the wrong way!" he replies. "Well, I guess it is my turn to make up a dare?"

"Normally it doesn't go on turns, but just whenever a good opportunity comes," I tell him. "But for the sake of learning, try to dare me now, yes!"

William examines the surroundings. It's not easy to find a good dare on demand, and clearly, I'm not the only one feeling that way. Another moment of silence. William occasionally lets out a few thinking-sounds. I'm not sure he's aware of it, but I somehow like it.

"Okay!" he suddenly shouts. "What are the odds that you will sleep on that bench for the rest of the night?"

He points into the restaurant yard next to us. There's an outdoor bench, still with its cushions on. It would actually be fun to sleep out here, though I'm not sure the owners will appreciate it, and I have no idea of when the restaurant opens.

"You realize that you also have the risk of sleeping there alone, right?" I ask William, a little confused.

"Yeah, of course. So what are the odds?" he asks.

Hmm… This is a difficult one. I kinda want to do it, but not alone. The rule of the game is to do the dare alone, else it wouldn't really be a dare game, but just suggestions of what to do together.

"Okay, the odds are 1 in 10," I decide.

He nods and gives me a look that informs me that I'm the one to count again. Here we go.

"Ready?" I say. "One… Two… Three…"

"NINE!" William shouts.

"TWO!" I shout at the same time.

The result makes us giggle. I got out of the dare perfectly.

"Okay, William. Your turn. Time to see if you need to sleep on that bench tonight," I say.

The smile on his face fades away like he just realized the situation he put himself in.

"Okay…" I say. "One… Two… Three…"

"FIVE!" He shouts.

"TWO!" I shout again.

Aw, he passed it too. He exhales and bends down, hands leaning on his knees. A relieved young man.

"I guess we'll both have to sleep in our bed tonight then," I say, giving him a light poke on his shoulder. "That was an impressive first dare."

"Thank you. I almost got myself into some mess there," he says.

I give him a curious look.

"What? You were gonna do it if you lost, right?" I ask, surprised.

He glances at me before moving his attention to the ground. If he's about to lie, he's an awful liar.

"I am not sure, to be honest." He luckily admits. "I did not think it through. Or I did not think that your odds-number would be that low."

Okay, that is an honest guy. I admire him for that. Not for considering cheating in the game and not doing the dare himself, but he's new and still learning, so I guess a single mistake would be alright.

"It's okay," I tell him. "I'm just glad that you wanted to play with me. And I respect your honesty, cheater."

I give him a light push and let out a short giggle.

"Hey!" he shouts, giving me a small push back. "I might have done it."

"Right," I say, giving him a quick wink. "But let's try out the bench anyway. I guess the owners wouldn't mind us sitting there watching the lake for a while."

"Good idea," William says and finds his way to the bench.

William

So, here we are. When I took my seat on the bench, I did not expect Iris to sit this close to me. Our arms are touching each other! It makes me nervous, yet I do not want her to move away. I am not sure if she sees anything in me other than a friend. She is probably just doing her free-spirited hippie thing, being used to having physical contact with friends.

"So, William, what's your story?" Iris asks me, while still watching the moon's reflection on the lake surface. "What is up with your Vietnamese background?"

I stay quiet for a moment. Where do I begin? How much does she want to know? People rarely ask me about the Vietnamese part of me. I guess they are afraid of sounding racist or whatever, so I'm not used to talking about that.

"Well, my father is from Vietnam. My mother is from New York and has lived in the city her whole life," I begin. "They met in Hanoi, the capital of Vietnam, during a case of investigating a murder. My dad was the lawyer of the victim's family, and my mother was hired as a lawyer for the American guy accused of the murder."

"What?" Iris interrupts. "They started as enemies?"

"I guess you can see it that way," I reply. "Though my parents call other lawyers as colleagues. But yeah, they fell in love, moved to New York and had me."

"That's a wonderful story!" Iris exclaims. "What happened to the accused guy?"

"The case kind of solved itself a few days after my mother arrived in Hanoi. The real murderer turned himself in, and the accused American was released. My parents had only met once when the case closed, but somehow they kept the contact," I tell her.

"I see," Iris says. "What a fairytale."

A sudden noise of crickets spread all around us. Usually, I would think of it as annoying, but at this moment I actually find it peaceful. Maybe even a little romantic. Iris lets out an exhale and puts her head on my shoulder. Woah. Her head fits perfectl. I feel my hands getting moisty. Am I supposed to do something? Should I put my arm around her? I feel like just going for it and kiss her. Maybe I can dare her to kiss me? She can simply make the odds bad, and I could say it was a joke. If she wants me, she can make good odds for the kiss to happen. Is that too desperate? Will I just ruin our new-gained friendship, make things awkward, and make her leave the group?

"So what about you? How much Vietnamese and how much American are you?" Iris asks, pulling me out of my dilemma.

So I guess it is more talking. Maybe *she* will make a move at some point. She is the extrovert after all.

"Much more American than Vietnamese," I tell her. "My parents always worked a lot, so they did not have a big influence on me in my childhood. All the Vietnamese that my dad ever put into me was Vietnamese food and a single trip to see his part of the family in Hanoi."

Iris removes her head from my shoulder.

"So you don't know anything about Vietnam?" she asks, sounding almost sad.

"I know a lot about Vietnam, to be honest, but not from my dad. He put Vietnam behind him. I have been researching a lot, only because of curiosity. I can even speak a little Vietnamese." I tell her.

She puts her head back on my shoulder. This time I dare to lower my head down to the top of hers. The hat she made me wear makes her head feel like a soft pillow. A really calming, soft pillow.

"I've always wanted to go to Vietnam," she says all dreamy.

I feel her yawning silently. I could easily fall asleep with her here at this moment, even with the crickets' shrill noise burning my ears. I might be falling in love with this girl.

"So what about you? Are your parents both Icelandic?" I ask her.

She stays mute for a moment. I notice a sudden low humming from her, sounding like she is thinking.

"Ehm... I... lost them three years ago," she says silently.

Everything suddenly turns quiet. Even the intense noise from the crickets fades away. At least it feels like that in my head. Iris lost both of them? I already feel tears forming in my eyes, even though I have not heard the story yet. As a sensitive person, this information, in this situation, is not the best. I am lost of words. Somehow the situation triggers an instinctive reaction, and I take her hand in mine.

"How?" I ask her, nearly whispering.

The volume of my word is at minimum to not start crying, and I am not even sure if Iris heard my question.

Another minute of silence passes.

"I'll tell you another time." She says all calm.

She squeezes my hand and moves herself closer to me, rearranging her head on my shoulder. I give her a short squeeze back and keep holding her hand tight. We sit like that for a long time. I desperately want to know the story. However, I understand why she does not want to talk about it now. I wish that I could change the subject and make the mood enjoyable again, yet that would somehow feel wrong. There is only one word that I can find to say right now:

"Sorry," I whisper, with a tear escaping my eye.

Iris

I literally killed the mood. Why did I tell William that my parents are dead? However, it felt right to let him know at that moment. The last word he said triggered me. *Sorry*. Even though I rarely cry over the loss of my parents anymore, that word was a door to my memories of them. *Sorry*. It was the last word my mother got to say to me before she passed away. When William said that word, tears silently started to fall from my eyes, just as it did back then. I have been traveling ever since, in an attempt to get my thoughts moved from my loss, but now and then something reminds me of my parents, and the feelings that I'm trying to hide away return. Especially now when my secret is also getting real. I've been so unlucky in the last three years. However, I often compare my life to other people around the world, and to be honest, I can't complain. Not even with all the terrible things happening to and around me. So many people are living a tough and challenging life, so honestly speaking, mine has been great and still is.

We have been sitting in silence for a while now. I close my eyes, feeling the tiredness in them. William is still holding my hand tight, which has an incredibly calming effect on me. I realize how attracted I am to him right now. I feel him breathing silently by the movement of his shoulder and his head on mine. Deep, calm breaths. Realizing that my hand is getting sweaty, I kindly try to remove it, but he won't let me. He keeps holding it tight. Am I seriously beginning to have feelings for this guy? Why shouldn't I? A handsome, clever and emotional one, sitting here holding my hand. How should it not trigger some kind of feelings in me? Oh no, that's not good. It wouldn't be right, either for him or for me. Not in the long run. In the last few years, after I lost my parents, I have been terrified of getting too close to people. Even before that, I was never good at keeping friends. I always just found new friends when the old ones disappeared, but somehow, I always felt a little lonely. Losing my parents made me realize that I have no control of keeping people in my life. I'm aware that it might sound silly, but I don't want any more sadness and loss in my life. It wouldn't be good for William either to get too close to me at this point in my life. In the end, it would only lead to a loss for him as well.

Usually, when I feel attracted to someone, I would just go for it. Just give him a kiss and see whatever happens. But it has been years since I've felt this way for someone. I'm not sure that kissing William would be a good idea. I have to get out of this situation before I do something stupid.

"I'm tired, William," I tell him. "Are you up for an escort home to the hotel?"

He releases my hand and removes his head from mine.

"I am," he replies. "But first, you need to get this back."

He takes off the Nepalese hat from his head and pulls it down on mine.

"Hey, what are the odds that you will sing a little song for me on the way back?" he asks.

He is actually quite good at getting the mood up again. Going to bed with these depressing thoughts would not be the best.

"Oh, you're going to regret that dare," I tell him, feeling a bit happier. "My odds are 1 in 1."

William gives me a confused look.

"So that means? You will just do it?" he asks.

"That's right. I'm gonna destroy your ears with my singing, so you will be able to sleep through Tom and Noah's snoring," I inform him.

He laughs.

"I appreciate that!" he replies.

With that decided, we start walking, and I begin my singing.

chapter two
THE ADVENTURE
BEGINS

- Day 1 -

William

10.00 in the morning. Yesterday, before bed, we planned to wake up at seven o'clock, pack our stuff, find breakfast and get a taxi so we could have an early start at the mountain. None of us remembered to set the alarm, though. We woke in confusion and panic half an hour ago, ate some cereal bars for breakfast, packed up, and now we are here, looking for a ride outside the hotel. The night with Iris feels like a dream. I am still unsure if it really happened, though I do have her singing stuck in my head. She does not have a lot of singing experience, that is for sure, and luckily she knows that, but her voice has something unique to it.

She did not say much this morning, though, hopefully because of tiredness and lack of coffee. That is my excuse at least. I hope we find coffee at the starting point at the foot of the mountain. I need it.

"So how far are we hiking today?" Iris asks.

Tom picks up a map, unfolds it and points at our taxi destination.

"*Kande*. That's our starting point. The plan is to take a taxi to Kande, here, and go all the way up here, through here and end up here in Pitam Deurali," he informs while moving his finger along a trail on the map.

"A little too much information without coffee," Iris says, rubbing her face.

"Well, this will be an easy day," Tom says while folding his map and putting it back in his pocket. "Not too many hours of hiking. At least according to the map."

Iris gives me a quick look. It almost seems like she is avoiding me. Well, I might have put more meaning into last night than she has. For me, it was a romantic night, filled with emotions. For her, it was most likely just another night of traveling with some new backpacking friend. Noah and Tom were not awake when we got home, so they do not even know that we were gone. Maybe I should talk with them, just to have them telling me that I should stop whining and get over her. They might actually have some advice for me.

"There's a taxi!" Noah yells out of excitement.

Great, one step closer to coffee time. We drop our packs in the trunk, find a seat and inform the driver of our destination. On we go.

Iris

The taxi driver is not very talkative. His English skills are not the best, I believe. The boys sit in the back, joking about something. The engine and the music from the car radio make sure that I can't hear the jokes, so I guess this ride will be some alone time for me. I'm pretty tired, so that's fine. We got back to bed quite late this night, though I didn't check my watch. Not a fan of time. Time pulls me out of the moment, just making me think about what will happen at certain moments in time. Like "soon bedtime" or "I need food soon" or "ten minutes to the next bus." I like not knowing what happens next and especially when it will happen. Just doing things that I feel like doing at the moment.

Well, except with feelings, as I found last night with William. I wanted him. I wanted to hug him and to kiss him. I wanted to explore this newfound attraction for him. But my logic for once won over my desires. I'm not sure if it was the location and the situation that got me that emotional, and I haven't dared to check up on my feelings this morning. It's best not to think about it, and hopefully, everything will be alright.

Anyway, I've got some time to kill. Man, I hate that saying. I look down at the book in my lap: *Into the Wild*. A classic. People have been telling me to read it for years, but I'm not good at reading books after seeing movies. I compare them too much, and the surprises are not really surprising when you expect them to come, like when you know what will happen and somehow when it will. I was told that this book is very different from the movie, though. We'll see.

William

Coffee! Finally! Kande is a small town with only a few houses, but here is an incredible view of the surrounding mountains.

This house has a small bar outside, with coffee. We all order a cup of coffee and buy a couple of cereal bars to eat with it. It feels great to be here, and the weather is just perfect today. The taxi hunks us goodbye behind us and drives away. The driver was actually an amusing man when he first began speaking. A funny, honest man. He informed us, in an ironic way, that we should always know the price before entering a taxi, else he could just demand whatever he wants after the ride is done. When we arrived here in Kande, he demanded an insane price for the trip. We all laughed, though we were still unsure if he was kidding or not. Luckily, he was, so we ended up doing a reversed haggling with him when he told us the actual price. Let's just say that we gave him a lot of tips for excellent service and honesty. For us, that kind of money is not a lot, but for him, it goes far. He gave us his phone number in case we need a taxi for the trip back when finished with the mountain. Taxi drivers have to fight for customers here, he said.

Well, coffee and cereal bars are in my body system now. On with the backpacks and start moving. The mood in the group is strange, yet satisfying. It is like all four of us are trying to understand that we are here now.

We walk for five minutes before I realize what I brought, but completely forgot about. I open up a pocket built in the hip belt of my pack and pull out a pocket-camera.

"Hey, let us have a *day-one* picture!" I shout.

Iris claps her hands from excitement, Noah laughs in agreement, and Tom puts his hands to his head. So we found the posing-hater in the group. When that is said, I hate posing for pictures as well, so Tom is not alone in this. But a group picture like this is almost mandatory. We take off our packs and put them on the ground in front of our posing position.

"Oh, we should take a picture when we get back down as well," Iris suggests while getting ready for posing.

"Good idea!" Noah joins in. "Before and after our trip. Looking like gods now and like crap when we get down!"

I set the timer function on the camera and place it on a large rock. Inspecting the small camera screen, I see the group standing ready for me to run over to them.

"Okay, here we go!" I shout while starting the timer.

I run to the group, getting a spot next to Iris. She puts her arm around my shoulder. I put mine behind her back, making sure it is not going too low. Three short flashes and a long one emit from the camera. The picture mission is done. I kindly remove my arm from Iris' back, while she slowly moves her arm from my shoulder, down my back before pulling it away. Something within the touch triggers me, giving me goosebumps all over my body. Not being sure if she intended to touch me like that, I push the thoughts out of my head and run to the camera. As I pick it up, I turn it off instantly.

"Wait, what? Aren't you going to check if it's okay?" Tom asks.

I return to my pack and put the camera back in the front pocket.

"Nope. Let us keep it old fashioned. We will see the pictures after the trip. Or at a time where picture-looking fits,"

I say.

The actual reason for this decision is that I do not want to see how I look. It merely destroys what is left of my confidence. I always appear stupid in pictures. This trip is about exploring new sides of me, and I do not want to be stuck with the old me by seeing pictures of what I might see as the old me.

"What a silly idea," Tom exclaims.

Iris gives him a sudden shoulder punch.

"Hey, what's up with you?" she says. "It's a great idea!"

Tom can't help it and puts a smile on his face. He probably realized how negative he unintendedly sounded.

"Oh, of course, my lady. Now, let me carry your luggage for you," he says and grabs out for Iris' pack.

She slaps his hand away.

"No, kind servant! You will most likely break something," she says in a formal tone. Or at least what probably should sound like a formal tone.

She puts on her backpack, as do the other three of us.

"Listen up, my three humble minions!" she continues. "We have a mountain to climb. Let's go!"

Iris

What is up with all these stony stairs? We've been climbing stairs for more than an hour, and William just showed on the map that we're only one-third of the way. *One third*! Only one-third of the altitude increase too, so it will be two more hours of stairs. *Why do they build stairs in the mountains?!* Okay, I'm just tired. They built them for a reason. William *did* warn me about this now that I think about it. My backpack is just so heavy. The guys seem to be doing fine with all that special lightweight gear that they brought. Now I'm regretting that I didn't do my gear research, instead of just bringing whatever was in my wardrobe. I'm used to be traveling with this backpack and the weight, but not when climbing up stairs for several hours. I'm sweating like a pig while trying to keep up with the guys. Luckily we will reach the first mountain restaurant soon, where we will have a long eating break, and not only these five-minute stops every half hour.

While walking, Tom inspects the strange, golden orb he bought from a magic shop in Kathmandu. He rotates the upper half and it begins ticking. Without any explanation of what that orb is, he continues the conversation I've had with him the last ten minutes about his girlfriend at home.

"Emmy was actually the one making me go on this trip," he says. "She told me that it's better that I'll get it done now than when the baby comes."

"That sounds fair," I tell him. "Do you have a date for when you'll become a dad?"

"Not yet. Emmy is quite early in the pregnancy, but I can't wait for it to happen," he says, grinning happily.

He puts a hand in his pocket and pulls up his wallet

before opening it up and dropping it in my hand. There's a picture of an incredibly beautiful young dark-haired woman.

"That's Emmy," he informs me.

"She's beautiful, Tom," I have to admit. "That's a keeper."

I give him back the wallet, and he takes a long look at the picture before putting it back in his pocket.

"I know. I really love that woman. Missing her every day," he says.

I would never have guessed that Tom had such a grownup side, having this amazing pregnant girl at home and being so open about how much he loves her. I suppose that Tom and Noah are actually more serious when apart from each other. They just never really progressed on their childhood friendship, simply keeping it as it was when they were kids when life was all about having fun and no worries.

"So you don't want kids? How come?" he asks me.

"I've always wanted kids when I was younger. But I've had a lot of bad things happening to me in the last few years, which made me unsure about the whole getting-children thing," I tell him. "Besides, I'm not a planner, as you know. Maybe I would have given it more thoughts if I've had someone to plan it with."

He looks concerned at me. Please don't ask about the bad things. *Please.*

"Well, you're still young. Plenty of time to find that one," he says, morphing his concerned expression into the relaxed, natural one he uses to have.

"I guess," I whisper without realizing it.

He doesn't know. I might never get to try planning babies or having a future with someone I love. My heart tightens up a bit now. It feels like millions of tiny needles stab it. Feelings like these are precisely what I try to avoid. It hurts so much when thinking about all the things I'm gonna miss in life, and it doesn't help me in any way to go through these thoughts and feelings. One day someone will come to collect me, and until that day, I'll be happy. Even after that day, I'll be happy. That's it. Always happy.

"Hey, who wouldn't want you?" Tom says, poking me with his elbow.

"You got a point," I say, almost cheered up again.

Tom inspects the golden orb in his hand. It's still ticking. I want to ask about it, but figure that I will get an explanation whenever the ticking stops.

"Anyway, now that you're unemployed, how will you support your family, you old man?" I ask instead.

I suddenly become unsure of how mature Tom actually is, and if such a question will offend him. I didn't think of how severe that question could be for some people. Having a child to support is an important thing. For me, unemployment has never been something serious. I have always managed fine when not having a job and only having to support myself. It's not that easy when you have to support a whole family and when the child's growth depends on that.

"Oh, don't you worry, young girl," he begins, clearly not offended. "Emmy and I made a big saving before starting the whole baby thing. She'll do fine with me not bringing money home for a while. I plan to take an education in computer science and become a rich programmer. Hopefully coding big video games someday."

"Woah, you surprise me a lot today, being all adult-ish and having programming skills. That's like the opposite of me," I say with a low chuckling.

"I figured," he replies happily. "So, what *are* your special skills?"

My special skills? How can you ever answer that question without sounding too self-confident? If I tell him what I'm good at, it might seem like I'm bragging and thinking big thoughts of myself. However, I never gained any special skills. I have a lot of skills, but no *special* ones that I'm extraordinarily good at. Having this intense curiosity and lack of patience just makes me learn new things constantly: playing all kinds of different instruments, drawing, instructing yoga, climbing, crocheting clothes for children, training archery, knowing tons of different languages, etc. But when I reach the basic knowledge and experience, I lose interest and find something new to learn before I ever gain enough experience to call it a special skill.

"Well, I'm just good at living," I end up telling him.

"What? No, there must be something you're good at," he says, eager to hear a proper answer.

I shake my head in disagreement.

"I'm afraid not. I'm good at a lot of things, but there are no special skills inside this one," I reply.

A voice suddenly shouts in front of us. We have fallen long behind William and Noah, who now stopped and are waiting for us. Most likely, it's my fault with this stupidly heavy pack of mine. My shoulders and my back hurts like hell.

As we near them, Noah tells us that our restaurant break is just around the corner. He is also having one of those golden orbs in his hand, and now my curiosity can't handle it anymore.

"Are you okay?" William asks me before I manage to open

my mouth and ask about the orbs.

Oh no, I must look like I'm dying with sweat dripping from my head and the shoulder pain that might be glowing out from my eyes.

"This backpack…" I admit. "It might be too heavy."

"Your body will get used to the weight soon," William informs me.

"I hope you're right. If we're only nearly halfway in today's goal, and the daily treks will get longer, I'm not gonna make it," I reply, sounding a little too desperate.

Tom punches me on my backpack.

"You've been traveling so much with that pack. How are you not used to it yet?" he asks.

"I'm not used to hiking up and down mountains," I tell him. "Walking an hour or two from your transportation to your hostel is not quite the same."

"When inspecting it, it does not look like a pack that is good for long treks," William says. "Does the hip belt even support your shoulders?"

I stare confused at him. I'm aware that there are all these technical features on backpacks, but not if this one has it or how it even works. I just bought the pack, back in the days, because it was practical. The seller told me something about a 'suitcase' opening and showed me that the whole front could open. That alone sold it to me.

"No idea," I reply. "However, I didn't really pack light-weight, so it might just be a bit too heavy."

Noah shouts something in front of us. He seems eager to get to the restaurant and started moving again. William claps his hands together, turns around and begins catching up.

"Let me look at the backpack tonight," he offers me before

turning his head.

He catches up with Noah in no time. It takes me a while to get ready to walk again, but Tom waits for me.

I notice a few ants crawling on my boots. They seem so energized, sprinting randomly around with their tiny legs. I inspect the strange, S-shaped formation line, which their family members follow, from a patch of grass at the side of the stony stairway to my boots, and I suddenly wonder what the cause is for that formation? Which ant started this, and why not just a direct line? There are so many things I don't know about the world.

"Sorry, Tom, I'm ready," I tell him as I realize that I'm about to begin questioning how the whole world works, which often turns out to be hours of wondering.

We move on. For some reason, I look up at a mountain ledge in the distance and spot a short, black-haired girl sitting with her feet dangling loose. She has something in her hand, but she is too far away that I can focus on seeing what it is. It looks strange, and my nerves almost can't handle the thought of her falling. Thankfully, Tom reclaims my attention.

"So, Iris. Are you up for a bet?" he asks me.

Normally I hate betting. Gambling is not my thing. I always lose. But being offered bets always triggers my curiosity.

"I might be!" I reply. "What's the bet and what can I win?"

He doesn't need time to think about it. Either he has been thinking about this for a while, or he's just winging it well. No matter what, the reply comes instantly.

"We both need to gain one special skill. Not necessarily on this trip, but just in the near future," he says.

I study him for a moment, and a smile appears on my

face.

"That's a great idea!" I exclaim. "What skill will you train?"

This time he thinks for a while.

"You know what. I think it might be good for me to be good at connecting with children. You know, act like a parent," he says.

"Wauw, that's a big one," I say excitedly. "How will you train that before having your child, though?"

"Easily! There are kids living in the cities of this mountain. I'll just try hanging out with them. I'm not sure how I'll do it back at home, though. I don't know any children there, and people would probably find it strange if I started talking to their kids," he replies. "I guess I'll just read up on it and train on my son or daughter when he or she comes."

I nod. I'm out of words, again not expecting this side of Tom.

"So what should your special skill be?" he asks.

Man, how can I make up my mind? There are so many things to do. I have to choose only one. Choosing has been the problem of my whole life. I'll just go with a random one, I guess.

"Okay. I will train my drawing skills," I say.

"Sounds good. Have you got drawing gear with you?" Tom asks.

"Yep! I like to draw and always wanted to be good at it, but as usual, I never had the patience to develop any amazing skills in it," I tell him. "So that will be it. What are we betting?"

"If you don't gain that special skill within... let's say a year from now... you will have to climb this mountain again, but naked," he replies with a little grin.

There's the Tom I know. Not entirely adult yet, still making bets with silly risks. I know that this bet is just on the edge of being unrealistic for me, but somehow making the bet makes me glad. It gives me something to focus on.

"Seems fair," I say. "But we need to take the bet seriously despite the weird risk."

"Of course! Else betting wouldn't be fun. We just have to make sure that we reach our goals," he says in a tone telling me that this is obvious.

Suddenly the orb in his hand chimes a short melody and a tiny paper roll drops into his hand. He happily unfolds it and reads out loud:

"*Free as a bird. Flying high but falling far.*" he mumbles. "What is this nonsense? It was supposed to tell me my future! I become a bird or what?"

I laugh from his disappointing future-note while shouts come from in front of us. We reached 'Australian Camp', which I, for some reason, was informed is a popular camp-site for tenting. Nevertheless, the restaurant is there. Perfect!

William

"What! Our break has been on for an hour now!" Noah suddenly shouts.

I take a look at my watch and find that Noah is right. Where did the time go? The food was, to my surprise, delicious. Who knew that they cook such tasty food in these mountains? I study our empty plates only to see that they are all completely cleaned up from the momos and spring-rolls that we all had. Iris had her vegan editions, of course. I regret that I did not order vegan spring-rolls like her. It might have given me some bonus points, and I am used to having meat-free rolls from my dad anyway. He loves Vietnamese spring-rolls made with vegetables, wrapped in rice paper and fried on a pan like regular rolls. He does not like putting meat in them because of some traumatic episode from his childhood, where he ate rolls with rotten meat, which ruined spring-rolls for him. It almost killed him from food poisoning, he says.

"Should we get going?" Tom asks and gets up from his chair.

We grab our packs and get ready to leave. The Nepalese waiter, cook and owner of the restaurant tells us goodbye and wishes us a safe journey. Such a friendly person. His daughter comes running out from inside the restaurant and waves us farewell as we leave.

"Oh, she's so cute!" Iris says with a voice that gets my heart beating like crazy.

Iris and I did not say much to each other during the break. It was mostly Tom and Noah talking and joking, with Iris and I adding a few inputs from time to time. I can not stop considering if I am putting too much into last night. I feel insecure around her when I do not know if she has any feelings for me at all. If that night with her head resting on my shoulder was just another freedom-moment in her life. William, your thoughts are running in circles. Just quit it.

It seems that Noah and I are in front again. I have found that Noah has absolutely no patience. He is walking fast and not feeling like waiting for Iris with her heavy backpack. Not that Noah is mad at her in any way. He would do the same, whoever was slow. Even Tom. At least that is what he told me. I am just glad that Tom sticks with Iris, as I am not sure if it would be awkward for me to walk with her right now. I might need a little mental distance from last night before my insecurity fades around her. Maybe I could get control of some of these feelings I am seriously starting to have for her.

Something catches my attention, sprinting past me, almost making me fall. A cat, intensely chasing some weird bug. I wonder how life is for a cat up here. Does somebody own or protect it, or is it completely wild? It appears clean and healthy, so it might belong to the restaurant. Or belong to itself: it is a cat after all. Nobody really owns a cat. Iris would probably think that nobody owns any animal. Maybe even any living thing at all. I agree, to some degree, I guess.

"William! Do you know why cats are so good at playing video games?" Noah asks me.

It seems like Noah is ice-breaking every conversation with a joke. He has jokes about everything.

"No?" I reply.

"Because they have nine lives!" he says, all serious and monotone.

I laugh. As usual, not because of the jokes itself, but the

way Noah tells it. You never know what expressions he will use for it, and with his French accent everything sounds hilarious. Even when he is not telling jokes, he can not help but randomly change the mood or change the tone of his speaking, just for the fun of it.

"That is a horrible joke, Noah!" I inform him, still laughing.

"You're wrong. It might just be too much information for your small, little lawyer-brain," he replies while staring curiously at his golden orb, which has been ticking for quite a while now.

We reach another massive stony stairway. There is a mild afternoon sun shining down on us, but luckily also a fresh wind to cool us down. We are sweating waterfalls on these up-and-down stairways, but the conversation with Noah on the way up here distracts me from the sweat and pain. I had just dared to ask him about his past, right before we got interrupted by arriving at the restaurant. When we first met, he told me about how he has no problems with being adopted and all, but I kinda want to hear more about it.

"So you never got to tell me about your parents," I say, hoping that he is up for the talk.

"Ah! You see, when my African biological parents died, I was picked up by the French military who brought me to a center in Paris," he begins. "Luckily for me, I was only there for less than a year, so I don't remember anything from that time."

I can not help but notice the calmness in his voice when telling this. I might have found a subject here, which he does not want to joke about.

"So, your parents adopted you and brought you to Marseille?" I ask.

"Yep. To make a long story short, my parents couldn't have children of their own. Yes, I know, what a surprise when adopting…" he continues. "You know, it's not like they just went there for a zoo trip looking at trapped babies, and just falling in love with me, pointing and asking: can we have that one, please?"

A little smile appears on his face, but not the loud laughter that usually comes with a joke.

"No, to be honest, my parents told me that they considered adopting even before they knew that they couldn't have children," he says. "They are like… people of principle. Putting new life in the world doesn't make sense when there are so many lives already to save. So many children who just want parents, you know."

I stop walking for a second. Noah stops as well, sending me a confused look.

"Noah! Those are wise words," I say, all baffled.

He starts laughing.

"I know! They are not thought by me, though. Whenever I say something clever, it's just memorized words from other people," he replies. "However, everything is true."

"Oh, I know," I reply, giving him a clap on his shoulder.

The laughing continues while we move on. I find it quite interesting to hear what is behind the joking camouflage of Noah. I have been able to get a little deeper into the head of Tom the previous day, but with Noah it has been harder. I am glad that he is opening up. However, I still wonder why he is hiding behind that barrier, just turning conversations into fun every time it gets too personal. I mean, I do the same because of my shyness and introverted personality. I always have trouble continuing conversations. But Noah does not seem shy nor being an introvert. Can I ask him about this? No, that would be rude. And it might backfire. I guess I will have to figure it out myself.

Something else catches my attention and makes me glance up in the distance. A short girl, with long dark hair, is stretching her arms up in the air, standing on a ledge far away. The sun behind her blinds me, only allowing me to see the silhouette of her strange posing. The setting makes her appear extremely scary with her hair floating in the wind. A couple of the usual colored sparkles emerge and idle around her, which only makes the whole scenario even more horrifying. She bends down and jumps high up in the air, making my heart stop for a moment, fearing that she will fall off the ledge, which would definitely result in death. A terrible death! However, she finishes her stretching, strolls away and disappears out of sight, with the sparkles following her. Who the hell does something like that? I hope we will never stumble upon that psycho. I am a bit shocked by, somewhat, preparing myself to see someone die. Which raises a question in my head.

"Do you know how your African parents died?" I ask Noah, hoping it is okay to ask that question.

"Actually nobody knows. They might still be alive," he replies. "But if they are, the odds of ever finding them again is one in a zillion. A lot of information got lost when I was transported to Paris. They must have been important people since the French chose to take me with them. Anyway, my adoptive parents were just kind enough to raise me with the idea of my African parents being dead. It's like a closure to the story, so I wouldn't have to walk around wondering if I could ever find them, when that would be almost impossible."

"So you are okay with that?" I ask.

"With the decision? Yes, I appreciate it a lot, actually. Because of that, I never had the urge to find out who my African parents are... or who they were," he replies. "I have had contact with people who were transported to Paris with me on the same day. They are constantly thinking about finding their African parents because they were raised with the knowledge of them being alive somewhere. And you know, being a black kid in a white man's land will often make you think of your origins."

Again I am stumbled by what I am hearing. Such serious words are coming from Noah all of a sudden. It might be memorized words, but nobody would know if it was, if he did not inform about it first. I think that a lot of "smart" people are just memorizing other people's words. I found this myself in school, at least. Being a shy guy working in groups, sharing all the right answers, only to have the credit stolen by the talkative people in the presentation. I am not sure that Noah is like that, though. Behind his jokes, he seems like a caring guy.

"How is that like in France? Having a different skin color, I mean," I ask.

I know that a lot of people would think twice before daring to ask such a question, but with my semi-Vietnamese skin color, I have always felt it more natural to ask questions about race.

Noah runs his hand over his face, removing some of the dripping sweat.

"Oh, for me, no problemo," he says while making an

exaggerated sweat-removing shake with his hand. "My parents taught me to focus on other things when being met by problems. But not everybody finds it that easy, you know. I have been quite lucky most of my life. Also, growing up with a white friend like Tom probably made things easier for me."

"Namaste!" a voice suddenly says right in front of me.

I make a small jump from the surprise, not realizing someone was coming down the stairs. My eyes were most likely too much on the ground, and my mind was focusing on the conversation. Noah replies with a namaste immediately. Namaste: a Nepalese way of greeting. The voice-owner walk past us with good speed. A middle-aged backpacker. I guess he has completed his adventure and is returning down. He seems happy. I admire people for going alone like that. My short night-exploration alone, last night, was way out of my comfort zone. Going on such a long hike alone would kill me. Well, I guess you are not completely alone when other people are hiking the same route and sleeping in the same places, but still... I turn my head to see the man walk past Tom and Iris longer down the stairway, clearly giving them a namaste as well. Iris looks like she is fighting to keep up. I get a sudden urge to go hug her. To simply pick her up and carry her the rest of the way in a tight, warm hug. No! William, stop it! I turn my head back to Noah who is staring at his orb again.

"So, what is up with Tom having a baby coming?" I ask him.

Noah's happiness disappears within a split-second. Not the reaction I expected.

"Yeah, that's weird," he replies shortly.

I am suddenly not sure if Noah is joking right now with

the mood change, or if he is genuinely not happy for Tom becoming a parent. That is one of the downsides about Noah's jokes, I guess. Luckily he continues with an explanation.

"To be honest…" he continues. "… I'm happy for Tom, of course. But being a little selfish, I wish nothing would change. I wish that things would never change. I like how things are back at home right now."

He stops talking and gets a look on his face telling me that he is probably trying to figure out a joke or a way to change the subject.

"So, you are afraid of losing Tom?" I ask.

"I guess," he replies after some consideration. "But please don't mention it to him. I'm afraid of losing, yes. Afraid of him being a family-person with no time for me. On the other hand, I'm excited to be the cool uncle!" he continues.

"That is true!" I tell him, sticking to the cheerful uncle-subject. "You will probably be the funny, cool uncle, whom the kids want over to visit all the time. Tom might even be worried that he is losing you to the kids."

And with that, Noah is back to normal, bursting out in short but loud laughter.

"You're right! They might even hire me as their babysitter!" he says. "So that's what I will have to study when I get back home! Babysitting! Now I finally have a plan! Thanks, Will!" he laughs.

I can not help but think back on one of the first conversations we had, about him having no plans and no future. It makes sense why he is afraid of losing Tom. It sounds like Tom is more or less all that Noah has at the moment, besides his parents, of course. It suddenly occurs to me that Noah might suffer from a lack of self-esteem. He told me more than once how he is not good at anything, and how he does not know what to do from now on after he and Tom lost their jobs. He joked that he was waiting for Tom to figure out what to do so that he could do the same, but now I begin to think that there is some truth to that joke. A lack of confidence would make sense as to why Noah turns everything into fun. I have heard of people doing that. Well, I guess it is hard to know. I might be curious because of my own small self-esteem problem. Anyway, if I am right, it does not change Noah as a person, I know. It just gives an explanation which might be of no use after all.

Suddenly Noah releases an evil laughter, as the orb in his hand starts playing a scary melody. Two paper notes pop out and he opens up both of them:

"*Destiny is yours to decide,*" he reads from the first note. "*Make a choice,*" the other one says.

For a moment, it looks like someone pressed the pause button while pointing the remote at Noah. Only his mouth mumbles the text from the note a few times.

"Nope, I give up!" he finally exclaims.

He drops the two paper notes, which get caught by the wind and fly away. Did Tom and Noah seriously believe that the orbs would tell the future? They are weird.

"Oh, I guess we're here," Noah says, as he looks up in front of us.

Indeed, it seems like we have already reached our first sleeping destination.

Iris

Those twenty minutes of lying in bed definitely removed some pain from my back. It appears to have gotten dark outside as there's not much daylight left in our four-person room. Being used to huge dormitory rooms, having a private one like this is a significant upgrade that I didn't expect. It seems like there are only private rooms in the mountains and no dorms. The rooms are basic with nothing in them but beds, but still.

A low snore sounds from my side. Noah and Tom are still napping, but William is not in his bed. I wonder what he is doing? Time for me to explore, I guess, else I won't be able to sleep tonight. I get up from the bed and put on some warm clothes, before silently sneaking to the door.

The air is fresh and goes perfectly along with the warm, orange light coming from the small village. *Pitam Deurali*, Tom said was the name. I hint some smoke from the little restaurant building, which adds to the coziness of the place. A few stars have begun to show in the sky, but I can't see much of the surroundings. Everything seems quiet, except the talking from a group of Asian people on the wooden benches around a long table in the center of the village. They're having a warm camping lantern placed in the middle of the table, illuminating their faces. Five women, it seems. Oh, wait, no, one of them is William!

"Hello," one of the women greets me as I get nearer. "Come sit. You want sum tea?" She asks, clearly not that good in English.

"Thanks, that would be great," I say as I sit down on the bench opposite William.

The woman gets up and walks inside the restaurant building while I greet everyone around the table. William gives me a nervous, but cute, greeting-smile and a nod. Somehow I feel my return-smile to be wider than usual.

"So you must be the girl from Iceland," one of the other women concludes. "William told us everything about you," she continues ending with giving William a small wink.

"Is that so," I chuckle, sending William an exaggerated curious stare.

In his somehow shy panic, he denies it with a head shake. A sudden desire of him actually telling these women about me appears. A hope that he cares about me. I suddenly feel my plan of not getting too close to anybody breaking down. That's not cool, Iris! Wake up! Don't be foolish!

"Where are you from?" I decide to ask the women.

The same woman answers almost before I end my question.

"We're from Malaysia. We all just met two weeks ago at the briefing meeting and are now on a booked tour. Ten people in all. All women. One male guide. Poor guy, haha. We're trekking to the Annapurna Base Camp and down in fourteen days. People in our group are between 30 and 42 years old, so we have to take it slow. Not like you young people. You can just run up and down easily. I remember when I was young…" she informs almost without breathing.

While she continues babbling, the woman who went for tea returns and puts it on the table in front of me. I thank her and put my hands around the warm cup, still trying to look focused on the ongoing one-way conversation with the unusually talkative woman. The three other Malaysians initiate a discussion of their own in Malaysian.

"…so have you ever seen anything like that?" I suddenly realize being asked by the talkative woman.

Man! Anything like what? What could she have talked about while I was unfocused? Well, I could take the easy way and just say *no* and hope for it to end there. But that could eventually get me in trouble if she continues giving me questions about the subject. What to do?

"Oh, there is nothing Iris has not seen on Iceland," William suddenly says. "I bet she has seen those Northern Lights a million times."

Iceland! Northern Lights! Okay, I didn't expect the conversation to be about me that sudden. William sends me another cute, shy smile. He must have seen the panic in my eyes when I got the question. Oh, how I owe him for this one.

"That's right," I say, returning what I hope looks like a discreet thank-you expression to William.

The woman starts her monologue "conversation" again before I can even open my mouth to say anything more. I let the woman continue while taking a sip of my tea. Masala tea! The mixed feelings from when I first tasted it in the hotel yesterday returns. The surprise of having that incredible unexpected taste, but with the downside of the tea containing milk. My gaze jumps to William again. He is giving me yet another cute smile and a jump with his shoulders, either telling me that he's sorry for not preparing me for the milk, or as a *'sorry for baiting you out in the claws of this extremely talkative woman'* gesture. The light from the lantern gives a special glow in his eyes. Like a soft sparkle. I now conclude: this is a handsome guy. We hold our eye contact for longer than I have ever had with him before. He keeps the cute smile on his face. Somehow I can't stop staring into those two sparkling black pearls. I hear low, weird giggling coming from myself. Immediately I wake up from this... weirdly paralyzed state, and watch the talking woman, afraid of being rude to her. I suspect myself of showing that I'm not listening to her babbling. Well, she doesn't look like being offended in any way. It's like she doesn't even care if people actually listen to her.

Somehow I'm just not in the mood for one-way conversations right now, so I close my eyes and take another sip of my tea. MAN! Still masala tea. Hmm... Actually, I think I will drink this one. I mean, it has been made already, and it is getting kinda chilly out here. And it would be rude of me not to drink it after this friendly Malaysian woman walked inside to get it for me.

Taking another sip from the cup, I begin to enjoy drinking this milky tea. My eyes wander to Williams' yet again. My heart starts pounding this time. A light breeze moves by, giving me goosebumps, but my eyes are locked at his. I get an urge to throw away my cup, jump over the table and kiss him. I need to gain control of myself before I do something I will regret.

ARGH!

A pair of hands clash down on each of my shoulders, making me jump in my seat. I turn my head, only to be met by a laughing face with a bunch of orange hair on top. Tom!

"So, we've stopped napping," he says. "Are you up for dinner?"

Noah shows up from our room with a big yawn. As my shock-level lowers to normal, I feel the hunger. The talkative woman stopped talking to greet Tom and Noah, so William and I get up from our seats simultaneously while we're still free from the monolog-conversation. I have no clue if she was still going with some long story when Tom interrupted us by "awaking" me, but I'm not staying to find out.

"We're about to have dinner as well," the talkative Malaysian woman says as she realizes that we're leaving.

"Perfect," I tell her, trying to sound excited. "See you in the restaurant soon then."

Waving the women goodbye, we find our way to the restaurant, ready for some proper food.

William

I put down my fork and inspect my watch. 8 pm exactly. Now, after getting full from this surprisingly delicious meal, I feel like I could sleep instantly. The atmosphere in the restaurant is quite cozy, even though it is basic and built of plastic. The owners of the accommodation lighted the little metallic fireplace, making the small room warm and relaxing. They told us that they only do this when big groups are visiting, so I guess we are lucky being here with the Malaysian group. When the group entered, the talkative Malaysian woman sat down, started eating and talking with her friends at the long table next to us. I am honestly relieved to get rid of her. Their guide sits with the two owners around a small table in the corner, next to the fireplace. It seems like they know each other pretty good. The rest of us took the last table and got the last candlelight in the village, so again a little luck for us. The owners' son is in Pokhara, getting candles and other supplies, and will return by foot tomorrow. That is how you do when no roads are leading to your small newly-built village, they said. It makes sense but sounds like hard work.

"So, how is your back?" Tom asks, looking at Iris.

She straightens her back, testing it fully before answering.

"Could be better," she answers. "I have to get rid of some of the weight if I want to survive this trip."

"I can help you out if you want," I offer out of the blue. "I even have space for more stuff in my own backpack, so you do not have to throw away too much."

She gives me a huge, warm smirk, which makes my heart jump.

"That would be great," she replies.

During the dinner, Iris and I got to talk a bit, making things less awkward between us. Since our minute of mesmerizing eye-contact outside, I have not managed to remove my eyes from her. Even though she looks exhausted and broken, she is still one of the most beautiful persons I have ever met. I can not find a single thing I do not like about her. Her soft voice, her cute Icelandic accent, her blue eyes, her wild blond hair, the sweet smell of her wild blond hair, her silly hippie anti-hiking clothes and the open, but mysterious, personality. I could go on forever. Everything is just perfect. And I still do not know if she has any of these feelings for me, or if she is just being friendly. I found that she has this thing of rubbing the nail-root of her thumb with her index finger when she gets tired. It is rather strange, but I like it. A discreet yawn sounds from her.

"Maybe we should get the repacking over with now so we could get to bed," she says, stretching her arms up in the air.

"Yeah, okay. Sounds like a good idea," I say, picking up my sweater from the bench.

Tom and Noah glance at each other and nod. I still admire the way they communicate without words.

"Seems like we're up for some dessert," Tom says. "Go fix that backpack."

"Yep! We had that long nap, so we're fresh and need sugar," Noah adds.

"Of course! Makes sense. You are the smartest guys I know," Iris says, putting a hand on Tom's shoulder.

"Do not stay up too long, kids," I join in as Iris and I leave the kitchen house.

As far as I understood, the payment for both food and accommodation will happen tomorrow before we leave. I guess that the guesthouse owners can trust people up here, as there is nowhere to run if you decide you run from the bill.

Wow, it has become cold outside. Cold enough to see our breaths. It feels like hitting a wall of frost after being inside the heated kitchen house. However, the sky has become filled with stars. It is a fantastic sight. I have never seen stars so bright. Never been so far away from the light pollution that dim the light from the universe. Iris is somehow not that impressed by this view and continues towards our room. I try to catch up.

"Hey, I'm sorry to be a stone in your guys' hiking shoes," she says as she opens the door to our room.

"What? No!" I reply to my surprise. "You are not! You are part of the group just as much as any of us. Even though we only met a few days ago, I can not imagine this trip without you."

"Thanks, William. I just had a feeling that I split you guys up today because I'm so slow," she says in the dark, searching her backpack for her flashlight.

I can not believe that she feels that way. If I dared to, I would give her a gigantic hug to show that she is wrong, but as usual, my shyness overcomes my feelings.

"Iris, that is no problem. Actually, I could use a slower pace than Noah's myself," I tell her, maybe lying a bit. "And now when we fix that backpack of yours, you might even be faster than any of us."

There is no electricity in the room, and Iris' flashlight is not doing good, so I find my camping lantern and turn it on. To my surprise, it is powerful enough to illuminate the whole room. Do not tell me that I did not do my research on equipment well. I did read and watch reviews of everything to find the best before buying it. Seems like a good idea now.

"You're sweet," Iris says and puts her flashlight on the floor.

She opens her backpack, and before I realize what is happening, the pack is rotated bottom-up, leaving everything that was inside it in a messy pile on the floor. I move myself to the mess and find myself putting a hand to the back of my head.

"Now, what do I need and what don't I?" Iris asks and starts messing with the pile.

She throws some underwear and a couple of t-shirts to the side while mumbling *need* with every throw. A quick image of Iris wearing that underwear passes through my head. *Quit it, William!*

"What about this?" she asks to my relief.

She holds up a pair of thick, green pants with flowers sewed on it. Or shorts? No, wait, what is it? Iris laughs.

"It's pants. Made from hemp. Weights like a ton," she says, probably seeing my confused look.

"Ah, okay," I say. "Well, it will be good to have a pair of thick pants when not walking."

She browses through the pile for a moment and pulls up a similar blue pair.

"I got a spare one," she says, holding it up.

"Then definitely get rid of one of them," I tell her.

"Good for you that I'm not attached that much to my clothes. Telling a girl to throw away her clothes. Jees'" she replies laughingly. "So, which pair do you like the best?"

I take a good look at them. To be honest, I would tell Iris to throw away both of them if she did not need warm pants in the cold. I have not seen her in any of them yet. Maybe they look better on her body than when being held up in the air like this, just hanging loose.

"I like the blue one best," I tell her, hoping it was the right answer.

She thinks for a moment.

"Good! Away with you!" she says, throwing the green pair on the bed and the blue one into the need-pile.

I suddenly realize how many t-shirts she has in the mess-pile. I bend down to get an overview.

"You could easily get rid of some of your shirts," I tell her. "It is okay to wear the same shirt for several days when hiking like this. No need for so many."

She gives me a curious look. Does she not believe me? It seems like she is thinking.

"I believe you're right, Will," she finally says. "Not sure what I was thinking when bringing all this stuff. Old habit, I guess."

She makes another browse through the pile and ends up with five t-shirts. Almost without inspecting, she throws two in the need-pile and the rest on the bed with the green pants.

"Wow, you are definitely not attached to your clothes," I conclude in surprise.

"Yeah, I know. Not that I'm gonna need it anyway later in my life," she says with a sudden change in mood.

What does she mean by that? I guess this is some of the mystery about her which attracts me. I cannot figure her out. It is like she is carrying some sort of pain inside that she will not tell. I inspect the messy pile and see two large books that were hidden under the shirts.

"Do you need both of those books?" I ask, pointing at

them.

She picks them up and smiles.

"Man, of course not," she says, all embarrassed. "I'm sorry, Will. I must be the worst packer in the world for a hiking trip in the mountains."

She puts the biggest book in the trash-pile and keeps the smaller one in her hand: *Into the Wild*. I have seen that movie. Not a surprising pick for a person like her. She throws it in the need-pile while I bend down to browse through the rest of the mess.

"Seems like the rest is needed," I conclude after we finish browsing, and after she insisted on keeping the pencils and thick paper-block. "I can have your fluffy, green sweater and warm flower pants in my pack to save you some weight."

"Thank you so much, William," she says. "I really owe you one. Or two."

As I pick up her huge sweater, something drops out of it. The small, metallic object brightly reflects the light from the lantern. It looks like a necklace of some kind. Iris picks it up, and an enormous smile appears on her face.

"There it was!" she yells out of happiness.

She opens the locket attachment and stares down into it for a while.

"It's my parents," she says, almost whispering now.

I move to her bed and sit down next to her. The locket contains two pictures. One on each side. Her father on the left and mother on the right. Iris is like a copy of her mother. With her father's eyes. It feels strange to think about them being dead.

"She got cancer," Iris says.

I am out of words, not prepared for this. But she is opening up to me, that is something.

"Three years ago. We got the bad news in January," she continues. "After that, my father got very ill. He kept his head up, though. I am not sure how I could survive the news without him. Such a brave man. He was in his car, on the way to the hospital, the day my mother died. But he drove too fast, lost control of the car and..."

She stops talking while a tear runs down her chin. My heart has completely frozen from the story. Still out of words, I take her hand and hold it tight. We sit in silence for a while.

"I am so sorry, Iris," I finally get myself to whisper.

She turns her head and looks into my eyes. Her eyes are wet from tears, shining from the reflection of her flashlight on the ground. It feels like she is peeking directly into my soul, trying to devour my heart, yet in a delightful way. Another tear escapes her eye and runs down her cheek, and I instinctively catch it with my free hand. Iris releases our handholding and puts her arms around me. I hug her back and hold tight.

Please never let this hug stop.

Iris

I can't hold it in anymore. The tears fall from my eyes. I haven't told this to anyone in two years. I needed this. I needed this hug. Aw, this is such a perfect hug. I pull William even tighter. He pulls me in tighter as well. The pressure from the hug hurts a little, reminding me of my secret. Should I tell him about it? Now that he knows about my parents, he could learn about me as well. No, everything would just be weird. That's why I kept it a secret in the first place. I get so emotional around him. I feel safe. Since I lost my parents, I have tried to suppress the pain of losing them by being free and out there in the world. I first realize now how much I miss feeling safe. I focus on the tight hug, which I do not intend to end any time soon. I want to press myself hard enough into him to merge and disappear into nothingness, being safe and happy. I get an urge to kiss him. To pull his soft, dark hair and press his lips into mine. My heart jumps from the thought, and my tears suddenly stop. William kisses my neck through my loose hair but keeps the hug tight. I didn't think it was possible, but I manage to pull him even closer to me, my breath becoming heavy.

NO! I cannot do this! No matter what I do, it will end in sorrow. It would be bad for me and especially for William. I can't do that to him. I have to stop this…

William

Iris suddenly releases her grip and pushes me away. She wipes the remaining tears from her cheeks and puts her hands into mine.

"I'm so glad I met you, William," she says softly and smiles, still keeping the eye contact locked.

I know that I am optimistic when hoping for another hug, but I would like one. And a kiss. An infinite kiss. Oh, William, what were you thinking?! Did you seriously hope for a kiss after hearing about the death of Iris' parents? Did you really kiss her neck while hoping for a kiss back? Get control of yourself!

I open my mouth to say how glad I am that I met her too, but I am interrupted by the door opening and two laughing guys entering the room. Iris and I pull our hands to ourselves and pretend like everything is normal. Clearly, our acting is not that impressive.

"Did we interrupt something?" Noah asks grinningly.

The sudden change of mood- and energy level in the room is a little strange, and I struggle to find words, but luckily, Iris is a better actor than me.

"Actually, you did," she replies. "We were just fighting over who of you two will be the lucky owner of these fine, manly trousers."

She picks up the green flower pants from the bed and throws it to Noah.

"Now you two can fight for them yourself," she continues.

"You know what, Noah," Tom says. "I'm going to be a gentleman and let you keep them."

Somehow we all laugh, clearly affected by tiredness. I

check my watch. 9.30 pm. I guess it is time for bed. We need to get up early and start walking. That's how you do in the mountains, to walk in daylight and avoid avalanches. Well, that's what I read, at least. I give Iris one last glance into her dark blue eyes, and we exchange a quick smile before getting up from the bed.

"So I guess it's bedtime," I say, picking up my lantern and my toothbrush.

- Day 2-

Iris

"Is it six in the morning already?" I ask after the boys' alarms started ringing simultaneously.

I hear one of them mumbling *yes* from what sounds like a still sleeping state. Despite the early time, I'm filled with energy, excited for what's going to happen today. I get up, slip on a warm pullover and find my way to the door. As I open it up, I lose my breath. I didn't see this yesterday when we arrived. All around the village, there are icy mountains on the horizon. The sun is still rising behind one of them, yet, the sun provides enough light to see everything clearly. It's not as cold anymore as it was in the evening and throughout the night. My pullover and long underwear are more than enough to keep me warm now. I step outside and close the door behind me, taking in a big breath.

"Good morning, Iris," I hear someone say from my side.

The talkative woman is awake too, enjoying the incredible view just as I am.

"Oh, good morning," I reply with a smile. "Not a bad thing to wake up to, huh."

It's brave of me to reply with more than just a *'good morning'* when it might trigger this talking machine, but I don't care right now. I'm feeling good. Before the woman gets the opportunity to answer, all of the doors to the rooms of the Malaysian group opens up and out comes the nine other women. They all either grin, nod or wave at me as they leave their rooms and move to the restaurant house for breakfast. The talkative woman gives me a small wink as well and follows the group. I take in another breath of the fresh air and enjoy the view and the silence.

Suddenly something pokes my leg, making me do a small jump forward from the unexpected touch. Aw, a dog! I have never seen this kind of dog before. Dark medium-long hair with beige spots. A medium-sized dog. It looks scared from my sudden jump away from it, so I get on my knees to greet it with my arms open. Its tail wags like crazy before it runs straight into my arms. Aw, a massive hug to you, sweet dog. I do a silly cannot-control-myself petting all over the dog. It, or he, as I see, begins what I would describe as a happy dance. We're like two individuals with a sudden cannot-control-myself happiness-disorder. I laugh out loud as he makes a jump onto me and I fall on my back. The door opens behind us.

"Iris! Are you making new friends behind our backs?" I hear Noah yell.

The dog stops to stare at him, preparing to flee. I guess that not everybody who comes around here likes the dogs, just chasing them away instead of greeting them. Noah instantly runs out and gets on his knees as well while the dog sprints over to him, ending in them doing the same exaggerated petting. He greets the dog in French with words that I don't understand. Behind him comes Tom and William, looking kinda tired. Without saying a word, they walk like zombies over to Noah and the dog to say hello and do some petting as well. This is simply the happiest morning I have had in a long time. William gets up from his knees and realizes the surrounding mountains. The surprised expression on his face makes me giggle. He is cute with morning hair and a surprised morning-face. The sound from my giggling catches his attention, and he looks at me. A smile appears.

"Ready for some coffee?" he asks, keeping the smile on his face.

William

"That breakfast was something, wasn't it?" Noah asks Tom and me while checking the last straps of his backpack.

Mountain pizza for breakfast is hard to disagree on being a good breakfast, even this early. I check my watch: 7 am. Perfect timing for our plan. The sun is already heating the air around us, so we're back in our regular hiking outfit. Everything seems so calm, especially after the Malaysian group left half an hour ago. We will probably catch up with them at some point, though. Now we are just waiting for Iris to pay her part of what we owe for the overnight. I see her through the window to the kitchen house, handing over the clothes that we sorted out from her pack last night. It seems that the owners are pleased to receive it. The woman gives Iris a short hug and the man is good with a handshake. Happily, she leaves them, exiting out the door and saunters towards us.

"Are we ready to go then?" Noah asks.

I can hear the impatience returning to him.

"Yep! Let's go," Iris replies, picking up her backpack. "So much lighter than yesterday," she says, putting it on and making a few quick knee-squats.

"Witchcraft!" Noah yells and points at her. "It's not our Iris! Vegans cannot be that strong!"

Nobody is, strangely enough, falling for this joke, creating a moment of silence. That does not stop Noah from chasing the laughs.

"Tom, do something!" he continues. "Look into her memories and see who possessed this girl!"

Tom plays along this time and puts a hand toward Iris.

"I see… I feel… The possessor is…" Tom begins. "It's…

129

A woman... Middle-aged... Name... Starting with a B... It is... It is... William, help me here! Who is it?"

What? Did this end on me? Middle-aged, starting with B? Who can it be?

"William! Quick!" Tom continues.

Stress! Panic!

"Ehm... ehm... BOB MARLEY!" I suggest, instantly realizing how wrong that is.

Tom, Noah and Iris stop and stare at me like I am a complete idiot, before bursting into a huge laughter.

"What? Bob Marley? Are you stereotyping me, William?" Iris asks teasingly.

"No, no... I mean... You know... You got his nose... His eyebrows... His curly hair... You are basically him," I tease back, realizing how bad I am at winging this.

"Haha, that makes no sense, Will," she replies.

"Oh, don't be so sure," Tom falls in. "I see physical similarities in you two as well."

We finally decide to stop the awful silliness, let the laughter die out and start walking. We walk for 10-15 minutes before realizing that something is following us. I look back to see the shadow of something coming lingering towards us: the dog. I guess he likes us then. We all greet and pet the dog before moving on, now with the dog officially following us.

"Seems like we have a new companion in the group," I say, putting my hand down to let the dog sniff it. "We should give him a name."

"Yeah, let's do that!" Iris says.

"No collar and no dog tag, so I guess we can choose freely," Tom declares.

We continue in silence for a minute, thinking, before Noah finds the perfect name.

"Let's call him… Bob!"

Iris

Tom folds the map and puts it back in William's backpack while still walking along the wide mountain road.

"We hiked for three hours now, and we're almost half-way," he says. "We're doing good."

"Great. I *do* feel my body hurt a little today though," William says.

"Good!" Noah says. "Then I'm not the only one."

"Well, it is normal, until we get used to carrying the weight at least," William informs.

With the lighter backpack, I am able to keep up with the boys today. I feel like flying compared to yesterday. Today it's the boys' turn to be the ones struggling.

Suddenly our newest companion, Bob, stops abruptly. He has been happily following us since we left the small village this morning, and we've fed him and given him water in exchange for being our guide. He scouts out in the distance in front of us. We spot a group of small people bashing each other while ambling down the road. We move towards the group, who is walking towards us with good speed. As they get closer, we see that they are local kids. They stop in front of us as we reach them and we stop as well to greet them, while Bob stays behind us.

"Choclat?" one of the boys asks and reaches a hand out.

His hand is empty, so I guess he asks to get chocolate from us, and not offer it. One of the girls in the group of kids walks up and asks the same.

"Choclat?"

I haven't got any chocolate, or any more snacks to eat for that matter. I was planning to buy it in the next village we will pass. However, Tom takes off his pack and finds a small box of dark chocolate. He counts the number of children in the group.

"Six people, huh?" he says, breaking the chocolate into six pieces.

He hands out a piece to each of the kids, and they instantly start eating it with satisfied looks on their faces. I wonder if they have ever managed to get chocolate by begging from backpackers passing by. Tom gets down on his knees.

"English?" he asks them.

The girl asking for chocolate takes a step forward.

"Little," she says proudly.

"Are you on your way to school?" Tom asks.

I first realize now that all the kids wear little rucksacks and that one of them is carrying a small book in his hand.

"School!" the girl answers with a little nod.

It seems that Tom is doing an excellent job already with training his upcoming special skill: learning to be good with kids.

"That's good," he says, holding out his hand for a high-five.

The girl gives him a quick high-five and giggles. One of the boys in the group steps forward. He seems shy.

"Pen-cil?" he asks silently.

Tom smiles at him.

"Pencil? You don't have a pencil?" he asks the boy.

The boy doesn't seem to understand and gets a scared look on his face, taking a step backward. Aw, it's brave of him to ask. He must be desperate for a pencil. Tom turns his attention to the girl who knows a bit of English.

"Lost pencil? No pencil?" he asks her, elegantly pointing

at the boy.

"Pencil gone," the girl answers and points at the boy as well.

I imagine that pencils are worth a lot up here. Kids could probably get in trouble with their parents or teachers for losing such writing materials. I put down my backpack and pick up my collection of pencils: a container of ten professional pencils from hard to soft. They are dark-blue with golden writing on them and look just as expensive as they were. I'm not going to need all of them, so I pick out one of the harder ones. I like the soft ones the best anyway.

"You can have this," I say, handing it out for the boy.

He stands his ground, clearly not sure if it's for him, but keeps his gaze locked at the pencil. The English-knowing girl says something to him, and he moves towards the pencil, step by step, until he's close enough to reach it. He carefully takes his hand out, and I put the pencil in it.

"Thanks," he says silently and rapidly returns to the group of children.

He still seems shy, but I see a glow in his eye. A glow is telling me that he already loves that pencil. He keeps staring at it. It's strange how such a simple thing can be appreciated so much. I fear that the other kids might envy the pencil, but they just seem to be happy for their friend.

"School," the girl says and points on the road from where we came.

"You have to go to school now?" Tom asks. "Sounds like a good idea."

He gets back up and returns to us. The kids talk for a moment and simultaneously shout '*thanks.*' They happily begin walking, and Tom takes his hands out for another high-five. William, Noah and I do the same and get a high-five from each of the kids as they pass us. We turn around to see them leave and they wave at us yelling something in Nepalese. We wave back at them before they turn around and get up to running speed, maybe a little late for school now. They start singing some Nepalese song, which sounds so incredibly happy and sweet. We stand there looking amazed until they're out of sight. Bob rejoins us. He's not too fond of locals, we've found.

"Hey, buddy. Are you up for some more guidance?" Tom asks and gives him some head petting.

Bob barks consentingly a few times with his tail wagging like crazy.

"About an hour left until we reach our lunch-break village," William informs as we move on. "*Landruk*. It should be a quite large village.

William

I can not believe that we are having pizza yet again. But here in the mountains the cooking people, without doubt, cook the best pizzas I have ever had. Fresh tomatoes and local cheese are so tasty. Only Iris chose something different than pizza this time: noodles. I slowly move my gaze to her. She left our table when the food was served, and are now sitting on a rock, drawing and eating, with Bob lying at her feet. I cannot stop but wonder what she is drawing. Tom told me about their agreement of some *special skill* which just made me curious to see how skilled she is *now*. She keeps her attention on the paper, not even removing her eyes from it when she takes a fork of noodles to her mouth, clearly drawing something from her imagination. Although the sky is full of clouds, she found a spot with constant sunshine, illuminating her up like an angel. A noodle eating angel.

"Go kiss her," Tom suddenly says.

I turn my gaze to him, probably appearing somewhere between surprised and scared.

"What?" I giggle nervously.

"You are obviously falling for her," he continues. "It's been clear ever since you told us about her the first time. You know, when you told us about the time when you met her on the plane, holding hands and all."

"And you are not good at hiding your in-love face when you look at her," Noah adds teasingly.

As usual, I'm about to deny everything and just keep it cool. Finding out that people know things about you, that you wish to keep a secret, is rarely a pleasant feeling. For some reason, I feel like talking about my feelings right now, and get it out of my system. Maybe that will let me have some control of what I feel for Iris.

"Do you think she knows?" I ask the guys.

"That's hard to say. What do *you* think?" Tom asks me.

I take a glance at the two slices of pizza I have left on my plate. Watching my food helps me concentrate when talking over dinners. Does Iris know? I poke one of the slices with my fork while thinking it through.

"I am not sure. I constantly feel that there is some kind of connection when I am with her, but that could all be in my head," I finally answer.

"Dude, she is probably drawing you now!" Noah says a little too loud.

Loud enough that Iris might have heard it. She is looking over here now at least. Hopefully, she just heard someone speaking loudly, and not what was actually said. Noah waves at her. Before waving back, she puts a fork of noodles in her mouth, making half of them hanging out, dangling around and dripping soup. Now she waves back, showing an exaggerated smile with noodles hanging everywhere. *Noodle angel*. Bob sends her a questioning stare. I do not blame him. At last, she sucks up her noodles and continues drawing like nothing happened. In my head, I picture a drawing of me and her hugging on a bed of noodles. Somewhat an illustration of last night. However, I believe that her drawings are based more on her parents. Or maybe it is just weird hippie art. Who knows.

"I think she loves you," Noah continues and points at Iris with his fork.

"We don't know that," Tom adds. "It's best to see for yourself, William."

"I guess you are right," I say. "Hey, you guys could help me convince her to love me!" I joke, trying to change the seriousness of the conversation.

"I can do some magic," Noah says. "But it ain't free."

"No, Noah. Please don't do that to William!" Tom, says all frightened. "William, he wants to devour your soul in exchange for her love! It's such a perfect soul! Don't let him!"

"Oh, do not worry, Tom. If Noah can make Iris love me, my soul is his," I add to the horrible joking.

I hear a bump coming from where Iris is sitting. She closed her paper album and is on her way over here now. I guess we will begin our hike again soon then.

"Can we see your drawings?" Tom asks as she nears.

She shakes her head.

"Nope, not today. Another day, I promise," she replies.

Iris

"Oh no no, just keep walking, I'll catch up," I tell the guys and begin tying my boots.

"As you wish," Noah says and keeps walking.

Tom follows him, while William decides to be a gentleman and waits for me, along with Bob. Stupid, dumb, thick-witted laces! I almost tripped because they keep untying themselves.

"Why am I so bad at tying these boots properly?" I ask myself out loud.

"Good question," William replies. "Maybe it is just bad laces, you know."

"Yeah, that's why," I agree, giving the new-tied boots a light punch.

As I get back on my feet, I see that William is feeding our little companion with some crackers. They are becoming quite good friends. It always makes me happy to see humans and animals bond like this. Bob eats up, and the three of us start moving again, but Tom and Noah are out of sight already. We're currently on a curvy road, which means that they might be just around the corner. We walk side by side in silence for a moment with Bob roaming happily around us, sniffing every tree on the right side of the road. On our left, there's an amazing view of the surrounding mountains.

"What are the odds that you will let Bob sleep in your bed tonight?" William asks me.

He understood the game correctly.

"Well, let me see," I reply. "Bob *is* a handsome dog. He most likely doesn't snore that much. However, he might have some uninvited, small guests on him, if you know what I mean, which I rather not want in my bed."

"But you are vegan," William interrupts. "Are you not supposed to invite all living things up in your bed? Even small bugs?"

He gives me a teasing look.

"Of course. You're right! They are welcome. But I wouldn't want to make you jealous," I tease back. "So my final odds would be 1 in 5."

William stares at me.

"Make *me* jealous? You mean that you don't want to be jealous for me having Bob in my bed, right?" he asks.

I like his mood today. It's like the mountains are making him more open. Bob might also be part of the reason for him being so glad. And of course me. No, just kidding. Right? The apparent attraction that I felt for him yesterday, with the connection I think that we had... I somehow believe that he returns the feelings. Doesn't he?

"Well, let's say that if one of us loses, or *wins* if you like, and get to have a night of napping with Bob, the other one of us will just have to be sad and jealous, okay?" I say.

"Seems true," William replies.

"Okay, ready? This one is for having Bob in *my* bed," I say. "1... 2... 3..."

"FIVE!" we both shout simultaneously.

Oh really! Did I just win the rights of having a dirty, but cute, mountain-dog in my bed? I didn't think this through before making the odds. Anyway, maybe Bob will get tired of us at some point before bedtime and wander off, who knows.

"I am sorry, Iris," William says, poking me lightly with his elbow. "Seems like you won Bob for a night."

Bob comes running over to William for some reason.

"Ow, you are a lucky one are you not," William says and

pets him.

I can't help but smile from the cuteness of those two new best friends. They both look so happy at this very moment.

"You can have him another day," I tell William.

Suddenly they both stop and look to their right. A path is going up through the trees. However, the bigger road that we walk on is continuing straight.

"They might end up in the same place, but there is no way to be sure," William informs.

"Don't you have the map?" I ask him.

"No, I gave it to Tom when we had our lunch break before," he replies, actually sounding a little nervous.

I study the road. Then the steep path through the trees.

"That way looks the most fun," I say, pointing in between the trees.

William scratches his head.

"I'm not sure, Iris," he says, for sure sounding nervous now. "Being lost up here is not the best situation to end up. If you ask me, it would be better to stay on the bigger road."

He is right, I know. It's just my curiosity coming up in me... Wait, I see something!

"William, there's a mark on that tree!" I say and point at a red and white arrow which points in the direction of the forest path.

I can see the dilemma in his eyes: stick to a more significant road *without* markings or going with the smaller path *with* markings. Both options seem like a logical choice. Before he can say anything, Bob is happily sprinting up the forest path.

"It appears that Bob knows the way," I say, trying to convince William that we should go the exciting way.

"Yeah, well. It *does* look like Bob has been here before," William says after some consideration. "Let us follow him then."

I take a final glance at William to check if he is sure about this, but his confused expression is gone. We get eye-contact for a moment, but he breaks it again. The short moment made my heartbeat raise like an explosion. Okay, Iris, it's better to get going now. I start walking up the path, trying to catch up with Bob. William follows right behind me.

William

"There is another marking," I say, pointing at a tree marked with a red and white arrow.

We have not yet reached Tom and Noah. They might have followed the more significant road. If not, they are walking this way as well, but with Noah's speed. Nevertheless, they are giving Iris and me some alone time. I am glad that we decided to go this way. It is almost like hiking in a jungle. A very steep jungle. It has been going up, up and up for at least thirty minutes, so both Iris and I feel pain in our legs and feet. Bob does not seem to mind, of course. He still roams around us, happily sniffing everything. Despite the pain, I enjoy walking alone with Iris. Being just the two of us probably makes me just as happy inside as Bob looks on the outside. We have been talking and having fun all the way, almost like we have known each other for years. Not much awkwardness, though we have not had any real eye-contact nor physical contact, which makes it easier to stay focused on the conversations. I notice that Iris sounds tired.

"This is a good spot for a five minute break," I say as we reach a couple of big rocks.

We have been searching for a proper place to have a break for the last ten minutes, but only now something came up.

"It's perfect," Iris says. "My feet are killing me."

She drops her backpack on the ground and throws herself down on one of the rocks. I do the same, finding my seat on the opposite one. We both immediately untie our boots and take them off, and I can instantly feel the fresh wind going through my socks and cooling my feet. It's such a refreshing feeling after having my feet trapped inside the sweaty boots for hours. I notice that Iris is barefoot. Well, she is an Icelandic girl, after all. Being barefoot is too cold for me, so I better keep my socks on. I find some crackers from my pack and give a few to Bob who almost swallows them whole before I put one in my own mouth and ask Iris to have one. She has already opened a bag of raisins and gives me a friendly *no*. As she shakes her head, I notice a spark of light coming from her neck. It's the necklace with images of her parents. I have been thinking a lot about her story of losing her parents. I feel like wanting to know the rest of it. The details that might make me understand her better. I can not force it out of her, and I do not *want to* force it out, for that matter. But asking will hopefully not hurt.

"Iris," I begin. "Your Mother. Can I ask what kind of cancer she got?"

She automatically grabs the necklace and holds it tight.

"Of course, Will," she replies and gets herself ready for some explanation. "Well, my mother had different health issues for a long period. She didn't really like doctors, so she just kept ignoring it, saying that she would heal by living healthy and happy. Only when she started having trouble focusing on daily tasks, and at the same time lost some mobility in her right arm, she went to the doctor. They scanned her and found a large tumor in her brain. They told her that she only had a few weeks left. It was horrible. She lived for two months, though. Two happy months."

Iris does not seem as affected by telling me this now, as when she talked about her parents last night. I, on the other hand… Already fighting to keep in tears.

"Are you okay, Will?" she asks.

Okay, I might make weird faces when trying to look

tough.

"Yes, sorry, Iris. I am just sad to hear about this," I say.

"It's okay. I've been going through everything so many times in my mind. I have accepted the facts again and again. I'm just glad to let it out on you."

She smiles at me, half teasing, half serious. It eases me to know that she *wants* to tell me this, and is not feeling like she *has to*, just to be kind to me.

"What about your father?" I ask after some consideration.

She thinks for a moment and puts her bag of raisins back in her pack.

"My father…" she begins. "My father had some health issues as well. But they were suppressed when my mother got sick and the focus was on her. He couldn't handle the thought of losing the love of his life. I often heard him crying in the nights, yet he always managed to stay positive when I was around. One day he got a call from the doctors. They told him that his wife was dying, and that he had to come immediately to say goodbye. I didn't have my phone near me that day. When I saw his eight missed calls, it was already too late. He drove too fast in his car, didn't see the traffic light change…"

"…and he died in the crash," I find myself interrupting silently.

Both Bob and Iris send me surprised looks. Iris' look is most likely from having me interrupting her. Bob is probably confused about my tone, hoping that I was talking to him.

"Well, exactly. I'm glad that you listen," Iris says smilingly, this time like she means it entirely.

I try my best not to feel embarrassed by interrupting her in the middle of telling me this. I have to focus, but a million questions pop into my head at the moment.

"You mentioned that you had accepted the facts multiple times," I say. "But are you not angry about this happening to you? Losing both of your parents so sudden?"

She shakes her head.

"Most of the people I have talked to get angry on my behalf. I *was* angry at the world at first, thinking that wasn't fair. I cursed at God so many times, even though I'm quite sure that he, or she, doesn't exist, just to be sure that if he for some reason does exist, he's a complete idiot for letting this happen. My family and I didn't deserve this. We were never evil or did anything wrong..." she says.

She pauses and inhales, calming herself down.

"Anyway, after thinking everything through, I concluded that being angry wasn't going to do me any good. It wouldn't bring back my parents. I made this necklace and promised myself that whenever I would think of the loss, I would look at it and focus on the good times we had together and how good people they were. Even though I don't truly believe in spiritual stuff, I somehow feel the presence of their souls in this necklace. When you found it last night, it was like a surprise party. I feared that I forgot it at home, especially as it's the only object I own to which I'm attached. It made me so happy to have them with me again. I know it sounds weird," she says.

I get up from my rock and move to hers to sit down next to her. Carefully I put my arm around her and press her against me. Somehow it just feels like the right thing to do.

"It does not sound weird, Iris," I tell her. "Not at all."

She puts her head on my shoulder, and we sit in silence for a while. Everything is tranquil around us. Even the light wind that was before is gone.

"I miss them," she says silently. "They were such loving people. So open-minded. Friends with everyone around them."

Another moment of silence. Silence seems to be the best reply.

"The tumor in my mother's head made her delusional and confused. But it also made her honest. I couldn't believe that either of my parents could be more honest than they were before that, but she suddenly just said her thoughts out loud. Sometimes literally all of her thoughts were spoken. One day she told me about things that she never got to do. Things that she always *wanted* to do, but never did. Places that she always *wanted* to see, but never took herself. She told me about how she regretted the days and the periods of repetition. Going to work and getting home all tired. She was not ready to leave this world. She hadn't finished what she came for. She told me that she was so happy to have me and my sister. So happy to have met my father. So happy for hanging out with us after coming exhausted home from work. But so sad that she and my father didn't take us to see more places, or didn't have the energy to do fun things with us away from home in general. I tried to tell her that she and my father were always good at taking us to exciting places during the holidays. I told her how perfect she had made my life and how thankful I am. I said to her that she shouldn't regret anything. I reminded her that she had already done more and seen more than most people, but she just started being sad for those people. She wished that these people would realize that they should live their lives *now*. She cried and got frustrated when she told me about how sad it is that people save up money to retire, as she did herself. *'Why don't people use the money and time now and not when it's too late? Why didn't I do that myself?'* "Iris says.

She pauses and thinks for a moment.

"Oh, I'm talking much," she continues. "What I'm trying to say is that she inspired me to live in the moment. You never know when it's too late to realize your dreams. My dream is simply to be happy all my life, so I focus only on positive things when thinking of my parents. Life is short, and sometimes it's shorter than you expected. So there's no need to walk around being angry. I would just regret that someday, you know," she says.

I rarely hear such an inspiring and emotional speech. I am still out of words, so I let the silence do the talking for another moment.

"Did you fall asleep, William?" Iris suddenly says, removing her head from my shoulder.

"What? No, I'm… I just…" I mumble, still not sure what to say.

"I'm just kidding," she continues. "People usually don't know what to say in emotional conversations like these. They don't want to say wrong or hurtful things. And trust me, I know the feeling myself."

A little relieved, I finally find some proper words in my mouth.

"Yeah, it *is* hard finding words," I say. "You have been through a lot. You have so much life experience. For me, I…"

Bob suddenly raises his head, letting out an interrupting wonderingly sound. He looks alarmed. Getting up on his paws, he sprints up the path until he is gone. Iris and I glance at each other and instantly get up, put on our boots and packs and start running after him. After a minute of running, we reach the hilltop, stop abruptly and stare down at a bigger road a hundred meters in front of us. Bob is running towards a couple of walking backpackers.

"Is that…?" Iris mumbles.

We continue running. Bob already reached the backpackers who greet him happily. Yep, it is clear now. Noah and Tom. They must have taken the bigger road. I guess we made some kind of steep shortcut then. Finally, we reach them as well, both of us trying to catch our breaths.

"Where did you come from?" Tom asks. "And what's up with the untied laces?"

Iris

After finishing that delicious meal, I'm delighted that we decided to stay in this village instead of continuing to the planned one. It would only be an hour of hiking from here to our intended sleeping destination, but we all ended up being exhausted. Also, the owner of this village stopped us and asked if we wanted a free cup of tea or coffee, and who can say no to that? It's not actually a village. It's only what people around here officially call *tea houses*. Here's a small restaurant building, a small accommodation building and a small private home for the owner. It feels like a small, cozy village, placed in a beautiful valley surrounded by mountain trees. On top of that, we're the only ones here, so it's nice and quiet. In other words: it's the perfect conditions for a group of tired people.

The owner, an elderly man who calls himself *Baldeep*, told us about a big group of Chinese people passing by his tea house just before we arrived. We told him that they were probably Malaysians and not Chinese, and he couldn't stop laughing. I think he's happy to have some company. His tea-house is only a tiny dot on the map, so I could imagine that there's not a lot of people who plan to stay here, even though it's a great place.

While having our free cup of tea and coffee, Baldeep showed us a spiritual tattoo on his back, aligned with his spine, and told us about legends of magic and powerful gods. He told us about myths that were spoken in the temples that he worked in before moving up here with his brother to build the tea house. His brother died last summer, but Baldeep often sees him in his dreams. "There's *a link between our souls,"* he said. *"The energy of my brother is translated into dreams."* I could listen to his stories all night, but he had to go to bed. He has an appointment with his brother, he informed us happily. Then he told us to just close the door to the restaurant building when we left for sleeping in the accommodation building. Nobody would come to steal from him, so locking up the place is unnecessary. People around here are scared of him, fearing that he will make a curse upon them if they do him wrong, he said chortlingly while leaving the restaurant. What a sweet, elderly man.

"Now *I'm* ready to sleep," I finally tell the guys. "The toothbrush can wait till the morning."

They all agree. We stack our plates and move to our room, yawning all the way there. Noah and Tom enter, but William stops me at the door.

"I think you are forgetting to invite someone inside," he says with an evil smirk on his face.

I forgot everything about that! I turn my head and find Bob. He is still lying in front of the restaurant house, watching us with sleepy dog eyes. Well, I'm not the one to bail out on a dare.

"Bob, come here!" I yell clapping on my knees.

He lifts his head and stares curiously at me. I repeat my call, and he jumps up and runs up to me. With some convincing, we get Bob inside the room.

"Ehm, what is Bob doing in here?" Noah asks as he discovers that our new companion is happily sniffing everything in the room.

"He will protect Iris from being cursed by Baldeep," William giggles.

I guess that William is waiting for me to bail out at any

moment, so I take off my thin sweater and warm pants before slipping into my sleeping bag.

"Come here," I call out to Bob, lightly bouncing my hand on the foot-end of the bed.

He looks at me like I'm crazy. Again I try to repeat my call, but he just keeps staring, clearly not understanding the odd situation. I hear that the guys are finding the scenario funny.

"It's okay, Bob. I know you haven't slept in a bed before, but this is your big chance," I tell him while doing another round of hand bouncing.

Nope, doesn't seem to work. Bob sneaks to the corner of the room to lie down there instead. I check to see if William is going to help me out with completing the dare.

"Okay, we can not force Bob to sleep with you, so it seems that you will have your bed alone tonight anyway," he says.

"What a shame," I say, putting myself longer into the sleeping bag.

I pick up my pencils and paper album from the floor. I will have to finish this drawing before being able to sleep.

"Goodnight," I tell the guys and start drawing.

- Day 3 -

William

Baldeep enters the dining building with a wooden tray and places it on the table. On it is a pot of "morning coffee" and five cups, which he hands out to us one by one. Also, there are five plates with large, puffy flat-breads called *gurung bread,* which he cooked in his private kitchen. When we asked him what he would recommend for breakfast, he suggested this right away. Noah and Tom ordered them with melted cheese on top. I am trying the honey and salt version that Baldeep is having himself. Iris sticks to an oil and salt version. I even saw that Baldeep made a cheese version for Bob as well, throwing it to him before entering the dining building. Our friendly host hands out our plates and finds a seat for himself. It is kind of him to have breakfast with us like this.

"Bon appétit," he says after we are all done filling our coffee cups.

I take a bite of the warm bread. Again I am amazed by how tasteful the food is, which these Nepalese mountain people make. I have never tasted anything like this. It is not healthy for sure, but we need energy for walking, so it is just perfect. I glance around to see Noah, Tom and Iris having the same glow of amazement in their eyes. As we did not drink our coffee yet, people are just too tired to express themselves with words, I believe.

"I'm glad you like it," Baldeep says with a proud smile.

"It's amazing, Baldeep," Iris replies for all of us.

As we went to bed early last night, we decided to get up even earlier than usual this morning. I look at my watch: it is only 5.30am and still dark outside, and I am sure that the darkness influences our current tiredness. Baldeep is fresh and energized. He told us that he is used to getting up at 4 am, to enjoy the silence. Then he naps for a few hours in the middle of the day before having new guests, if any guests show up that is.

Iris clears her throat.

"Do you have any more stories about legends or myths from the temples?" she asks Baldeep.

He takes a sip of his coffee. Then a bite of his gurung bread, giving himself good time with the chewing before answering the question.

"I do indeed," he finally says. "Have you heard about the Royal Massacre?"

None of us says anything.

"It seems not," he continues. "You see, Nepal was once a kingdom. Actually, we were until 2008, but that's another story. Seven years before that, nine members of the Nepali Royal Family were shot and killed, including the king and queen. To make it worse, it happened in their own residence, and there have been circulating many rumors about who the killer was. Most rumors say that the murderer was the king's son, the crown prince. He was also shot, probably by himself, and died a few days after. However, some of the traveling monks I've met, believe that the real killer is still alive. Or that he is still habiting this world, to be exact."

Baldeep takes a suspense-generating pause. He takes a sip of coffee, bites a piece of his gurung bread, and chews it slowly before swallowing. He is a great storyteller and for sure knows about teasing suspense tricks.

"So…" he finally continues. "The monks believe that the

real killer is, in fact, the spirit of an ancient monk called Bandhul, who possessed the crown prince and killed the members of the royal family. Bandhul, an ancient monk filled with anger and hatred against the royal family, who's ancestors kept him imprisoned for performing what they called black magic. He finally got his revenge, knowing that such a massacre would help in ending the era of the royal kingdom. His evil spirit lives on through possessed people. If the possessed person dies, his spirit will die as well, which is why he left the crown prince deadly wounded and not dead. He needed to find another host to possess before the prince would turn over."

Baldeep gives us another suspense pause, grabbing for his cup. But Iris won't let him do that this time.

"So did he find another host?" she asks, eager to hear the end of the story.

Baldeep puts down his cup.

"Indeed…" he says silently. "Indeed he found a new host. An unknown backpacking traveler, innocent as can be, just passing by. The possessed backpacker fled to the mountains, camouflaged between all other backpackers. Nobody knows for certain who the backpacker is or if the spirit of Bandhul has found new hosts."

Baldeep takes his teaspoon from the table and stirs his coffee.

"Well, the rumors tell, that the ghosts of the nine royal victims are on a never-ending hunt for the spirit of Bandhul. They are led by the ghost of the real crown prince, on a quest for revenge. The legend says, that they kill *one* random backpacker in the Nepalese mountains each night, hoping that one day, the victim will be the one possessed by the ancient monk, whose spirit will then die with the backpacker," Baldeep says almost whispering creepily now. "So if you listen closely at night, you might hear the screams of the vengeful ghosts. And if you do, there is nothing you can do, but hope that you are not their next victim."

All of a sudden, he slams his hands onto the table, making everything on it jump. It creates such a loud sound that all of us jump in our seats as well.

"Aaand, now you're awake!" he says with loud laughter.

We can not help but agree with him. I surely feel awake now, and realize that the sun is rising outside, spreading a violet light which makes the valley outside look like a fairytale forest. I can even hear a few birds that started their morning twittering.

"Are you going to visit the Jhinu Danda hot spring today?" Baldeep asks.

I remember reading about that, but have not yet discussed it with the group. It was supposed to be a surprise when we arrived in Jhinu Danda: the village in which we were initially supposed to stay.

"Ah, yes, the hot spring. I think we will make time to go there, now that we are up early," I reply.

I receive curious stares from the guys.

"I will tell you about it on the way," I inform them. "It is not far from the next village."

Baldeep eats the last of his gurung bread and drinks his coffee before we ask if we can buy some bottles of water for today's hike like we did the previous day.

"Oh, I'm sorry," he says. "Selling plastic bottles is not allowed up here in this part of the mountain. It's an environmental thing. We don't want plastic bottles lying all around.

We are not allowed to burn wood either. We need to protect nature. Anyway, didn't you bring any bottles of your own?"

Noah, Tom and I read about this from home, so we did, of course, bring our own expensive hiking water bottles.

"Ehm… I'm afraid not," Iris says. "Wait, I'll be right back."

She runs out of the dining house and into our room before coming back with two crumpled one-liter plastic bottles that she bought yesterday.

"Well, I already crumpled them and put them in the trash, so I hope they still function," she says, trying to uncrumple them as good as she can by blowing air into them.

"Good, we can check for leaks. Crumbled plastic bottles usually work fine," Baldeep says. "From now on, all the water that you will find is boiled and filtered water."

He picks up a jug of water from another table and pours some into our empty coffee cups.

"Think of this as the wine of the house. Taste it, and if you like it, you can have more," he says.

We play along with him and taste the water like you would taste wine in a restaurant before buying it. It tastes like normal water, though.

"What a remarkable blend of water. You can clearly taste the fresh notes of pure minerals. Can we buy some of that please?" Noah asks.

We find our bottles and Baldeep fills them with his filtered water. Luckily Iris' bottles are still functional and do not leak. Baldeep tells us that he will be in Kathmandu for a wedding in two weeks, so if we are there at that time, we should see him. He gives us the address of his cousin's place, where he will stay himself, so that we can find him there. We pay him for the food and accommodation, and leave a big tip in our room as well as a handwritten note saying:

—

As compensation for protecting us against
THE EVIL SPIRIT OF BANDHUL.

Thank you for the stories and hospitality.
See you in Kathmandu, Baldeep.

-Tom, Noah, William & Iris.

—

We say our goodbyes to Baldeep, put on our packs, give Bob a petting, and start walking. We have a long day of hiking ahead of us.

Iris

I examine the stairway to the hot spring. It's going downward forever. We've already been climbing downstairs for ten minutes and have no idea how far we have left. The stairway keeps turning, blocking the view to the bottom. What I fear is the fact that we will have to do the climb back up again to get back on the trail so we can reach today's sleeping destination. I cross my fingers that the hot spring will be worth it. Also, I hope that relaxing in the warm water will remove some of the pain I feel today. I try to touch my shoulder gently. Ouch! It's been a while since I felt pain like this. I hate it! I hate being reminded of things I just want to forget.

"Finally! Here it is," William suddenly says.

That was unexpected. We take off our backpacks, which we were stupid enough to bring in the first place. We didn't expect the hot spring to be so far away.

A guy comes running towards us and wants to sell us tickets to get into the water. There's nobody else around, so I guess we will have to trust that this man is a legit, official ticket seller, and not a random guy tricking money out of us. Anyway, we pay him the small price he demands, and he hands us five handwritten tickets, which is just a slip of paper with a number on it. I tell him that he probably made a mistake, and gave us one too many tickets, as we only paid for four. He shakes his head and points on us, one after one. Tom, Noah, William, me and then Bob. Then a thumbs-up.

"Aw, you gave us a free ticket for Bob," I say to him. "Look, Bob, the nice man gave you a dog ticket."

I show the ticket to Bob, who sniffs it and produces a small sneeze, which results in awkward giggling from all of us. The friendly ticket seller gestures that we can get into the hot spring now. The hot spring is made as a square pool built of stones, where warm water is running into it from a stone pipe. Natural hot water which comes somewhere from the ground. A light mist is laying on the surface of the water, making it look very cozy.

"Well, I'm ready to get in," Noah says, starting to take off his clothes.

All of the guys strip immediately, and I realize that they are going to bath in their underwear. I spot a couple of small plastic changing-rooms, yet, I figure that I will use my underwear as well. I'm not the one to kill the underwear mood. Within a split-second, my clothes are on the ground as well, and I can sense that the guys are doing a visual inspection of me. Some people would call it creepy, but I don't blame them. Curiosity is a good thing. To be fair, I set off my own inspection. Noah and Tom: average non-muscular young-man bodies, I would say. William, on the other hand; For some reason, William offers what appears like quite a well-trained body. Anyway, enough inspection for now.

We all move to the edge of the water. I dip a toe into it. It's warm. Then my whole foot gets in. Perfectly warm. One moment after and we're all floating around in the pleasing, misty water, except Bob of course. The relaxation begins. I close my eyes and enjoy the moment. I listen to the birds in the trees and the water from the stone pipe falling into the pool. The memorizing sounds and the temperated water puts me in a meditative state. I think back on my childhood when having fun with my sister and my parents. I picture us going on a trip to see the geysers near Reykjavik. The first time my parents showed me Northern Lights was on that same day.

My mother made sandwiches, which we ate while watching the bright stars and those vibrant Northern Lights. I have always remembered that as the best day of my life. I'm often in conflict with myself, if already having had the best day of my life sounds depressing. But to be honest, it makes every other day easier to enjoy. I don't have to chase the new best day of my life. I never have high expectations. Small things make me happy because I know that small things are enough. I rather want every day to be *good* than having this *best* day and some dull *preparing-the-next-best-day* days, which might end in disappointment. No expectations, no disappointments. Without expectations there are only surprises.

William coughs, halfway pulling me out of my meditative state. I close my eyes again, and for some reason, my thoughts go to him. How does *he* feel about *his* past? How is it to live on another continent and having parents from different continents as well? Personally, the idea of having a part of my family in Asia, whom I could visit, makes me excited. It might not be that exciting when you're actually in the situation and have been in it your whole life, but still.

William said that he has only been in Vietnam once. I wonder how much William's parents have affected who he is today. When I compare us, we're actually very different from each other, exactly like our parents where. We are somehow reflections of our parents. My parents always gave me the freedom to do whatever I wanted to do. To go wherever I wanted and to be whatever I dreamed of being. William's parents are both lawyers, who expect him to be a lawyer as well. From what I have understood, they have never given him the option of following his own dreams. His path was always chosen. It makes sense that he gets nervous when being outside his comfort zone. Well, most people do, but he gets more than *nervous*. He gets *scared* or even *terrified*. My first experience with him was seeing him scared in the airplane to Kathmandu. So cute. And to be honest, it's brave to end up in the situations in the first place. Even though he gets scared, at the end of the day, he is tougher than those "cool" people who claim not to be scared of anything. Those people rarely have to face their fears. Facing fear is a tough job. Being scared and overcoming the fear is much cooler than just doing scary things without feeling it. I guess I'm kinda jealous. I have always been one of those "cool" people, but I never felt like it. I have never been proud of it. My comfort zone has gradually been enlarged throughout my whole life, so I have only had to conquer small scary situations all the time. When the scariest part of my life happened to me, I had no idea what to do with my fear. I had never faced this much fear. The fear of losing the two people I love the most in the whole universe. At that point, I wished that I was one of those people who often struggle to find the strength to overcome anxiety; one of those people who know how to control the fear a lot better than me. And when my fear turned into sorrow, I had no idea how to overcome that either. Not until I realized what my mother said to me on her deathbed. I should *live in the moment. Happily.* I tried so hard to learn about overcoming fear and sorrow. Feelings are so hard to control. When I learned about my secret, I was both broken and relieved. It restarted my feelings of fear, but it made me learn about *time.* There's not enough time in the world to do everything. You have to choose wisely, how you want to spend your life and for what experiences you want to trade your time. My new choice was to not focus on my painful feelings and emotions, but focusing on living in the moment. So I hid my feelings and never learned about control. The control that William finds every time he faces his own fear. He would probably think the opposite. We would be a good match if things were different.

Someone pokes me on my shoulder. William!

"Iris? Are you awake?" he giggles. "We need to get going. We have a long way in front of us still."

Confused, I sit up in the water. How long have pasted? The pain in my body is gone, but I feel sleepy from the relaxation. I could easily sleep for hours now, but as William said, we have to get going.

William

No, no, no!

Is this for real? I look at the others. They seem cool. How can they be cool about this? I take a step forward towards the bridge. Beneath it is a deep drop into a broad valley with a narrow dried out river, which makes everything appear dead and lifeless. A rush of nervousness runs through my stomach, and of course, a couple of bright, colored sparkles appears in the distance. I can not believe that we have to cross this. It is made of nothing but thin steel-wires and wooden planks, that is it. It is way too long and narrow. How will this ever hold us? I keep picturing the bridge snapping and throwing us down into certain death. Already when just standing at the edge, I notice the bridge swaying crazily. I am sure that the bridge will swing 360 degrees like an amusement ride once we reach the middle.

Deep breath, William.

Bob is watching us, probably waiting for us to take the first step. He knows about this bridge. How many it has killed. He knows about it being a death trap for unlucky people like me. Even if nobody has died here yet, I am certain that I will be the first one. Would it be crazy to give up and return? Of course, it would.

I take another small step towards the bridge, and I suddenly feel a wind punching me in my back. The evil spirit of Bandhul is pushing me to my death! More sparkles appear in the air around me. Stop it, William!

"Well. Let's go," Iris says and starts walking.

Tom and Noah follow her right away. Even Bob is okay

with just entering this deathtrap. Well, I guess that I can do this as well then. I move to the beginning of the bridge and put my foot down on the first plank. It seems to be stable. Then my other foot goes to the next plank. Deep breath. My first foot to the next plank. Deep breath. More sparkles. Next foot to next plank. Breath. Sparkles. This will take forever. I have to focus on something else. I check how the group is doing: almost halfway, with Iris still in the lead. *Iris!* I should try to appear strong and brave when she looks back at me. She will be my focal point. I take another step forward and try to think back a few hours on the moment in the hot spring; Iris in the water. Iris, swimming around only in her underwear. I have never been a physical person, but seeing her like that awoke something in me. The few girls I have dated in the past were technically a bit overweight, but I never saw that as a problem at all. I found them very attractive. Iris is no photoshopped supermodel either, yet she is the most beautiful person I have ever seen in my entire life. It fits her sweet, mysterious free-spirited character perfectly. To be honest, I believe that I would be interested in that girl no matter how she looked. I might even blame her personality for being the cause that I find her so beautiful, who knows. She is just… amazing.

Shit!

I suddenly find myself flying. I tripped! This is my death coming!

Death!

The sound from my body hitting the planks on the bridge awakes me from my panic. Sparkles fly in all directions before disappearing in tiny explosions. I did not die yet. I feel the bridge wobbling and swinging. Did my slamming body break a wire? Will the bridge collapse? In confusion, I manage to get up on my knees, feeling the weight of my backpack, heavier as ever before. I see the group coming running back for me. That might explain the bridge's movement. Something wet drops onto my hand. I look down and expect to see a drop of sweat, but my hand is soaked in blood. Blood is literally raining from my nose. I notice a slight pain, which makes me fear if I broke it. Oh no, my skull might have fractured up into my brain!

The blood might be coming from my brain!

William, relax! Deep breath. I feel Tom grabbing me, asking if I am okay. He puts a cloth on my nose and tells me to hold it there to stop the bleeding. As I do so, the guys lift me to stand on my legs and carefully walk with me. Why are they so brave? They fear nothing. I honestly wished that I had that courage, being able to do anything. No thinking, just doing. I should stop over-thinking everything. I should stop planning and researching everything and instead just take things as they come.

On the other hand, I also feel good with the safety of being prepared. I just wished that I was just a tiny bit less anxious about things. That would at least give me a little more hope of ever impressing Iris. She does not want a guy like me. If only I were strong enough to trash my feelings for her, only seeing her as a friend, I would not have to try and impress her all the time. But the image of her in that hot spring keeps popping up in my head now. This beautiful girl who was lying silently in the water, with her blond hair floating around her like an angel. In my memories, I see holy light glowing from the water around her. Music plays in my head as well when replaying the scene. It is like a fairy tale. She is an angelic, happy fairy.

"William, are you okay?" Iris asks me, snapping with her finger.

I realize that we have crossed the bridge already. I sit on a rock, still holding the cloth on my nose, staring into her deep blue eyes. I could not be more okay.

Iris

I empty my last bottle of water while waiting for William to finish inspecting the map. We already travelled a long distance now, so I guess it we are near.

"We should reach our destination any time soon," William says and folds the map.

We start moving again. I'm happy that William is okay now. For a moment, I was afraid that he broke his nose or got a concussion. The poor guy seemed so confused. Anyway, he's alive, and the bleeding stopped ten minutes after the fall, so I guess he will survive. Bob, on the other hand, has been acting weird ever since. It's like he is afraid that William will trip over his own feet again, so he keeps focusing on William to check if he is okay. It's lovely. It makes the mood happy like a fairytale where humans and animals communicate with nothing but pure love. Or something like that.

I put my hands to some backpack-straps that hang near my armpits. I found that they perfectly fit my thumbs, making my arms dangling all relaxed. For some reason, this feels like a great way of walking when I'm in a good mood. I make a little happy walking-skip.

"Hey, what do you think is the thing with Bob?" I ask the group.

They look at me weird, which they, for some reason, often do when I speak.

"I mean…" I continue. "What is his story? Who sent him? What is his epic purpose in the world?"

They finally seem to realize what kind of conversation I'm trying to start.

"I'm sure his purpose is to guide and protect us," Tom

says. "He was sent by the spirits of our Nepali ancestors."

"He is protecting us from…" Noah interrupts.

We all know what he is about to say, but it doesn't stop him from trying to make somewhat a weird zombie-move and what should most likely be a creepy voice.

"*The evil spirit of Bandhul!*" he completes the sentence.

Bob suddenly freezes as the sentence is said. He gives Noah a frightened look.

"It seems like Bob understands human language," William says. "Maybe he *is* the spirit of Bandhul, just waiting for the right moment to devour us all."

He puts a hand down to pet Bob, who is instantly cheered up again.

"You better take that back, William," Noah says. "Bob might be a magical dog who grants us wishes if we protect him and show that our souls are clean."

"Ah, yes! Sorry, Bob, I was just joking," William excuses.

"Actually," I add. "I think that Bob ran away from home. Away from his crazy owner in Denmark, when he found that Danish people are all robots, which scared him. Then he took the first flight away from there toward Thailand so that he could get drunk at a full moon party with pretty thai-dogs. However, the plane crashed on the way. Bob managed to get himself out of the plane with a parachute, yet the remaining people in the plane survived and were taken as hostages from alien people. Now Bob is trying to hang out with human people, to see if he can learn our language and one day be able to explain how to save the survivors of the plane. Just then, Bob will become a real hero. Right, Bob?"

Bob returns me a happy bark, which makes us burst into laughter.

"Such a silly story, and yet Bob agrees with you," Tom says. "Bob, I will be honored to teach you to speak human language. Especially if you grant me magic wishes after your mission is done!"

Also, Tom gets a happy bark. I think Bob knows that we are talking about him, and he likes the attention. I'm so glad that we got him as a companion. He is a solid part of the group now.

He suddenly sprints ahead of us. I hint a building on the horizon. Perfect timing, just as my body slowly starts to hurt.

William

I inspect the wooden sign as we enter the village.

-Sinuwa-

2360m.

Nearly two and a half thousand meters above sea level. We are slowly getting somewhere. Also, we are just below the 2400 meters, which is the usual limit of risking getting altitude sickness. I am a bit scared of reaching this point after reading about how fatal altitude sickness can be, but if we take it slow in the next two days, until we reach Base Camp, things should be fine. The base camp is at around 4100 meters, so if only considering the altitude, we are only a little more than halfway there. The altitude has been increasing and decreasing until now, but from here, it should be mostly up-going.

"Namaste, my friends," a woman, with a familiar voice, says as we near a teahouse.

It looks like the Malaysian group is here as well. The talkative woman is standing outside her room, with a cigarette in her hand. It is nice to meet a familiar face again, even though I am not in the mood for one-way conversations. I will suggest that we head for another tea-house in the village.

"You are lucky, my friends. There are exactly four beds left in the whole village," the talkative, Malaysian woman informs. "And it's right here."

Somehow I get a sense from Iris, who is standing right next to me, that I am not the only one being disappointed with the news: we will have to stay with the Malaysians again. Well, if we are lucky, the woman is too exhausted for talking at this point.

A heavily bearded man shows himself from the kitchen house.

"Hello and welcome. I'm Jack," he says and shakes our hands.

He does not look Nepalese at all and has a very British accent. He is a big guy in a loose t-shirt and large shorts. He even wears sandals despite the air being quite cold in this altitude and at this time of day. He finishes his firm handshake. Almost too firm. Ouch.

"Do you want accommodation, lads?" he asks us while giving Bob a gentle handshake as well.

"Yes, please. We heard you had exactly four beds left for us," Tom replies.

Jack turns his head to the talkative Malaysian woman. She nods at him, and he winks flirtingly at her.

"I might hire that woman," he says, smiling. "Now well, yes, I have four beds. I have no four-person rooms, so you will have to do with two double rooms."

Jack shows us our rooms. Without any discussion, Tom and Noah call dips for the first room, which lets Iris and I share the other room. I try to hide my excitement of having a private room with her. The thought of it makes me nervous, but in a good way. However, I know that it will most likely be no different from having Noah and Tom in there too. Nothing will happen between us anyway. It is just the same, but with less snoring. We drop our backpacks in our rooms and go to the kitchen house right away. Jack wants us to taste his *dal bhat*, which he claims to be the best in the entire Annapurna region, even though he is from London and not Nepal. I am excited to see what it is.

Iris

Trying to look eagerly content, I nod at the talkative Malaysian woman who sits in front of me. Her mouth hasn't stopped talking since we entered the restaurant building ten minutes ago. Whenever I give it a try to concentrate on her talking, all I can manage is to stare at her extremely bright red lip gloss that she apparently decided to wear tonight. Besides the talkative woman, it is nice and cozy in here, with candlelights everywhere. Everything is glowing with a warm orange light, combined with the cold blue afternoon light entering from the windows. Unfortunately, the Malaysian group chose to have dinner at the same time as us. Well, they were actually in here first, so it's probably the other way around. We didn't know.

Nevertheless, Jack has a lot of food to prepare all of a sudden. Luckily for him, everybody in here agreed to have his *dal bhat,* whatever that is, so he's only cooking one massive portion of the same meal. *The most significant portion of his entire history*, as he said. I sit next to William who does the same pretending-to-listen nodding as I do. Noah and Tom were lucky to get seats at the other end of the long table. I realize that the talkative woman is waiting for an answer to some question that I didn't hear. I pretend that I couldn't hear it from the noise of the other people in here, putting a hand to my ear.

"How long have you two been together?" the talkative woman asks again.

The question puts a smile on my face. This woman thinks that William and I are a couple. Why wouldn't she? She hasn't seen us apart from each other yet. I open my mouth to tell her the situation, but William gets to answer first.

"We have been together for… what? Almost five years now, right honey?" he asks me with an elbow push.

It takes a moment for me to realize what is going on before I remove my confused face and play along with the joke. It should be better for the curious woman to hear a sparkling romance story than the boring truth, and she will never find out the truth anyway.

"Six years, Will! How can you not know this?" I ask him with an offended tone.

"But… I…" William begins, probably trying to come up with a good reply.

I realize that the talkative woman has a huge, evil smirk on her face. It seems like she likes to watch couple-fights, and I suddenly suspect her to live for drama like this.

"It's our honeymoon," I tell her.

William's hand is on the table, so I put mine on his to make it look real. He instantly grabs hold of mine and squeezes.

"That is right," he says. "I asked Iris' father for her hand a few months ago, and he thought me to be the best son in law that he could ever imagine. I proposed the same evening."

I fight to hold back the smirk that is slowly forming from how absurd this is. I know that it's normal to ask for permission or blessing from the father in some places, but not where I'm from. Second of all, my father wasn't here a few months ago.

"Sorry," I suddenly hear William whisper in my ear.

Aw, he realized his mistake. I give his hand a squeeze to indicate that I forgive him. The talkative woman doesn't know about that either anyway.

"How did you propose?" she eagerly asks William.

He takes good time thinking this time. I'm probably just as curious as the talkative woman, if not more.

"Okay…" he finally begins. "As you know, I was in Iceland visiting her and asking her father for permission. After dinner, I drove her up to this mountain just outside of Reykjavik. What was the name again?"

"Mount Esja," I add, impatient to hear the rest of the story.

"Mount Esja, yes," he continues. "I knew that on this particular day, there would be a good chance to see the Northern Lights, so I wanted us to get away from the city's light pollution and to be completely alone. Mount… Esja… was the perfect place. We sat there, just watching the Northern Lights for hours. Long story short, she said yes and we got engaged."

What? I find myself feeling a little disappointed about not hearing how the actual proposal went. A romantic story, though.

"You forgot to mention the wine you put into me first, to make sure that I would say yes," I tell him.

He looks at me.

"But the wine wasn't for you, dear," he admits. "It was for me. To make sure I would find the courage to propose."

I give him a silly elbow punch. The acting is maybe getting a bit too real.

Jack shows his head from the kitchen. Food time. He brings plates to all of us, two at a time. William and I release our hand-holding as Jack puts down our meals in front of us. *Dal bhat*: rice, thick lentil porridge, something looking like yellow potato curry, some spinach-stuff, something red and spicy and a slice of flatbread. It's much more than I expected. Jack was confused when I told him that I haven't had this

Dal Bhat meal yet and that I never heard about it until now. Apparently, people in Nepal eat it all the time. Especially in the mountains. For sure, it's not fancy, but there's a lot of it, and everything turns silent as we all start eating simultaneously. It's so tasteful! Everything in these mountains has a unique, fresh taste. They most likely use fresh, locally produced vegetables. A thing that I'm not very used to in Iceland as the transportation time removes the taste of the food.

The silence stays for the whole meal. Now that we've eaten up, I feel the fatigue building up. Even the talkative woman seems too tired for conversation now, and it's time for the Malaysian group to go to bed. We'll do the same.

"Goodnight you two," the talkative woman says as she gets ready to leave for bed. "Sleep well."

She gives us a smarmy wink and leaves the building. Either she knows about our acting, or she thinks that *things* are going to happen in the young-people honeymoon-room. Silly woman. I hope the latter. Or I don't hope that things are going to happen. I hope that the reason for the wink was the latter. Never mind. It's time for us to get to bed too. We say goodnight to Jack and leave the restaurant building as well. Outside we see Bob sitting in the dark, with his bowl of food. An empty bowl of course. We pet him goodnight, and he lies down to sleep. I'm glad that he's okay with being alone like that. What a brave dog. William and I say goodnight to Noah and Tom as well. Then we enter our room.

William

I look up from my e-book. Iris is sitting against the wall on her bed, drawing. The room is lit up only by our two camping lanterns, so it's dark and cozy in here. When we entered, we briefly joked about the act that we made with the talkative woman, before we went to our beds. I was about to get ready to sleep when I realized that Iris was not going to do that just yet. She wanted to draw. Something made me pick up my e-book for the first time on this trip. Perhaps to continue the small hope that something *will* happen in here. There is an unusual tension in the atmosphere when being alone just the two of us. At least for me, that is. I want to talk to her, but I am afraid of being annoying and just disturbing her drawing. I have been opening my mouth to speak several times now, yet every time I do so, I regret and shut it again. What the heck, I guess it does not hurt to give it another try.

"What are you drawing?" I finally ask her.

Iris replies without removing her eyes from the paper.

"You will see when we reach Base Camp in a couple of days," she says, still concentrated on the drawing.

She puts a hand to her shoulder. I have seen her do that before. I wonder if she is hurt. I did not see anything painful on her skin in the hot spring, though I did not look *that* closely. I am not a pervert. Or am I slowly reaching the limit of being a pervert when not being able to take my eyes from her? All of a sudden, she glances up from her drawing, and in a panic, I forcefully look back down on my e-book. This is stupid. She saw me staring at her. In an attempt to save myself from humiliation, I raise my head again, smiling.

"Hey, do you have any photos of your family with you?"

she asks and puts down the drawing block.

I pick up my wallet and take out a small picture of my family and me posing in front of our house.

"Yeah, actually I do," I reply.

Iris immediately throws her drawing gear on her bed, gets up and jumps over to my bed, sitting next to me. She is sitting close enough that I can smell her hair: a fresh scent of flowers. She takes the picture from my hand and inspects it.

"They look sweet. How old is this picture? You have such long hair," she asks.

"It is only a few months old. I got a haircut just before leaving for this trip," I tell her.

"You look cool," she says, handing me the picture back. "So your parents are lawyers who want *you* to be one as well, but you don't want that. So what *do* you want to be?"

This question is new to me. Nobody ever asked me that. Everybody just assumed that I would become a lawyer like my parents. Even I believed that myself.

"That is one of the reasons why I went on this trip," I tell her. "To somehow find a new start. To figure out what I should do with my life."

She nods.

"That sounds like a fair reason for going on this adventure," she says.

We sit in silence for a moment before I see the hint of a smirk on her face.

"So you're in a rich family?" she asks.

I give her yet another timid elbow push. A lot of these have been given out between us today.

"Yep," I say fake proudly. "But that only means that *my parents* are rich. I never felt their wealth much myself. Only when I had birthdays, I got bigger presents than my friends, but besides that, my parents taught me to work hard for the money myself. I am glad they did, to be honest."

"I am too," Iris agrees. "I wouldn't like to see you as a spoiled kid."

She slams her hands on her thighs and gets up from the bed.

"Sleeping time," she informs while returning to her bed.

Somewhere inside of me, I feel a slight disappointment about this night alone with Iris ending already. But what did I expect?

"Goodnight, Iris," I say.

"Goodnight, Will," she says back.

We get into our sleeping bags and turn off our camping lanterns. Everything becomes dark.

Iris

Darkness and silence. Cold and moisty. Not the ideal sleeping conditions for me. I try to tighten all of my muscles to generate heat to warm up my sleeping bag. I was taught to do that on a tent-trip with my school once, and it works. Get as naked as possible and use energy to warm your sleeping bag. Easy as that. I release the tension and lie on my side to face the wall. Or what should be the wall, but is just total darkness. I listen to the silence. It's been a while since being surrounded by such little amount of noise. It almost results in a lack of pressure in my head. It's scary, yet quite pleasant. I close my eyes, ready to fall asleep.

Wait, what is that?

I roll over on my back and listen. Some strange sound is coming from outside. At first, it sounds like a wolf howl, but the sound doesn't stop, so it's obviously not a howl. It can't be Bob. I listen closely and hear some kind of whistling on top of it. Three tones repeated over and over. What the hell is this? The volume of the sound increases and decreases randomly. Creepiness gets to me. I find myself thinking back on the story that we were told this morning: the story about the evil spirit of Bandhul. My heart starts beating like crazy. I'm suddenly sure that there's more to the world than we can see. Maybe people here know things, and perhaps the story about Bandhul is actually true. Is this the sound of Bandhul coming to kill a backpacker? I slide the rest of my body into the sleeping back. I'm scared.

William

I look into the black space above me. I cannot sleep. The thought of being alone with Iris is haunting me. I want her so badly. She is right there! Forget it. I close my eyes for yet another attempt to sleep. I focus on the weird sound coming from outside. What is that anyway? Could it be wind? The volume has only increased since it started. I find it disturbing, not knowing what it is. I never heard anything like that. Suddenly a loud bump sounds from outside. Then another bump. What is that? I sense some movement coming from Iris' bed.

What the...?!

Someone stands in front of my bed. Is it...? Yes, it is just Iris. What a shock. She gives me a gentle push, making me move closer to the wall, and she lies down next to me, with her sleeping bag pulled up over her body. She lies with her face towards me. What is this? Should I make a move? I roll onto my side, now with my face just in front of hers. I can sense her breathing, but it is too dark to see her. My heart beats from the thought of me making a move. *We are ten centimeters from kissing!* My hand reaches for her face, heart beating like a thunderstorm. I want to feel her soft skin. To caress her elegant libs and go for a kiss. However, I retreat before reaching her. What if she just got scared from the sound? That would make this very awkward.

On the other hand, is this not a good excuse for finding out if she likes me or not? Everybody could misunderstand a situation like this, you know. I slowly move my head toward hers. Touching foreheads is a subtle way of testing if it's a misunderstanding or not. That could either lead to kissing or be excused by doing it half-asleep. Our heads are nearly touching now. She makes a movement. My heart jumps to my throat. I hold my breath to see what the movement brings. Iris exhales and rolls 180 degrees and lies on the other side, with her face away from me. A slight relief hits me, being more relieved than disappointed. My nerves almost could not handle the tension, though I would have liked a kiss. Just a single one. Iris leans back, takes my hand and wraps it around her. She keeps holding my hand, and I squeeze her closer to me. This is probably better.

"Goodnight, Will," she whispers.

Goodnight, Iris.

- Day 4 -

William

Here comes breakfast. Gurung bread again. Yum! It looks and smells delicious. What a wonderful morning. I can not remove the smile from my face. I slept so well this night, waking up early with Iris in my arms. Best morning ever! When her phone alarm rang on her bed, and she had to get up to stop it, I sincerely hoped that she would return to my bed. Well, she did not. Instead, she threw her pillow in my head and told me to wake up, without knowing that I was secretly awake already. It sort of stopped the romance, but also made it less awkward. I would have liked to talk about why she decided to join me in my bed, but I will find a better time for that conversation.

"Good morning, lovebirds," someone shouts from the door behind me.

The talkative, Malaysian woman has entered the kitchen house. It seems that she is the only morning-person in her group. Noah stops chewing his bread and stares confused at the woman. He does not know about the relationship joke, and I imagine that Tom would have the exact same reaction if he had returned from the toilet yet.

"So how did you two sleep?" she asks, giving Iris and me another of her smarmy winks.

Noah moves his confused look to us.

"A perfect honeymoon night," Iris answers with a wink back.

The woman laughs and takes a seat in front of us while Tom enters the kitchen house, returning from the toilet. Noah moves his confused face from us to Tom, like he is searching for an answer. Tom finds his seat and stares back at Noah.

"What is up, Noah?" he asks when he notices the confused expression.

Noah does not reply, but moves his eyes back to Iris and me.

"You never told me about how your wedding was," the talkative woman informs us. "Sorry, I just live for this kind of stories."

I see that Tom figures out the situation immediately and joins the conversation.

"Oh, that was the most amazing wedding I have ever attended to," he answers on our behalf while I try to come up with a good story.

Noah has still not realized what is happening, so Tom helps him out by whispering in his ear. A huge Noah-laughter is released. He says something in French and Tom shushes at him, but with no effect. While the laughter fades to a reasonable level, I start telling my wedding story.

"Africa," I begin and take a bite of my gurung bread. "We had a wedding in Africa. We wanted it to be a small wedding only with the two of us, so we found this small tribe village in Northern Africa, where we became friends with the inhabitants. Actually, we did not plan to get married there, but they offered to do a wedding ceremony for us, and we liked the idea. It was there we met Noah and Tom."

"That's true," Noah interrupts.

The talkative woman looks excited about the story.

"So how was the ceremony?" she asks eagerly, changing focus to Iris.

"It was amazing," Iris replies. "Both of us were

individually welcomed into each of our own new African families like we were adopted. The two families completed the traditional rituals for us, where the families traded two blankets to welcome each other into their families. The two families had actually already merged, as a marriage between the families had already taken place, but they were nice and felt happy to do it again. Anyway, in the evening, there was dancing and a final blood-sharing ritual. We had to put a drop of our blood into each side of a bowl. When the drops met, the spirits of our ancestors would know, that two became one. Then we were officially married."

I am not sure if Iris knows anything about actual African wedding procedures, but this could sound plausible. At least the talkative woman buys the story.

"That is incredible," she comments. "My husband would never do this. He is scared of everything."

She tells this with a cheerful tone, but I sense the seriousness behind it. To be honest, I somehow wish that this wedding had happened for real. That Iris and I were married now and could excite other people with this true story. What happened in our room last night has planted a slight hope in me, even though the reason for her lying with me could still be the scary sounds. What was that anyway?

"Did you hear that weird sound last night?" I ask everybody around the table.

It is probably best to change the subject from our marriage before the truth comes out.

"Yes, it honestly scared me," Noah says.

Tom shakes his head.

"Noah cried like a little baby from that sound. I'm sure there's a logical explanation," he says.

"Indeed there is," our host, Jack, suddenly says, stepping out from the kitchen. "You guys are far from the first people who found the sound weird."

He returns to the kitchen, leaving us without an answer. What is it with people in this mountain? They love stretching things out for suspense.

"Jack?" the talkative woman yells.

"Yes, my darling?" Jack says, sticking his head out from the kitchen.

"Could you please tell us what you know?" she asks in a demanding tone.

"Alright, my love. You see, we are in some sort of a valley. As you know, there are mountains on both sides of this humble village. Somehow the mountain wind creates this hollow sound that you heard last night. Nobody has ever been able to figure out exactly why the sounds appear though. It doesn't sound like anywhere else in the world. I have even had professors and scientists up here, who couldn't explain the sound, other than guessing that the wind somehow is the source. I should brand my little village with this: '*Experience the unexplained, mysterious sound of Sinuwa!*'" Jack suggests.

If this is true, that branding idea is not a bad one. Jack mumbles something and returns to the kitchen while the entrance-door behind me opens, and a short Asian girl with long black hair walks in. Without saying anything, she saunters to the end of the long table and finds a seat. She looks tired. I did not see her at dinner last night. Maybe she went to bed early or came in late. She peeks around the room. Her gaze stops at me. She smiles. I smile back expecting her to remove her eyes from me, but she keeps her gaze. My shyness comes up in me, and I break the eye-contact myself. I am not up for a staring contest. However, I can feel that she keeps staring at me. It does not scare me, but it makes me uncomfortable for some reason.

"Are everybody done eating?" I ask.

"Yep," Iris concludes. "Should we get ready?"

We all agree to leave the kitchen house and get ready for walking.

"It was nice to meet you again," the talkative woman says. "We might see each other again today or tomorrow."

"Definitely. Nice to meet you too again," Iris says while getting up from her chair.

We nod at the Asian girl on our way out. She keeps her eyes locked at me until I am entirely out the door.

Iris

I enter the small public toilet booth but keep the door open to let in some fresh air from outside. As usual, I'm brushing my teeth just before leaving. The guys mocked me at first for using this kind of natural herb toothpaste, but when they saw how cool it was, they suddenly wanted to try it themselves. I press some of the black toothpaste out on my toothbrush before putting the toothbrush in my mouth and looking at myself in the mirror, enjoying how the black toothpaste magically turns to white. I still giggle inside from the memory of the guys' surprised faces when they saw that for the first time.

"Hello there," someone with a cheerful voice says.

It's the Asian girl from breakfast.

"Oh, hey," I mumble with my toothpaste-filled mouth.

The girl gently pushes herself in front of me, rinsing her toothbrush in the sink, even though there's a free toilet booth just next to this one. She backs out and starts brushing her teeth as well, making exaggerated brushing movements. At first, I'm surprised by her weird behaviour, but she offers me an enormous, exaggerated grin and begins brushing the visible side of her front teeth, which she is clearly flashing energetically to me. As I move my head over the sink to spit out some toothpaste, she immediately pushes her way to the sink again and spits just at the same time as me. This girl is crazy. I like it! I keep brushing while taking a closer look at her. She has long, black hair and beautiful black eyes. Her brown, soft skin jacket is a few sizes too big, but it suits her. My best guess would be that she is Japanese. Her age, I would say, around twenty. She most likely appears younger than she is, so twenty years is a fine guess. I spit in the sink and rinse my toothbrush. The girl spits on the ground and stretches out her arm for a handshake.

"I'm Ayame. But you can call me Aya," she says while shaking my hand.

"Hey, Aya. I'm Iris," I greet her back.

She pulls her hand back and put it to her face along with her other hand. She opens her mouth to make an exaggerated surprised-pose.

"No way! Are you for real?" she asks.

I wonder what she means with that, but I tell her yes.

"This is insane!" she says with a mix between a cool and a sweet accent. "*Ayame* means *iris* in Japanese! My name is Japanese Iris! It's like destiny!"

I can't figure out if she is lying or if it's true, but it's a cute story anyway.

"So you're from Japan?" I ask her.

She puts down her hands and tries to act normal.

"Yes! Japanese girl here," she replies. "And you are... Let me guess... Macedonian!"

Macedonian? First time I have ever been guessed to be from Macedonia.

"Nope, I'm from Iceland. Nice guess though," I tell her politely.

She laughs. What is funny about that?

"Sorry," she says. "How's Iceland?"

"Well, it depends," I reply. "If you, like me, are from Icela..."

"Yep yep yep yep," she interrupts.

I can't help but stare amazed at her. I can't figure out this girl. She is a little crazy for sure, but that only makes me even more curious. I already like her a lot.

"You're with those guys?" she asks and nods at the boys. "Where are you going today?"

She flicks her finger against the bristles of her toothbrush impatiently.

"I think William said something about a village called Himalaya," I answer.

I realize that she hasn't removed her eyes from mine the whole conversation. Did she even blink?

"William? Is that the Vietnamese guy?" she asks while still flicking her finger.

I nod.

"Yes, have you met him?" I ask.

"Nope," she replies shortly.

She must have guessed his Vietnamese part from his appearance then. I'm not sure what to do with this girl. We stand for a moment, just watching each other. Then she puts her hand up for a high-five. Yeah, why not. I give her a high-five, but she grabs my hand and holds it still in the air.

"Would you mind if I joined you just for today?" she asks smilingly.

I consider if the guys would be okay with this. Can I make decisions for the group alone? Actually yes, I want her with us. And if she's only joining for a day, the guys can't complain. To be honest, I think they will be happy with some new company.

"Yes, of course, Aya," I tell her. "We'll leave in 20 minutes if you can meet us out here."

William

"Everybody ready?" Tom asks as we all stand outside with our backpacks on.

Bob barks.

"Guess that's a yes," Tom says. "Let's go."

The sun is intense today, which is perfect as the temperature up here is quite low. As Jack told us, we are walking in a mountain valley, with mountain walls on each side. The new girl, Aya, only has a small denim rucksack and kinda dances as she walks, like there is no weight in it. What did she even bring?

"Are you ready for some altitude sickness?" she asks, making a slow pirouette.

"We're taking it slow, so hopefully we won't experience that," Tom replies.

I have the feeling that Tom does not like her. Myself, I find her funny. Her energy level is motivating.

"So, do you have a girlfriend, William?" she asks me out of nowhere.

The immediate question baffles me.

"Ehm, no," I answer shortly, not sure what to say.

"Good," she just comments.

I wonder what this is. I feel Aya's eyes on me, but still, my shyness prevents me from making eye contact. Instead, I pretend to be focused on watching Bob, who is clearly doing good on his own. Aya suddenly runs over to a big rock, which stands tall on the ground, and she hugs it. Noah, Tom, Iris and I look at each other for an answer. Aya is hugging the rock tightly for a while until she lets it go and joins us again without a word. I expect her to explain, but nothing comes.

"So… What was that about?" I ask her since nobody else dares to.

She finds a walking position next to me before answering my question.

"Normally I would do my hugging on trees," she says. "But there aren't many trees at this altitude, so I show my love to the rocks instead. Mountains are dangerous, and I would like to survive the avalanches, earthquakes, snow-storms, hurricanes, lighting-strikes, altitude sickness and whatever can kill you up here. If I show my love to the rocks, they will protect us. Trust me."

She lifts her hand to my head and runs her fingers through my hair.

"You don't want to die, do you, William?" she asks.

Feeling the fingers in my hair gives me unexpected goose-bumps. I get eye-contact with Iris who looks concerned at me. The night with her pops up in my head again, and a huge smile appears on my face, but she just looks away.

"I guess not," I answer Aya without removing my gaze from Iris.

I still have to talk to Iris about last night. I cannot stand it any longer. I need to know if there is anything between us. That settles it! Tonight I will find alone time with her and ask!

"Ow, there's another one!" Aya yells.

She runs to another rock and hugs it. This one is twice as big as her.

"Iris, come, join me!" she yells.

The expression on Iris' face tells me that she was long gone in her own thoughts, while Aya's yelling awoke her, now being present again. Without thinking, Iris runs to the rock as well and gives it a hug from the other side.

"Guys, come on!" Iris shouts to us.

Noah and Tom decline right away. They are having a *Tom & Noah day*, being in their own little world, joking about intern stuff. I take a few steps towards the rock, and Iris moves to make space for me to join in. I try hugging the rock as well. It is actually not bad. I try to squeeze the rock harder, and I realize that Iris has her hand on mine, so I spread my fingers to make space for our fingers to hopefully intertwine. I can not see her face from the rock, but I imagine her amazing blue eyes sparkle from happiness.

I suddenly feel a hand squeeze in between my back and my backpack, and I turn my head to see the arm of an over-sized, brown skin jacket. Aya's hand purposely crawls downwards on my back. What the hell is she doing?

As her hand reaches my butt, I panic and release my grip on both the rock and Iris' hand. I take a step back from the rock in an attempt to get rid of Aya's hand, only to find her standing right in front of me, still with her hand planted firmly on my butt. Her height is too short for me to see her face, but I feel her kissing me on the chests and squeezing my butt before removing herself from me. Then she winks at me and returns to the stony path we are following. I check if Iris saw this, but luckily she is out of sight, hidden from the rock. Is Aya messing with me? I get a fear of Aya destroying things between Iris and me. Things which I am still not sure even exist. William, that is silly. Aya is just having fun. She is a crazy, fun girl. That is all.

"Are you coming, Will?" I hear Iris call from behind the rock.

Iris

Besides the happy input from Aya, I'm not feeling good today. I feel pain, and I'm already exhausted. Adding to that, we have only been on the move for a little less than an hour! Maybe the air pressure has something to do with my mood and fatigue. Thankfully, Aya chose to walk with a speed that I can manage to keep up with today. We just agreed with the boys to meet them at our eating break destination, if we don't catch up. I'm happy about this agreement, as I can walk at my own pace today.

"William is so handsome," Aya suddenly tells me. "I think he wants me."

This information is not really what I expected to hear. Yes, William *is* handsome, but I'm not sure about that last part.

"Why do you think he wants you?" I ask.

She puts her arms up in the air, stretching her whole body.

"Why wouldn't he?" she says. "And if he doesn't want me yet, I will make him want me! Just wait and see!"

I feel my heartbeat accelerating. Not from the exhaustion, but from the thought of Aya and William together. I realize that my feelings for him might be stronger than I thought. When I went to his bed last night, it wasn't because I wanted him, but because I was scared. However, as we lay there, it felt so comfortable. I felt safe and relaxed. I didn't want it to stop when my alarm rang. I wanted to return to his bed and lie there a few more hours, before I was reminded about my situation and how it wouldn't be good for any of us to make things complicated. I never thought about William being with other girls, and it scares me to figure out now, that the thought hurts.

"I had a boyfriend a few months ago," Aya continues. "But I beat him up so hard! Such a jerk! William seems better!"

"Why did you beat him up?" I ask surprised

She picks up a stone from the ground and throws it hard back on the ground before replying. The stone explodes into tiny fractions flying in all directions.

"I caught him cheating on me with another girl!" she says. "At first, I wanted to smash *her* face, but he was closer, so he got the punch. I couldn't blame her either, as *he* was the one with a girlfriend, not her."

I can clearly sense the anger within her. She must surely have liked that boy.

"I'm sorry, Aya," I say. "How long were you together?"

"A couple of years. Well, we weren't actually official," she says. "So maybe I was wrong when punching him in the face. I don't care. He deserved it,"

She chortles. A strange chortle. A combination of a crazily evil and a happy one. While still walking, she takes off her rucksack, zips it open and takes out a small glass flask with some blue liquid inside. She removes the lid and drips a few drops out on her neck. Perfume... It smells like oranges with a twist of cherries, in a quite refreshing way.

"This magic liquid will make boys fall in love with me in a second," she says while replacing the lid and putting the flask back in her rucksack.

"It sure smells delicious," I admit.

Aya's face shows that she enjoyed that comment, and she does a small pirouette.

"Hey, how's it like to be a hippie?" she asks.

It's not the first time someone calls me a hippie. I liked it when I was younger, until I read about what a hippie actually is. I'm no hippie. I don't want to be titled. I just want to be myself and do what makes me feel happy. And yes, maybe my attitude and clothing seem *'hippie'* to some people, but that's just my preference. And I am happy about who I am, hippie-title or not. Anyway, I can go along with it this time.

"It's powerful, man," I say with a slow hippie-like voice.

Aya laughs.

"Seriously, do you ever smoke weed?" she asks.

I begin wondering if Aya is high right now. That could explain some of her behavior, other than just being a bit crazy.

"Ehm, well, I tried it, yes," I admit. "But it's not my thing, to be honest. I like to be in control, you know."

She hums a few tones like she knows what I'm talking about.

"Me neither," she says. "Tried it only once, and it just made me crazy."

Can she be more crazy? Something in me would have loved to experience that. Nevertheless, I'm glad that she's not high right now, after all. People become so distant when doing drugs, yet I'm not against smoking weed. People can do what they want to, as long as nobody is hurt or annoyed by it. So if Aya is *not* high at the moment, I guess that she's just… open-minded then… Or let's call her crazy... in a cute way.

"Hey, a rock!" She yells. "Hugging time!"

William

Break time! Pizza time! We did not have pizza for days. It is time for sure. They lie right there, smoking hot, smelling delicious! The sun is shining bright and provides enough heat to sit outside. I am about to take a bite of my slice before Aya stops me.

"What are you doing?" she yells. "We need to pray our thanks before eating!"

I put my slice back on my plate and see that Noah, Tom and Iris do the same. Then we await guidance from Aya. I do not know anything about Japanese traditions, but I respect that she wants to pray before eating. I would never have guessed her to do it, though. She slams her hands together loudly. The rest of us put our hands together, as well. She then closes her eyes and whispers a lot of unknown words. The words are coming fast and do not sound like how I imagined Japanese. It sounds more like she is calling for a curse. At least it is similar to what I have heard from horror movies. The other guys have their eyes closed as well, so I decide to do the same, but just as I close them, I feel a hand on mine, which makes me reopen my eyes immediately. It is Aya's hand. She still has her eyes closed, so I move my hand away from hers. The whispering of fast-paced words becomes talking, which becomes loud speaking which becomes yelling. I have never experienced prayer like this. On the other hand, the only dinner prayer I have experienced is from thanksgiving, so I am no expert. This is surely something different.

"Guys I'm kidding," Aya suddenly laughs. "Did you seriously believe in this, you freaks?"

She picks up a slice of her pizza, rolls it and fills her

mouth with the whole slice. Bob looks scared at her before putting his head back on my lap. I tell him that everything is okay and give him a piece of meat from my pizza, which he swallows like he never tasted food. Before I get another try to have a slice of my pizza myself, Aya jumps up from her chair, takes my arm and pulls me up from mine.

"I have to speak with you!" she says eagerly.

She drags me to the opposite side of the kitchen house, where the toilets are located. She stops right next to the toilet door and pushes me up against the wall. Everything happens so fast that I do not even realize what is happening. Aya gets on her toes and kisses me while alternately pulling my shirt and pushing me into the wall. She presses her tongue into my mouth. I kinda want to stop her, but something makes me let her continue this. I find my hands around her waist, pulling her closer to me. Her lips are soft against mine. She smells like minty oranges. Both our breaths get heavier for each second. I can not control myself. My hands move up and down her back. I hear a silent moan. She runs her hands down my chest and stomach until she reaches the top of my trousers. What am I doing?

"Aya. No. Sorry, I can not do this," I tell her and gently push her away from me.

I am not that kind of person. I do not have feelings for Aya. It would be stupid to go with a moment of temptation. What if Iris found out about it? That would definitely not be worth it.

"Cool," she replies with a smile. "Let me know if you change your mind."

She runs a hand over my chin and catwalks away in the direction from which we came. I stand for a moment, trying to understand what just happened. A familiar giggle comes from around the corner of the kitchen house.

"What did I just see?" Noah asks. "Are you doing Japanese girls now?"

My heart jumps to my throat. Shit.

"Noah? What are you doing here? I…" I mumble, not really knowing how to escape this situation.

He points at the toilet door.

"Making space for more pizza, if you know what I mean," he replies.

I have to make sure that there are no misunderstandings. Most importantly, that Iris will not know about this. I panic for a second from the thought of Aya telling her.

"Noah, this was not supposed to happen. Please. Let it stay between us," I almost demand from desperation.

He runs his hand over my chin, just as Aya did.

"Don't worry. I won't tell anyone, loverboy," he giggles. "But now I have business to do."

He waddles to the restroom and shuts the door with a slam behind him. I take a deep breath and return to our table on the opposite side of the kitchen house. Please tell me that Aya didn't mention what happened. As I sit down on my chair, Iris' eyes jump to me. Oh, no, no, no, she knows! With a little help from the sun, a drop of sweat appears on my forehead. She opens her mouth to say something. Here we go.

"I didn't know you were such a love guru?" she says.

From her happy mood, she seems to take it very well. I feel like throwing up. Did I just destroy my chances with Iris? I can not find the right words to excuse what I did. Am I even supposed to excuse?

"I…" is all I get to say before Aya interrupts me.

"Yeah, I told Iris about the tips you just gave me for how to get over my ex-boyfriend," she says, giving me a quick wink.

"That was great advice, Will," Iris adds.

"Thank you," are the only words that I manage to find.

I am baffled. Simple as that. Aya did not tell the truth. When I think about it, why would she embarrass herself by explaining that I rejected her? I can not believe that I still might have a slight chance with Iris. Nothing has changed. I get an urge to drag Iris to the toilet and do the same all over with her. Or at least tell her how I feel and ask about her feelings. But I have to control myself. I will ask her tonight as planned. But now it is pizza time!

Iris

So we're back in our formations: the boys in front with Bob, and Aya taking the back position with me. My exhaustion has gotten worse, but knowing that we are more than half-way of today's hike gives me strength. Also, the incredible, open view with icy mountain tops in the horizon is motivating. Aya and I have been talking a lot about the difference between living in Iceland and Japan. We agreed to come visiting each other someday, though I know that I might have promised more than I can keep. She also assured me that she was serious when she said that the name *Ayame* means *iris* in Japanese. When I told her that I am lacking energy today, she handed me a gigantic chocolate bar, which I'm still trying to eat my way through. Even though I don't like her talking about William the way that she does, I like everything else about her.

"Wow, look at that!" she says and points at a Nepalese man coming towards us.

He is carrying three huge backpacks on his back, supported by a strap on his forehead. It seems like he holds a lot of the weight with his head and neck, though he walks with his shoulders hunched. The packs look just as heavy as he looks tired. It must be one of the *porters* that William told me about. The ones who are hired to carry stuff for hikers who then only walk with water and food at daytime. I suddenly feel silly thinking about how exhausted I am myself. I can't imagine how this man must feel, and that he literally lives like that every day. As he comes closer, I see that he's only wearing thin flip flops on his feet. Incredible. I get a tiny bit angry at the people who hired *one* person to carry *three* peoples stuff. I hope that he gets paid well, but I fear that he's not. Aya finds another of her huge chocolate bars and hands it to the porter as he approaches. She realizes that none of his hands are free, so she swoops it into the front pocket of his pants. He makes a small bend at us and says something in Nepalese, which probably means *thank you*. Aya blows him an air kiss gesture with her hand, which seems to be lightening him up before he turns around and continues walking.

"That was very nice of you," I tell her as we continue our journey as well.

"Yup. I'm not good at being nice to people, unless they deserve it," she says.

As I have gotten to know Aya more, I sense a calmness within her. I can see it in her jet black eyes. She may be a little crazy all day long, but only hyperactive in the morning. She would make an amazing morning-porter with that energy level. She's quite short and skinny, but she could do the same trip *three times* with *one backpack* at a time. Just fire off that energy for sprinting several trips instead of one. I could use some of that energy right now. This is definitely not my best day.

"Hey, you *do* look tired now!" Aya informs me.

When I informed her about my exhaustion earlier, she was kind and told me that it wasn't visible. Now the honesty comes. She grabs my hand and holds it tight.

"Let me drag you!" she says energetically.

She keeps the same speed, though. No dragging, yet it helps my motivation. It puts me into the moment instead of focusing on the pain and tiredness. Oh, how Noah would joke if he saw this hand-holding. Sadly for him, they are out of sight and have been for a while. Aya's hand is warm, despite the humid air being cold. Her hand is quite sweaty, but the softness makes up for it. We walk in silence like this for a while. It's relaxing.

"Iris?" she asks, breaking the silence. "Have you ever been with a girl?"

Surprised by the question, I turn my head to her to check if she is serious. Before I can open my mouth to answer, she presses her lips against mine. Not sure what is happening, I gently try to push her away from me, but she insists on continuing, grabbing my head and forcing our lips to stay joined.

As my hand is released, it falls loose down my side. Aya wraps her fingers into my hair, and I suddenly smell the fruity perfume. The kiss doesn't feel real in any way. There are absolutely no emotions involved, hopefully not for Aya either. It's not a bad kiss, to be honest. And to answer her question, I *have* kissed other girls before, but only shortly for the fun of it while being drunk. Never like this.

I'm not truly into girls, but as the kiss continues, why not just let it happen. It won't kill me. And again, it's not a bad kiss. Oh, if Noah saw this. I'm not even sure that he would dare to joke about it. I suddenly feel a tongue on my lips. It tickles just enough to make my body react with a burst of shivering. The tongue tries to find a way into my mouth. Okay, this is getting too real. In my panic, I hear myself giggle. Aya removes her head and stares curiously at me before offering a huge smile.

"Well, that was fun," she says and gives me a push, making me stumble away from her. "Icelandic chick is now crossed off of the list."

As I thought, no emotions there. Just pure fun.

"And likewise: Japanese hottie... Check," I reply to

indicate that there were no feelings involved from my part either.

Something catches my attention from around the corner ahead of us, but as I manage to focus, I see nothing. Probably the exhaustion is messing with my vision. We should get going before I'm completely drained of energy.

"With that goal completed, should we move on?" I ask.

"Yep, but I will still drag you all the way!" Aya replies.

William

I can not believe this. How could I be so blind? I almost feel like crying. Iris and Aya. Kissing. Woah, I am shaking. Why did she not tell us? Iris is into girls! I feel so stupid. I was hoping for a positive answer concerning her feelings for me, when I was supposed to ask her tonight. Well, I am glad to have seen this now, so the embarrassment would not happen tonight. I am not sure if I am angry or disappointed right now. I just feel like… hiding myself a long distance from Iris. Tom and Noah, oh, how I hope that they will never know. They will mock me up like crazy. No, calm down, William. They are good guys, yet I imagine Noah holding back a huge laughter when finding out about it.

It should not be legal to make people fall in love with you like that, and not let them know that there is no chance because you are the wrong gender. Oh, man, I *LOVE* her. *LOVE! HER!* I would transform myself into a woman for her. Maybe she would actually like that? No, you are ridiculous now, William. Wake up! It is over! Perhaps I should take that offer from Aya, if not Iris has stolen her entirely now. It might help me to get over Iris somehow. Thinking back on all the things we have already experienced together makes me sick. The memories feel like a dream, which I awoke from just now. I want to be back in that dream! I want to hold her warm hands in mine. I want to sit outside, looking at stars and fire-flies. I want to fall asleep with her in my arms. None of this will ever happen again. It would not be the same anyway, now that I know that Iris is into the opposite sex.

Wait a second, Iris *could* be into both genders! Yet, when I think about it, she never spoke about boyfriends or guys in her life. I remember her saying that she never had a boy-friend, when we played Never Have I Ever in Kathmandu. And she *did* cry when saying goodbye to that English woman, Diana, at the bus station. They *did* hug for a long time. The hippie closing! The veganism! The no-makeup style! I might be wrong and generalizing, not knowing anything about this subject, but right in this moment, everything in my head goes for her being into females. With all respect, I just wa…

"Are you coming, William?" Tom yells at me.

I have been standing frozen since the moment I saw them kissing. What if I never checked if Iris and Aya were still with us? Would it feel better for Iris to tell me in person instead of me seeing it? Now the image will be drilled into my memories for the rest of my life. That is harder than hearing the words. It is for me at least. I finally return to Noah and Tom.

"The girls are still with us," I tell them while we start moving again.

I suddenly appreciate their company more than ever on this trip. Iris has been so much on my mind that I never fully enjoyed Noah and Tom's presence. My focus was on the wrong person all this time. It is time to change that.

"Hoh, I could eat pizza again now! With a huge pile of cheese on it!" I tell the guys, trying to initiate a positive conversation.

Noah pushes me, almost making me fall.

"Man, don't say that! Now I feel like eating pizza too," he says in his standard happy tone. "Pizza and a good night of gaming, that's life."

I know that he is just messing around, though these guys have a sweet history of playing a lot of video games. They are slowly growing from finding time to actually play, but

I figured that they still love talking about it. And with this nerdy conversation initiated, I am sure it will go on for a while. An excellent way to get my thoughts moved from Iris to this, and it is just perfect that the hike today is a short one. We will be at the Himalaya village in only a few hours. Maybe even eating delicious pizza yet again.

Iris

Another day of hiking is done. And what a strange day. It will be good with some well-deserved food now. The shower I had when we arrived here in Himalaya village was quite refreshing, so I am energized enough to happily eat now. A couple of Korean people sit at a table in the corner of the restaurant house, else we are alone. There were no rooms for five persons, so Aya insisted on taking a room alone, even though I suggested to share with her. She wants her privacy, I guess.

The owner of this place said that he had never seen a dog follow a group of people for such a long time when he was presented to Bob. Usually, the dogs will follow for a few hours and then lose interest. Also, it has been a while since he saw a dog come up here at this altitude: 3200 meters, William said. We all agreed that we could feel the altitude when breathing while walking, but I'm not sure if it is just something we tell ourselves because we were told that it could happen. Sometimes you think that you sense something, but it was all in your head. Kinda like a placebo effect. It will be fun to feel the altitude change tomorrow. I can't believe that we will reach the Base Camp already. The goal is so close now, and then there's only our hike down and the horrible goodbyes.

The thought of not seeing these three guys hurts. Especially William. What is with him by the way? It feels like he has been ignoring me since we arrived here. Maybe he's ashamed of what happened last night? Thinking back on that situation again makes me smile. I feel like wanting more of that, just lying safe in his arms. I don't want to say goodbye to him and to never look into his dark brown eyes again. I have seriously started falling for him. I know that I promised myself not to do this, but I can't hold it back anymore. I want him. I need to talk to him about this when the right time comes. Something tells me that he likes me back. I just know it. The connection. The smile he gives me when I watch him. Or the smile he uses to give me, when he is not weird like now, whatever the reason is. This time my secret is *not* holding me back. I know it's selfish, but I'm going for him. Not today, though. I'm too exhausted. But when the right time comes!

"Dal bhat is comiiing!" our host sings out loud while bringing us our plates with dal bhat.

The guys wanted pizza again, but the host of this place didn't have pizza on the menu. The disappointment on their faces was hilarious, and luckily dal bhat is delicious. We all pick up our cutlery simultaneously, but just as we get ready to eat, Aya drops her cutlery back on the table, sticks her fingers into her pile of rice and starts eating with her fingers. We stare at her in confusion, and she gives us the same confused stare back.

"What? We're in Asia!" she says and continues eating.

For a moment, it feels like we are all frozen in place, not sure what to say. William suddenly drops his cutlery too and begins eating with his fingers as well. Seeing that Aya can make William do this kind of stuff makes me a little jealous. Aya and William look at each other with weird smirks on their faces. I have never felt this kind of jealousy before. It's a strange feeling. There's no reason for me to feel this way. They are just weirdly eating food. Aya made me do crazy things too. That's her thing: making people do all kinds of weird stuff. *People*. Not only *William*. It might be caused by Aya, or a result of jealousy, that I put down my knife and fork and start finger-eating as well, with Noah and Tom joining me. Great. Aya has already food all over her face. She is literally eating like a pig now, with her head on the plate. I wait to see if William is up for that too, but it seems not. He gets eye contact with me but removes his eyes again. I desperately would like to know what is wrong, but it has to wait until tomorrow. The rest of today is about eating up and going to bed, sleeping. That's it. Tomorrow will be a great day.

William

As I feared, I can not sleep. My mind is chaotic. The things I discovered today were horrible. To make matters worse, it is way too quiet and dark in this bedroom. I could use some kind of noise to focus on while falling asleep, even a weird, scary wind ambient. I try to hide myself in my sleeping bag. I am about to cry, just as I did for the first ten minutes when the light was turned off. The feeling of being alone in the world has gotten to me now. I feel lonely without Iris. And I never even had her to begin with. It was all in my head. Stupid, dumb, brainless William! A tear rolls from my eye down my chin. I should be happy about us reaching the Base Camp tomorrow, but I am simply not in the mood for it. All I want is either to be with Iris or completely forget about her. None of them can be done. I do not even feel like being with Aya, though it might help me get over Iris. It just feels wrong.

However, I am happy that Aya was with us today. I have never felt so open and spontaneous as she made me feel. Her energy level spreads to everybody around her. I wish that I could manage to stay spontaneous like that, but that is probably not going to happen. People at home would think that I have become crazy if I acted like how I did today. On the other hand, if it makes me happy, I should do it. Actually yes, I will try to put away my shyness and be more open-minded. I liked how I felt today. I felt like everything could happen. Literally *everything*. No thinking, just doing. That will become my motto. I will become a new William. A better one. William version 2.0. A William that does not fall in love with Icelandic girls without knowing about them not being into men. A William that will not hesitate to step out on wobbly bridges or to sit in shaky planes. A William that is open for doing things he wants to do, without being held back by shyness and panic. William version 2.0 will become my focal point, now that Iris is gone. Tomorrow will be the first day of the new William.

Goodbye Iris.

- Day 5 -

Iris

Yawning aggressively, I realize that it's still dark outside. What time is it? I check my phone: 05:40. Twenty minutes to planned wake-up time. I feel cold and dizzy, not able to sleep anymore. My mouth feels dry. I must be dehydrated, so I reach down from my bed to grab my water bottle, but it's not there. I must have forgotten to bring it. That means it's still attached to my backpack, which means that I am to get up from the bed if I want that water. Forget it. I close my eyes in an attempt to get the last bit of sleep, but it only makes my thirst and dizziness worse. Seriously? Okay, I'm going to get that water anyway.

With the sleeping bag removed, I get up from my bed, move to my pack and pick up my water bottle. A dim, blue light is entering from a gap in the window curtains, making me curious to look outside. Taking a few big sips of water, while peeking out the window, I realize that a lot of snow has fallen during the night. The ground is covered in a thick layer of the frozen, white material, which almost appears luminous from the moonlight. Footsteps from an animal are printed in the snow, almost in a circle. I hope Bob is okay in this kind of weather. I'm sad that he is not allowed in the room, but the locals said that we shouldn't worry and that dogs around here are used to all kinds of mountain weather. Nevertheless, I decide to check up on him. I put down my water bottle, and as I reach the door, I hint something on the ground in front of it. A paper note. That's strange. I pick it up and read the note to myself:

—

Hey, sleepyheads!
When you read this, I am long gone.
You know what I mean!
I'm probably already at the Base Camp.
I'M AWESOME - NOT LAZY AS YOU PEOPLE!

-Goodbye lovers-

STOP CRYING!!!
I will wait for you there!
See you!

—

It's not signed by anyone, but the drawing of a girl hugging a rock kinda gives away who wrote the note. Besides that, the only other companion who could have written this would be Bob. That would have been cool though. Just to be sure, I check if everybody is still sleeping in the room, but they are all here, so I conclude that the note *is* from Aya. I put it away and open the door to check up on Bob. He's sleeping happily under a small canopy, which has kept him clear from the snow. He looks all sweet and calm. A blow of freezing wind hits me and finds its way under my sleeping-shirt, so I slam the door shut again. Just as the door shuts, alarms start ringing from the phones on all of our beds. Time for breakfast it seems.

William

What a morning. The atmosphere in the kitchen house is quite unique, with warm candles on the table and the cold light from the snow-covered scenery outside the window. It is cold in here, but somehow I find it refreshing. I sip from my morning coffee. Delicious. Everything seems to be amazing right now. Everything but one thing: Iris. When I think of the things that I learned about her yesterday, I feel my heart tighten. For some reason, I compare it to the feeling of a breakup, even though we were never together. It is like waking up from a crazy dream. But I promised myself that I would not be let down by that. This is the day where William 2.0 comes to life. An open, happy William, who is ready to do anything. I already kickstarted the new William by ordering something different for breakfast: apple pie. It's not a significant kickstart of the new William, but I have to start somewhere. I grab a piece of pie with my fork and let it fly into my mouth. It tastes great! And who would have believed that you could even have apple pie up here? Everybody looked at me like a maniac when I ordered it, but to be honest, I do not find pie for breakfast more weird than having pizza for breakfast. Maybe people noticed the new William already. I smile from the thought. I already like William version two, even though I have not fully figured him out yet. If I want the new William to be more open and spontaneous, I will have to do something. Something like… talking about random subjects, maybe. Doing like a talkative extrovert and just talk and talk. At least until we finish breakfast. We have to leave soon, so I have to get started now. Yep, it is worth a try. Here we go!

Iris

Walking in the snow is crazily fun. The crispy sounds from our footsteps are like a sweet harmony to my ears. Bob appears to like the snow as well, jumping happily around. The boys complained about it being difficult and dangerous to hike in, which I found quite depressing to hear about, but I have been complaining today myself, so I shouldn't act like a saint. The altitude has gotten to me big time. I'm probably not suffering from actual altitude sickness, but I do feel my breathing to be shallow. Also, my body feels heavy, and I seem to have a hard time concentrating. It doesn't help to have the wind going against us and a light fog around us, which makes our line of sight only like 10-15 meters, yet not completely blinding us. We walk one by one in a straight line, with me in the rear end, and thankfully we go slowly enough for me to follow up easily. William is in front of me and I look at his footprints in the snow while passing them. The curvy prints from his boots are mesmerizing.

He has been acting strange today, but differently than yesterday. I think he talked more this morning than he has done on the whole trip. Random talking. It's almost like Aya injected a bit of herself into him and that she is now a part of William. To begin with, I found his babbling entertaining and inspiring, but then this thought of him being inspired by Aya came to my mind. I might be seriously jealous for the first time in my life. Especially because he still seems to ignore me for no reason. It kills me not to know if I did something to offend him without realizing it. I need to talk to him in private to know what is up. What is up with *us*? I want to tell him about my feelings for him. I wish for him to somehow return some of the emotions and let us explore our feelings together. If he doesn't return any feelings, I can hopefully let him go and think that it is probably for the best. It just hasn't been easy to find a good time for such a conversation yet.

I hear someone whistling happily in front of me. One of the guys is in a good mood. Why not. I mean, we will reach the Base Camp soon. I should feel excited as well, but again I find it hard focusing on that right now. The crispy sounds from our footsteps catch my attention again.

Woops!

I trip over something hidden in the snow, but I manage to stay on my feet and regain balance. I realize that I let out a weird sound from the fall. The whistling in front of me has stopped, and I glance up to see William giving me a surprised stare. He realizes that I'm okay and gives me a timid smile before turning his head away while continuing walking without saying anything. What a cute smile.

William

I begin whistling my song again: Jingle Bells. For some reason, the snow reminds me of Christmas back at home, and Jingle Bells is stuck in my head, and whistling it out feels great. It helps me to move my thoughts away from Iris and focus on the new William. She *does* look a little ill, though. I should stay close enough to not get out of sight, especially now when the fog is getting thicker. The snow is getting deeper too, but it is manageable when Noah and Tom step down the snow for us.

"What's up with you today, William?" I hear Tom say in front of me.

I spread out my arms and laugh.

"It is just a good day, Tom," I tell him. "Life is good."

Even though half of what I am doing right now is an act, it improves my mood. I honestly feel that this is a good day, and that life is good. If I could only turn my sorrow from Iris into joy as well. I will have to do something active for that to happen if I want it to happen now. If I can approach her as a friend and not as someone I want to marry, that would complete my day. I slow down my pace and wait for Iris to catch up with me. Noah and Tom disappear in the fog which is rapidly getting more intense. Bob sniffs my hand to check if I slowed down to feed him, but he seems to be content with a quick petting. Iris is right behind me now. Time for her to meet William 2.0. Time for the new William to meet his new friend.

"Is it true that all Icelandic people are feminists?" I, William 2.0, ask.

Iris

If all Icelandic people are feminists? I guess you could say that. I mean, we *do* learn a lot about gender equality in school, and we *do* have laws and a ministry for this, but does that make us all feminists? Feminism isn't only for females, and if males support equal rights, they are feminists as well. Now when I think about it, I haven't met anyone from Iceland who was against this kind of equality, so why not give William a simple answer.

"That's right!" I answer to his question. "And if you want to put more labels on us, just call us *'one big family.'* You know that we have to research each other before getting married to be sure that we're not related, right?"

"Seriously?" he replies.

I'm happy that he's finally speaking to me. He might not be mad at me after all. I suddenly can't wait to talk with him about my feelings, even though the result might end in disappointment. He is close, yet I can barely see him from the fog. It just began to snow too. Ow, and here comes the wind as well. That escalated quickly. I hear William yell something to me, but the wind blocks my hearing with a howling noise. The same strange sound that we heard the other night, generated by the mountains on both sides of us, flies through the cold air along with snow and hail. It somehow again reminds me of the story of Bandhul who comes to kill us. Silly story.

A cold blow from the wind hits me in the face. Nervousness slowly gets to me. I suddenly become much aware of my dizziness and my problematic breathing. Extreme weather is not what I need right now. Within a second, I find myself all alone in the fog. There's almost no visibility now. I try my best to follow the footprints through the blinding hail, but it's not easy. The wind intensifies and tries to push me backward. I'm blinded, deafened and fighting to not get disoriented. *Where did this storm come from?* The thought of hiding in my sleeping bag until this is over crosses me. I'm not sure what is more dangerous: to keep moving or to end up a frozen cube. I decide to stop to take off my backpack and think for a moment. Confusion. Panic. A gigantic, horrifying explosion sound comes from above me, echoing all over the sky. I freeze from fear. *Literally* freezing from fear. The ground shakes under my feet. I feel the blood in my face rushing to my heart, and I almost lose consciousness. All I want is to flee from this situation. I hear crackling sounds echoing all around me along with howling from Bob. My heart is beating like crazy. A violent blow from the wind hits my stomach and pushes the air out of my lungs. I lose control of my legs and collapse. This is not good! Something grabs my shoulder and pulls me hard. It all happens too fast. Another explosion sounds. Then everything turns dark and silent.

- Trapped -

William

No, no, no! Where are we?!

"Iris, are you okay?!" I yell at her in panic.

I am not sure exactly what happened, but I managed to pull Iris into this cave-like place just before the avalanche landed right at the opening of it.

"I'm okay," I hear her say all calm.

There is complete darkness in here, so I drop my backpack and fiddle in blind to find my lantern and turn it on. It illuminates most of the cave. There is nothing but gray and brown rock all around us. The entrance is blocked by huge rocks, just like in the movies.

Is this for real?!

I run past Iris, who is now sitting up, to the blocked entrance and try to move the rocks. Absolutely nothing happens. One more try. Still nothing. This is impossible!

"William?" Iris says from behind me. "Did you see the others?"

"The others?" I ask her, still considering what to do with the blocked entrance.

"Yeah. Tom and Noah?" she replies.

I stop my escape planning for a moment and go to sit down in front of her to try and calm myself down and avoid panicking. I see her nervously rubbing her nail roots again, which somehow helps me focus on the moment and our

221

conversation.

"Tom and Noah? No," I tell her silently. "But I am sure that they are okay."

I can not imagine them not being okay. I do not know how far Tom and Noah was from us or how big the avalanche was, but of course they are okay.

"And Bob?" she asks.

"I hope Bob is alright. He is a super dog, remember?" I tell her, trying to sound optimistic.

But to be honest, I fear for Bob. He followed *us* when the avalanche began. I lost sight of him, but I heard him howling right next to me all of the time. I do not want to think of this. Now it is more important how to get out of here. I set the light-setting on my lantern to low to save battery, in case we are going to be here for a while. Then I remember the extra batteries in my backpack. A quick thought of heating them up to make them explode, and create an exit, cross my mind. Nah, batteries probably do not explode *that* much. Maybe we should just wait until somebody gets us out.

I pick up a cereal bar from my backpack.

"Where is your pack?" I ask Iris as I realize that hers is not here.

"Ehm, outside I guess," she replies. "I took it off."

"Okay. No worries," I say. "We will share whatever I have."

I break the cereal bar into two and hand over the other half to Iris. She thanks me and starts biting off it instantly. I see that she is thinking so I leave her in peace.

Silence.

Iris

Nope, I cannot come up with a single solution for how to get out of here. We'll have to wait it out. How long can it take to reach us anyway?

Looking into the darkness around us gives me slight claustrophobia. A chilling feeling runs through my body and I make a freezing twitch.

"Are you cold?" William asks me.

I can barely see his face in the low light level, but his eyes reflect the dim light from the lantern in a magical way.

"A little," I tell him. "But my clothes were in my backpack."

William puts a hand in his backpack and pulls out a fluffy, green sweater. My sweater! How could I forget about that? He has been carrying my stuff since the first day in the mountains, and I forgot all about it. I remove the sweater from his hand and put it on. I don't even remember if I ever thanked him for carrying my stuff. Besides that, *he just saved my life!*

"William, get up," I demand.

Without question, he stands up, and likewise do I. I take a few steps towards him and throw my arms around him.

"Thank you, Will," I whisper in his ear. "For everything."

He put his arms around me and we hug for a while. My heart accelerates while the hug gets tighter for every second. He moves his hand from my back to my head, and I press my ear to his chest. I hear his heartbeat beating even faster than mine. This feels much better than I imagined. Here we are, trapped inside a giant mountain with no clue if anybody knows that we're here, and I feel completely safe in this hug. I realize that my hand is mechanically going up and down his back like I have no control of it. He brushes his fingers through my hair and I get a chilled sensation rushing through my whole body. I can't take it anymore. Within a split-second, I manage to remove my head from his chest and look him in the eyes before I find my lips against his. Our first kiss. *Magic*! No other words. Just *magic*. It's not as physically an intense kiss as it's an emotional one, but William's lips are abnormally soft, which matches perfectly with his gentle kissing.

Magic...

William

Is this really happening? I run my fingers through Iris' hair another time, just to be sure it *is* her. Oh god, this *is* happening. Colored sparkles begin to ignite everywhere around us, like sparks from a bonfire. I can not believe it. My heart is about to explode, while the sparkles are glowing and glittering like never before. I press her lips even closer to mine and the kiss intensifies. I try to control myself, but it is impossible. I want her. If I do not keep control of myself, I will probably end up eating her alive. A small moan escapes her mouth, and within a split-second, the million of colored sparkles accelerate and penetrate me in an explosion.

I feel complete.

Iris

Wow!

I pull myself away from William, ending the kiss brutally. What am I doing? The confusion on William's face says it all. I never made sure if he wanted this. I never had that conversation about my feelings. I have no idea if he is into me like that or if he just kissed me back to be kind. It *could* be that he didn't know how to stop me. Oh, this is embarrassing.

"Sorry," I say, accidentally closing my eyes with a regretful face.

"What? No, do not say that," I hear him reply.

I open my eyes again and somehow hope for him to start another kiss, but he just stands there looking confused and cute.

"I thought…" he begins, but stops again to find the right words. "You know… Ehm…"

His thinking makes me nervous about what he is going to say. Is this the time where he tells me that the feelings are a one-way thing? That the kiss was silly and will never happen again?

"I thought that you were into girls?" he mumbles to my surprise.

"What?!" is all I manage to exclaim.

He gives me a curious look, clearly trying to figure out exactly why I am this surprised.

"But…" he begins explaining. "I saw you… and Aya… kissing. I thought… with the veganism and all… Icelandic feminism… no boyfriend… I mean… you know… I…"

Wow, I have to end this suffering.

"William," I interrupt gently. "First of all, I'm not *into* girls..."

A big smile appears on my face for what I'm about to tell him. This is kinda absurd, yet cute.

"...when that is said, veganism and feminism have nothing to do with people being homosexual," I tell him and turn my smile into laughter from hearing how absurd this actually is. "Did you honestly believe that?"

It's obvious that William sees his mistake now as he lets out low, awkward giggling.

"No... or... When I saw you and Aya, I just thought..." he says, clearly not knowing how to end his sentence.

I love how awkwardness can fade away with laughter like this. Did William actually think I was into girls? Is that why he has been acting so weird around me? That's crazy. I would still be the same person. Well, I guess he deserves a short explanation then.

"William, the thing you saw between Aya and me," I begin explaining. "It meant nothing. It was all about the fun, that's it. I'm not into girls."

I'm into this amazing American guy!

That's what I should say. That's what I *want* to say at least. But I'm still unsure if there's more between us than ordinary friendship. I haven't told him about my feelings, and I don't know if they are returned. This would probably be a good time to find out, after starting a kiss like that.

"So... ehm..." I say, now knowing the feeling of not finding the right words. "Was the kiss okay?"

William

Was it okay?! I can not describe how amazing it was. Should I tell her that? I still have not yet fully understood that she is not into girls after all. I might still have a chance. Wait a minute! She kissed me, why did she do that? Was it also for the fun of it, or did she mean it this time? I fight to bring out William 2.0 to be able to get an answer in some cool way, but he does not want to show himself, even though I know he is inside of me somewhere. The new William was so good at hiding emotions and just doing things, but he has only existed for such a short period. Who am I kidding? Now that my feelings have exploded for Iris in this situation, the shyness from the original William is back. But I somehow like it now. I like that the original William can make me feel this way. I am falling in love.

"It was perfect," I admit.

She giggles nervously. Without thinking, I lean forward and kiss her again.

Iris

Magic.

William

This time it is my turn to end the kiss. I look Iris deep in her eyes. The dim light from the lantern flickers, but it does not wake me from this dream.

"I really like you," I hear myself saying.

Iris throws her arms around me again and we hug for a while.

"I like you too, Will. I really really like you," she whispers.

The lantern flickers some more, but right now there is nothing that can pull me away from this situation, especially not dying batteries. Iris steps back, takes my hand, and we lie down on the ground next to the flickering lantern. She stretches her arm and turns off the lantern before putting her arm around me. I find my hand moving to her hair again, and we lie on our sides, facing each other. It is total darkness now, but I still feel that I can see her face right in front of me. We move close together in the hug and our foreheads meet. I feel her breathing. Somehow I wish not to be found by anyone for a long period of time. If we could simply stay like this forever. I have never been this relaxed and excited at the same time. I could both fall happily asleep instantly, and stay awake, enjoying this moment for days. Nevertheless, I hope this is no dream.

- Escape -

Iris

"William, what time is it?" I ask him after realizing that we both fell asleep.

That didn't wake him up. I kiss his forehead in hope of a gentle wakeup, but no luck either. The thought of lying here with him fills me with uncontrolled happiness. It's still complete darkness, so I have only my imagination to see him with. His dark eyes. His cute smile. His sweet fright of everything. Which reminds me of my own fear when lying here with him: my secret. I will have to tell him before it's too late. That would be the best for both of us, even if it means that the thing between us will end.

"William," I say again, giving him a gentle push.

This time he awakes.

"Hey," he whispers, still half asleep.

"Hi there," I whisper back. "How long have we been sleeping?"

He removes himself from me, and a fizzling begins around his backpack. The dim light from the flickering lantern turns on while he still searches his pack for something.

"I never got to tell you this," he says without stopping the search. "I have not charged my phone for days. It is completely dead, and I did not bring a watch, so I have no idea if it is even night or day."

The thought of not knowing the time suddenly scares me. As William said, we have no idea if it's daytime outside or if we should ideally be sleeping now. I feel slight claustrophobia again. We're trapped inside this time pocket, with no clue what's going on outside this minute. At least I'm with William. This will be a good time for telling him about my secret.

"William…" I say nervously.

It strikes me that I have no idea how I tell him this without it sounding horrible.

"Yes?" he says after the long silence that came from my thinking.

He finally finds what he has been searching for in his pack: spare batteries for the lantern. He removes the old batteries, making everything dark again. A few seconds after, the cave is lit up brightly from the new-gained power of the lantern. William puts down the lantern and sits in front of me.

"You were saying something?" he asks curiously.

"Yes… Well, I…" I say, but am stopped by my own thinking.

I randomly examine the cave to try and restart my brain, just telling him without thinking of the consequences. The cave space appears bigger than I remembered. The rock almost looks like it's colored in red with this light. My eyes roam randomly around, inspecting the texture of the cave, but stop at a dark spot at the other end of the cave space. It almost looks like a crack in the wall. An enormous crack. William sees my focused inspection of the wall and turns his head to check.

"What is that?" he exclaims in surprise.

"I have no idea," I reply shortly.

He picks up the lantern and steps towards the dark area. There's no way I'm staying alone here, so I follow right behind him. As we get closer, I realize that it *is*, in fact, a crack in the wall and it's bigger than I first thought. It looks like a passage going away from the cave space.

"Why didn't we see that before?" I ask William, trying to make a mysterious thing out of this.

But I'm honestly only trying to make a game out of this to remove my nervousness and claustrophobia.

"No idea," he just replies.

We stop in front of the passage. I can't tell if it's human-made, made by some animal or made by nature somehow, but it's big enough for us to walk through. Not that I have any plans going in there.

"We should try exploring this thing," William says.

Seriously? Isn't *he* supposed to be the one being frightened?

"We might find a way out," he continues. "We can always return if we change our minds."

"You're right," I admit, though I'm not happy about going. "But let's take it slow, okay?"

He glances at me and offers a contagious smile. The smile comes with a quick kiss before he takes my hand and moves in front of me into the passage. The air here is moisty and cold, and besides the sounds from our boots, the silence is out of this world. The passage narrows, giving me a chance to run my free hand over the rocky walls. They are freezing cold and almost feel wet. I watch the rocky texture around my hand. There is something strange about these passage walls. Studying it makes me think of scratches from giant claws, but I can't tell exactly why. I better not think such thoughts right now, so I decide to put my hand in the pocket of my sweater. William leads me through the narrow passage in silence for a few minutes. Holding his hand is the only thing that stops me from running screamingly back to our cave space. I just hope for the passage to end blindly soon, so we can return and wait to be found.

"Wow, this is interesting," William suddenly says and releases my hand.

William

We reached another huge cave space. I take a few steps forward while looking around.

"Are we back where we started?" Iris asks from behind me.

"I believe that we are. It looks identical. However, my backpack is not here," I reply. "Wait a minute. This is new."

What is that? Bones? I find my way to the pile of white objects in the middle of the room. It *is* bones. This is *not* the same place. Iris lets out a weird sound behind me, letting me know that she is shocked from seeing the pile of bones.

"What do you think this is?" I ask her, trying to sound calm.

Please give me a logical explanation. Tell me that this is safe and normal.

"I've no idea," she replies. "Maybe we should go back, Will."

The fright in her voice almost triggers my own panic, but I manage to keep it cool.

"Okay, let us go back," I say and give Iris a commanding nod.

Just as we start returning, a deep sound echoes from the passage. I freeze and turn my head to Iris to see if she heard it too. Her eyes tell me that she did. *Fear.* The sound gets louder for every second. What the hell is that sound? It almost sounds like something is running. Something is definitely coming closer. By instinct, I pick up one of the bones from the pile to get ready for an attack of whatever this is. I regret not bringing my knife from my backpack. Stupid! The sound is close now. What can it be? Oh shit, did we enter the home of a leopard? Do leopards even live in caves? What else leaves bones behind? Thoughts are running in circles in my head. I position myself in front of Iris, giving her a sign to stay where she is. The sound stops within an instance. Reflections of two dark eyes are hovering in the passage. For a moment, it is like the whole world stops. I am not ready to die. I want to explore the world with Iris. I want to get to know her better and be with her every day. I finally had a chance with her, and now it all might end. It is not fair!

The creature in the passage releases a barking sound that echoes through the cave space like thunder. Then it begins sprinting towards us. I am not giving up without a fight! I lift the bone and run towards the creature, ready to give it a killing blow.

"William! Wait!" Iris calls behind me. "It's Bob!"

She was too late. I look down and drop the bone from my hand. It *is* Bob! I hit him in the head with all my strength. There is no sign of life.

"No, no, no!" I hear myself yelling.

I drop down to my knees while Iris runs to me. I put my hands on the poor dog. He is still breathing.

"Bob!" I hear myself yelling again.

A small whining comes from him. I check his head to see if there is any visible damage, but there is nothing to see. Iris moves her hand down his side to calm him. We sit like this for a moment. I am not sure what to do. However, to my surprise, Bob wakes up and tries to get back up on his paws.

"Wowow, take it slow, Bob," I tell him, running my hand over his head.

He licks my hand and gives me a low bark. He appears to be okay after all. What a relief.

"Where did he come from?" I ask Iris. "Do you think somebody found us?"

She thinks for a moment.

"Maybe," she replies. "But why didn't anyone run after Bob? They should know that he was tracking us."

We turn silent to hear if any other sounds come from the passage, but there is nothing.

"We should go back and check," I tell her after concluding that nobody was following Bob.

Bob finally gets up and shakes himself clean from dust. It is like seeing a broken computer reboot and then function perfectly. His tail starts wagging instantly. I am so relieved that I am not a strong fighter and that I did not hurt him more than I did. He lets out another bark and runs towards the passage.

"It seems like our guide dog is back in business," Iris says.

We immediately begin following Bob. Everything seems safer now that he is here. He is going fast, so we start running.

Iris

Too fast! The pain is too big when running. I slow down to walking speed, but William and Bob continue running. I try to call out for them, but no sound escapes my throat. The pain makes me dizzy, and I suddenly feel exhausted. The passage turns at a corner and William disappears with the light from the lantern. I have no clue where to step, so I put my hand to the wall and follow it the best I can. The light from the lantern is still slightly visible at the turning point of the passage, so I have that little clue for direction. I try again to call out for William to stop, but still no sound. A small rumbling comes from the rocky walls around me. The ground vibrates under my feet for a moment, then the rumbling stops. I try to speed up my pace, but my chest hurts from every inhale. The light from the lantern fades away completely, leaving me in total darkness. In my panic, I try one last time to call out for help. This time it works.

"*WILLIAM!*" I yell with a voice I have never heard before, almost sounding alien.

My voice echoes from all around me, both from the front and the rear, which makes me delusional. The light reflection from the passage turn reappears. Within a couple of seconds, William stands in front of me.

"Are you okay?" he asks, trying to catch his breath.

"I am," I tell him, though I'm not okay. "I just need to take it slow."

William grabs my hand and gently drags me forward.

"There is something you need to see," he says, sounding eager to show me.

We stop at a point where the passage splits in two

directions. I didn't notice that when we walked the other way.

"Which one did we come from?" I ask.

William stays quiet. The claustrophobia returns to me yet again. Are we trapped inside some kind of cave maze? I check the walls of the passages to see if there's anything familiar, but they all look the same. The ground vibrates again. This time the vibrations are strong enough to make small stones drop from above us. More avalanches? A bark sounds from the passage to the right.

"I guess we are following our guide companion then?" William asks, sounding relieved.

I agree, and we start walking into the passage that Bob chose for us. My body still hurts from every inhale, but it's tolerable now that the pace is slow again. I hear more rumbling. This time the ground literally shakes beneath our feet. The echoing rumbling is ear-deafening along with the small rocks dropping down all around us. Instantly we both speed up the pace, with William continually glancing back to check if I'm still with him. He's so protective. Could I be any safer? Roaming in a maze with my protector and my guide dog. Then who am I in this story? Well, that's easy: I'm the beautiful princess who needs to be rescued from her evil captor, of course. William is the hero and Bob is his awesome sidekick. Now I will be saved, and I will find out that William is actually a king of some magical town. We will get married and live happily ever after, with our kids, for a thousand years. My parents will even be there. No sorrows, no sicknesses, no pain.

I want to keep focusing my thoughts on imaginary stories, but the ground shakes yet again, pulling me back to reality.

This time the shaking is violent, and I fight to stay on my feet.

"Look!" William shouts in front of me and points at something.

There's a tiny dot of light at the end of the passage. The ground keeps shaking with more and more force for every second. The volume of the rumbling, and the amount of dropping stones, increases rapidly. Bob sprints fast towards the light. William turns around and pushes me in front of him.

"*Run!*" he yells, and we both instantly start running.

A large rock hits my forehead. For a second, I feel like losing control. This is surreal! The pain is unbearable, but I manage to keep running. The light is coming closer, but the ground shakes even more. It's impossible to focus and dizziness hits me yet again. It doesn't help that the light from Williams lantern behind me is wobbling like crazy as well. I realize the annoying small stones that are raining down from the ceiling, and I raise my hand to protect my head. I see my shadow on the ground copying me while gradually fading away, as we come closer to the light. The light is blinding now. I hear larger chunks of rocks falling behind us, echoing like bomb drops throughout the passage. William shouts behind me. *This is not real!* I speed up to unimaginable speed. The light is coming closer fast. Almost there! However, I trip and fall flat on the ground. William didn't see it coming, trips over my half-dead body and flies over me, landing hard on the ground. We are out! A gigantic explosion sound comes from the cave passage which we just escaped. I look back and see parts of the passage collapse in an inferno of rocks and dust. That was way too close.

Bob barks intensely in front of me. William! I jump to my feet to check up on him, but he is already getting up by himself. He seems fine. I check the surroundings to see if anything looks familiar, but I have never seen anything like this before. What is this place?

- Freedom -

William

The sun shines bright in the clear blue sky and warms up my face, with the fresh air cooling it down nicely again. The view is incredible. I look out on an open, stony field with snow-covered mountain tops in the horizon. A few turquoise pine trees grow here and there, though I have never seen trees growing from stone like that. After being trapped inside a dark and moisty cave, I feel a fantastic sense of freedom. An eagle roams around in the distance, probably searching for food. Listening carefully, I can hear it screaming. Something must be entering its hunting area.

Iris and Bob come up next to me. From the corner of my eye, something catches my attention.

"Iris, you are bleeding!" I exclaim.

She puts her hand to her head and feels the blood running out of her forehead. I turn around to find my first aid kit from my backpack, but am reminded that the pack is still lying inside the cave.

"Are you okay?" I ask Iris as I see that the blood is dripping out of her.

She nods, but looks confused. I take off my thin neck warmer and gently pull it around her head like a headband. We have no water to clean the wound with, so this is the best I can do. Hopefully, the bleeding will stop eventually. I decide to check her pupils to see if they are the same size, realizing how glad I am to have watched all those survival videos before leaving home. I put my hand in the air to block the sun and create a shadow on her face, before removing it again to make the sun-rays interact with her eyes. Her pupils appear normal, so I assume that she does not have a concussion. I move my hand down her chin to remove some of the blood that runs down her face. She puts her hand on mine, looking like she is going in for a kiss. Then she suddenly changes the expression on her face.

"William! Do you have the map?" she asks.

"I am afraid it is in my backpack in the cave," I tell her.

I check my jacket to see what I *do* have. I pull one thing up at a time as I find them.

"I have a chocolate bar... a cereal-, wait, two cereal bars... and I dropped the lantern when I tripped, so that one is gone," I tell her and nods at the broken lantern on the ground. "Oh wait, the compass from Tom and Noah! Maybe we can use that!"

Deep inside, I am concerned about not having any water, but I do not mention that for Iris. Instead, I open the lid on the silver compass and inspect it. I remember that we moved towards North-East on the map, but I have no idea where we are, compared to that. According to the compass, the blocked passage behind us is North-East. Well, it is not possible to go back that way. I check both left and right, but the mountains are more or less trapping us in a circle around us. There is absolutely no way we can cross any of them to get back on the trail. As I see it, there is only one way, and that is forward, in the wrong direction. I glance at Iris to know if she has anything to say about where to go, but she just stands there with empty eyes, staring out the distance with a hand rubbing her shoulder and the other one doing her nervous nail root rubbing. I look at Bob. He sits there watching me like he is just waiting for me to ask him for direction. He instantly gets up and waddles happily forward out into the open stony field.

"What do you say?" I ask Iris. "Should we follow Bob again?"

"I don't see any other choice," she replies silently.

With that decided, we start following Bob. I check the lantern one last time to make sure it *is* broken or if there is anything we can use from it, but it definitely is broken.

We walk in silence for a while. A colorful butterfly follows us curiously. At first, I wonder why there are butterflies in a place with no grass or flowers, but then it hits me, that there might be exactly that somewhere near. Something natural could be nearby! Again, I keep it to myself, as I do not want to spread hopes that might lead to disappointment.

Iris suddenly grabs my hand.

"I'm sorry, William. I never asked if *you* were okay?" she says.

"I am okay," I assure her. "No worries."

I do not want her to be embarrassed. She is the one that was injured, so it is not wrong of her to not think clearly.

"No, it's not fair," she continues. "You have been so protective and helpful to me. I haven't done anything for you. You know, I might even be dead now if you haven't been here. I feel like I owe you big time."

I squeeze her hand. Every word is like a tiny needle to my heart. Not a hurtful needle, but one who reminds me that my heart is existing.

"You clearly have no idea what you have done for me," I tell her. "Or what you mean to me. I am not like this normally, you know. The reason that I have not freaked out yet, or died from fear or whatever, is because I do not want to leave you alone. I know it is silly."

"It's not silly," she replies with a smile.

I decide to save the rest of my nonsense loving-her speech for another time. She will most likely run screamingly away from me, if I tell her that I want to spend the rest of my life with her, knowing that I have just met her like a week ago. Nevertheless, we walk hand in hand for some time, just following Bob who waddles in front. The landscape stays the same, and I doubt that we will ever reach those mountains we see on the horizon. Bob stops and sniffs the ground. Something shining is spread out, almost in a circle. It looks like some sort of silver and golden sand. I touch it lightly and examine the metallic sand that sticks to my finger. The sand glitters beautifully from the reflection of the sun.

"Have you seen anything like this before?" I ask Iris, hoping that it is some normal thing in mountains, and that she perhaps has seen something similar in Iceland.

"I've no idea," she replies. "But it looks like somebody put it there."

She is right. The circular shape is obviously human-made.

"That is good," I say. "Let us hope that these people are not far away."

I examine the area around us to check for more signs of human activity, but see nothing. Bob moves on. It gives me hope that he is so resolute on going that specific direction. I genuinely believe that he knows something that Iris and I do not, so we follow him yet again.

"You know what, Will," Iris says. "That kiss in the cave… That wasn't an impulsive thing."

"No?" I ask, not really knowing what to say.

"Nope. Okay, here's the story: I met this cute and scared hiker dude in a plane a week ago," she continues. "He had my attention from the moment I met him. But that's not weird when the first thing we did was holding hands. I didn't know that I was going to somehow fall in love with him back then. But it seems like I might have done that."

"You are in love with me?" I ask stupidly.

The conversation makes me nervous for obvious reasons. It is like an exam, where I am being told if I did good or should prepare to get home and tell my parents how I failed.

"What do *you* think?" she asks teasingly.

I take in a big inhale of the chilled, fresh air to calm myself down.

"Well, all I know is that I might have fallen in love with this crazy, Icelandic vegan hippie," I tell her, trying to make my love-speech sound not so serious. "That is it."

She laughs and gives me a quick kiss on my chin. Her eyes sparkle like fireworks, as if the situation was not grossly romantic enough already. The sun lights up her messy hair, literally making her appear like an angel. I notice some movement through her hair in the distance. It looks like goats. They are too far away to see us, and it seems like they are grassing, which means…

"Grass!" Iris yells and points forward.

Iris

It's getting rapidly dark. The sun glows warmly behind the mountain tops and casts long shadows from the increasing amount of pines that surround us. The white flowers which grow from the grass look like self-illuminating spots on the ground.

"This is a good place to camp," I decide for both of us.

"I agree. I will gather some firewood for us," William says and instantly begins his search for firewood around the pines, accompanied by Bob.

I remain seated and take one last hand scoop of water from the small water stream that we just found. The stream generates funny bubbling sounds every now and then, which is quite amusing. The relief we had, when we discovered that water, was out of this world. At least until my thirst was gone and my attention was back at the pain in my body. I never believed that the pain would increase this fast. For the first time in my life, I fear the future.

A pile of branches is dropped in front of me. That was quick.

"Could you please light it up?" William asks me with a smirk on his face.

I repeatedly look up at him and down on the branches.

"Are you serious? How am I supposed to do that?" I ask him.

"Well, how do you think?" he just replies and crosses his arms.

"Magic?" I ask after figuring that there is no way to light those branches without some tinder or a lighter.

He chuckles and drops something onto the pile of

branches: three big batteries.

"I took them from the broken lantern. Thought they might be useful," he says.

"But how are we going to start the fire with those?" I ask, now realizing how little I know about wildlife survival.

"I will show you," he says and arranges the small branches into a small hollow, wooden tower.

He grabs a hand-large stone and smashes it onto one of the batteries a few times, until it breaks, before he scrapes the content of the battery out onto the branches. Then he finds the chocolate bar from his pocket.

"Please hold this," he says, giving me the chocolate bar while keeping the wrapping himself.

He tears the wrapping into two long strips.

"Let us hope that this is actually metallic," he says and points at the inner part of the wrapping, which indeed does look like soft metal coating.

"Have you done this before?" I ask a little skeptical.

"Never," he answers. "But I have seen it in videos. I have seen other people doing stuff a lot more than I have done things myself, unfortunately. Let us hope it works in real life."

With that said, I'm getting ready for disappointment. Things rarely end out the way you expect them to. At least not for me. He puts each end of the strip on each end of another battery. Nothing happens. To be honest, I didn't expect anything to happen, so I guess that what I expected actually happened this time. William keeps the ends together, eagerly watching the battery. I wonder what *he* is hoping to happen. There is obviously not coming any sparks out of that battery. Maybe the wrapping wasn't metallic after all.

"William…" I begin to say, but he cuts me off.

To my surprise, a flame suddenly appears from the middle of the wrapping strip. William quickly lowers the burning strip onto the collection of branches, and the battery content ignites instantly, making huge orange and turquoise flames. It seems like we have a fire after all. William sits down next to me.

"I honestly did not think this would work," he says amazed.

"That was awesome, Will!" I tell him and give him a gentle shoulder punch. "Chocolate?"

I break the chocolate bar in two and hand him a piece. Bob comes running up to us and barks.

"I'm sorry, Bob. You're a dog. Chocolate is poison for you," I tell him. "Do we have something else?"

William finds one of the cereal bars from his pocket, unwraps it and puts it on the ground. I don't even manage to blink before the cereal bar is gone and Bob lies down in front of the fire, happy with his tiny meal.

"We only have one cereal bar left," William says. "If we save it for breakfast, let us hope that we find something to eat tomorrow."

We eat our chocolate in silence while watching the mesmerizing bonfire. I'm not sure how long we sit like this, but I like it. Time is not the same out here. Hunger is the stressful factor now, not *time*. Hunger can be controlled to some degree, just by eating, while time is constantly running. However, I *do* hope that we find food tomorrow.

"Are you hurt?" I hear William ask.

I realize that my hand is on my shoulder again, and I'm

suddenly aware of the pain. I won't find any better time to tell him. He deserves to know. It should not be a secret anymore, at least not to him. I inhale deeply to calm myself down while taking his hand in mine and looking into his eyes.

"I have something to tell you," I begin. "I'm not sure if you have any conjectures about why I feel pain or why I am abnormally tired from time to time, but there's a reason for that, which is also the main reason why I decided to go to Nepal in the first place. I wanted to find a good place to end everything."

I inhale again. There is no right way of telling him this, so I'm just going to let him know.

"I have cancer, Will," I say silently. "A bad one."

William's eyes tell me that he doesn't fully understand what he just heard.

"That's also why I have pain around my shoulder," I continue. "Normally I would take painkillers whenever it gets intolerable, but they are in my backpack so..."

"Cancer?" William interrupts. "What kind of cancer?"

He looks like he doesn't believe me. Or like he doesn't want to believe me. I keep looking him deep in the eyes, to make sure that he knows that this is not some sick joke.

"Well, it started with breast cancer," I tell him. "But it managed to spread before the doctors took me seriously. When I first went to the doctor with breast pain, I was told that it was phantom pain from the sorrow and loss of my parents. They told me to speak with a psychologist, so I could get over the loss and stop feeling the pain my parents felt. I was stupid enough to believe in them, so I was convinced that I could get control of the sorrow myself, without speaking with someone who mainly interacts with me because of the money. Nevertheless, a long time passed, and the pain only got worse, yet my cancer was only discovered by coincidence when I was in the hospital with a lung infection, and the doctors found my blood sample to be more infected than usual."

Thinking back on that specific time of my life for the first time in months gives me a freezing feeling, even though the fire is warming amazingly well. I shiver for a moment, giving William an opportunity to understand what I'm telling him.

"Then why are you here?" he asks. "I do not un… Are you not supposed to… be… you know… in a hospital or something? Are you cancer-free now?"

A feeling of desperation hits me. I don't want this to be real. I don't want to have to give William all of this sad information. I don't want to do this to him. I don't want to not be around him. Tears start running down my chin while genuine fear of dying from my cancer hits me for the first time in my life. First now, I truly understand how serious my situation is.

"No," I tell William, trying to find the right words. "I'm afraid that there's nothing to do. My cancer has spread too much and to too many vital parts. I was offered chemo to give me a little extra time, but I rejected that and went here to find peace instead. I'm dying, Will."

Seeing the shock in his eyes makes me cry out loud. I can't hold it back. I don't want to die. I don't want to be sick and feel pain. I want to stay here in the mountains with William forever, explore and experience surreal things. I see tears in his eyes. I know he's trying to find something to say, but I would prefer him not to say anything. I lean forward and hug him to stop him from searching for words. This is the best and most horrifying hug I have ever had.

William

I hug Iris even tighter. How could she keep this a secret all this time? So many questions are running through my mind.

"It is not true," I whisper in her ear, somehow hoping that she will agree that it is not, but she stays quiet. "You are not that sick."

"I am," she whispers back. "I can feel it getting worse every day. I didn't want to hear the doctors' prediction of how long I have left, but they said that it wasn't long."

I am still not convinced. I do not *want* to be convinced. How could Iris hide it this well, if she is that sick?

"Why…" I begin asking, but she stops me.

"I don't want to talk about it, please," she whispers. "I just wanted to let you know. Talking about it won't change anything. I'm sorry, but you would have to know sooner or later."

She is right. I can not do anything to fix this. She most likely already tried whatever she could to get rid of her cancer. However, I am *not* ready to accept it. She ends the hug with a kiss.

"Hey, what do you think Tom and Noah are doing right now?" she asks, obviously wanting to change the subject.

"Ehm, drinking beers and eating pizzas?" I say, in an attempt to help her change the mood of the conversation.

She giggles and wipes the remaining tears away from her chin. Her wet eyes reflect the flames from the fire, making her appear more radiant than ever before. That does not exactly give me reasons to stop believing that she will be fine.

She picks up a few branches and throws them on the fire.

"I hope they are not too worried about us," she says and

looks up at the moon which now shines bright in the sky.

"I am sure they are alright," I tell her. "I miss them, though."

They would be good to have now, making me think of other things than Iris' words that she is... *dying*.

"See the moon, Will," she says. "Whenever you miss somebody, whoever that is, if it's your parents, your friends or even Tom and Noah, then you always have a connection to them via the moon. You look at the same moon, and you see the same thing, but from different places. You are not psychically at the same location, but mentally you share the same experience. That thought normally helps me. It feels like I am much closer to people that I miss."

I turn my head to the moon. An image of Tom and Noah looking at the moon, from our last tea house, flashes before my eyes. A moment later, another image appears: I see my parents looking at the moon from their apartment back at home. They know what is happening to me, but they return their gaze to each other to continue talking about work, the way I have seen them do a million times before, not caring about helping or interacting with me. I don't miss being home right now.

"Well, I'm sleepy," Iris says. "Do you think it will be cold in the night?"

"It might be," I admit. "We are still high up in the mountains, after all."

If we did not have the fire, it might have been cold by now already. I better watch it throughout the night to make sure it keeps burning. Iris retracts her arms into her huge sweater.

"Take off your jacket and come here," she tells me.

Without questioning her, I take off my jacket. She pulls her sweater over my head, and to my surprise, it is big enough to fit us both. We lie down next to the fire, and I pull my jacket over us. Sleepiness comes to me along with the feeling that we will be fine tonight, even if the fire burns out. The sky is filled with bright stars. I have never seen so many stars in my life. Some are sparkling, some are white and some are colored with a pulsing red or blue glow. This must be what people talk about when seeing the milky way. I find it absurd to be in this incredible moment, in this incredible place, with this amazing girl, and at the same time knowing that she is *dying*. So much happiness and sadness at the same time. I close my eyes and enjoy the silence. Then the sleepiness takes me.

- The Path -

Iris

I wake up feeling the first rays of the morning sun shining onto my face. It takes a moment for me to remember where I am and why William is sharing my green, fluffy sweater with me. The fire is out and looks like it has been so for a while. Bob is still sleeping next to it, though.

I kiss William on his forehead in an attempt to wake him. It worked.

"What? What time is it?" he asks, almost still sleeping.

"Well, it's morning. Do you need to know more?" I say, smiling. "A new day is awaiting."

Waking up together in a sweater with someone that you fancy is an amazing thing. I don't get why it's not a common way to sleep. If we survive and find our way back from wherever we are, I *will* make it a big thing. On the other hand, if it becomes just as common as sharing a blanket, the feeling might not be as exciting. No, this will be a Will and Iris thing.

A dog head slams down between Williams and mine.

"Good morning, Bob," I say.

He licks my face, and I have no way to stop him as my hands are trapped inside the sweater, but I end up escaping by withdrawing myself from it. Bob attempts to wake up the still half asleep William by doing his licking-trick on his face as well. At first, there's no reaction from William. He actually looks like he is enjoying the free face-cleaning service. Then, out of nowhere, he sits up in shock, looking like he awoke from a nightmare.

"Good morning, Will," I say.

He mumbles something and rubs his face, while I find the last cereal bar from his jacket and breaks it in two.

"You made coffee?" he asks.

"Of course, my king. I will serve it to you as soon as your eggs and bacon are cooked," I tell him and throw him his half of the cereal bar.

We both decide to give a small piece to Bob as well. Our guide needs energy, after all. For some reason, I feel excellent and adventurous today. After telling William about my secret, a sense of freedom and relief has come to me. I almost know that something exciting will happen today and I'm eager to get going and find out what that exciting thing is.

We eat up and rehydrate ourselves from the stream of water before packing up our clothes and begin walking, again with Bob leading the way. We don't walk for long before we find another broken circle of metallic sand on the ground. Around it, the grass has been stepped flat recently. We follow the trail of trodden grass, which leads from the circle, until we reach the mountain foot. The trail changes to become a narrow path which leads up into the mountain. William and I haven't said much to each other this morning, but we have been communicating with our eyes and gentle, loving touches. We agree to be glad about seeing a more official path and that somebody must be near. Everything seems to be positive today, yet I also see the sadness in his eyes, which makes me stay mute. We hike up and up the path for what feels like hours. In my head, it would make more sense to go *down* from the mountains if we are supposed ever to get back home, but a path means people. At one point, we get high enough to enter a cloud, and our visibility is at a minimum, so we decide to go hand-in-hand and take it slow. The air in the cloud is cold and wet, however yet again also refreshing. That also reminds me of my thirst though. We couldn't bring water with us, so we haven't had anything to drink for hours.

Suddenly we exit the cloud and find ourselves at a cliff with a fantastic view. We look down at bright and wavy clouds which stretches as far as the eye can see. Only a few mountains tops stand tall from the clouds in front of the clear blue sky and brightly shining sun. This is a perfect place for a small break, so we sit down and enjoy the view.

"How are you feeling?" William asks after a while.

"I have a good day," I tell him. "How are you?"

This is what I hate about telling people about me being sick. I don't want to be treated differently. But by asking back, the questions become more of a general caring about each other, more than being questions focused on my health. William puts his arm around me.

"I couldn't be better," he says and puts his free hand on mine.

"What about you, Bob? How are you doing?" I ask.

He sprints over to us and begins another face-licking attack. His tail wiggles so much that he almost can't find balance. At one point, I fear that he will throw himself off the cliff, so I grab him in an attempt to calm him down, but it's not easy when I can't control myself from laughter. William produces a deep whistling tone and Bob stops his happiness-attack right away and stares at William with his head tilted.

"Another thing you learned from online videos?" I ask, maybe a little impressed.

"Nope, not this time," he replies. "I grew up with a hyperactive dog, so I learned a few tricks."

"That's cool," I admit.

"Yeah, I guess. Getting a dog in a big city while nobody has time to stimulate it was another selfish decision my parents made. They only got him to try and look like a perfect couple with the energy to manage a good carrier *and* a happy family at the same time. I was the only one who had time for him, but that was just not enough," he says.

It suddenly makes sense why Bob and William bonded that fast. William has been growing up being protective and helpful, taking care of his dog. That's why he's like that to me also. I can't get enough of learning new things about William.

Out of nowhere, Bob starts growling. He sprints past us and up a stairway that is carved into the mountain. Without thinking, we get on our feet and try to catch up with him. My heartbeat raises, both from the sudden running, and the small fear of not knowing what we are chasing. We finally reach the top of the stairway. My mouth drops as I see the shining golden village in front of me.

"Welcome, friends," a gentle voice says from behind us.

chapter three
MOUNTAIN SECRETS

- Welcome -

William

A young man ambles toward us. He is dressed in a beige robe with thin silver ornaments. With his completely bald head, except for the ponytail of black hair in the back of his head, he reminds me of the monks I have seen in Kathmandu.

"My name is Sumit," he says with a friendly young voice.

Just as he speaks his name, Bob looks up at him and goes crazy with happiness. The monk greets the happy dog and says something to him in a foreign language.

"You know this dog?" I ask.

"Of course!" the monk, Sumit, says. "He's my friend from when I was a child. He likes to run away for weeks, but he always comes back."

Sumit finishes greeting his old friend.

"Come, let me show you around," he says and walks past us towards the incredible mountain village.

As we enter the village, I am entirely lost for words. I feel like appearing in a dream. There are little houses built of stone, with silver and golden ornaments curling around every corner, appearing like shiny vines growing from them. The roofs are made from straw with the same ornaments on it. White strings hang between the houses, having golden triangles hanging on it dangling in the gentle wind. In the distance, I spot a golden temple with similar silver ornaments. Amazing.

An elderly man, with long gray hair, sits on a stool outside one of the houses. He waves at us and happily mumbles something as we walk past him. When he sees Bob, he laughs out loud and greets him in the exact same way that Sumit did. It seems like Bob is a popular guy up here.

"We are only two people in the village who know the English language," Sumit informs us. "We rarely find the need for speaking other languages than our own."

A group of kids runs singingly from a house toward the temple. They wear similar beige robes, but all with different bright colors on the ornaments. Bob runs after the children and disappears into the temple with them. So many questions are forming in my head, that I have no idea where to begin.

"What are your names?" Sumit asks us, cutting me off deciding what to ask first.

"I'm Iris from Iceland," Iris says.

"William from New York City," I tell him.

"Nice to meet you, Iris and William," he replies and claps his hands together. "I believe you have some questions now, and that you will likely have more as you learn about our village. I will explain over a cup of tea in my house, but first I want you to meet someone."

He yells out something, and a door opens from one of the houses next to us.

"This is Heena," Sumit says. "She is the Main Protector of the village. And my mother, of course."

A tall, black-haired woman in a similar beige robe shows herself in the doorway. She puts her hands together and bends at us. Then she starts a conversation with her son. The way they talk to each other sounds so calm and friendly. I almost suspect them for repeatedly telling how much they love each other. The conversation abruptly ends, and the woman nods at us and returns into the house.

"The Main Protector? Protector from what?" Iris asks

after the door closes.

"It is simply how we call it. I don't know the correct word in the English language. When something happens in the village, she will have to know. She knows everything and can help everyone. Now she knows that new guests have arrived and now the village people can go to her and ask about you. You will have the opportunity to talk with her another time," he replies. "Now let me invite you to my house for a cup of tea."

He leads us a few houses closer to the temple and stops in front of a house with the door open.

"This is where I live," he says and enters the house.

Iris

The small house is basically *one* room with a minimal amount of stuff. There's a small fireplace burning in the right corner with kitchen tools lying around it. In the center, there are cushions on the ground and a round wooden table-like platform in between the cushions. I look to my left and spot blankets on the floor, which must be the sleeping area. In the foot-end, there's a small wooden cupboard with golden ornaments, and a few books lying on top. That is all there is in here.

"Have a seat, please," Sumit says, and gestures at the cushions.

We sit down, and Sumit moves to the small kitchen area. He pours up some water in a black pot with the familiar golden ornaments. I have to ask about all this gold and silver. Mostly I'm curious if it is genuine valuable materials or not. Sumit picks up some leaves from a wooden box and throws them in the pot before he grabs the pot and places it in the fireplace. At first, I'm not registering what is happening, but then I see the pot hovering in the air above the fire. Wait, what? I double-check to see a reason for the hovering, but there's no explanation at all. Before I even find the words to ask, Sumit looks at us and smiles.

"No, it is not magic," he says. "Maybe magic as you modern society people would think as magic, but really it is just ancient knowledge with a scientific explanation. I'm not sure if modern scientists would accept this to be real, though. They are possessed with discovering new knowledge and following plausible theories."

William and I glance at each other for answers.

"But how are you doing it then?" I ask Sumit.

He adds some white flowers to the tea and stirs in the hovering pot with a wooden stick.

"I will explain later, my friend," he replies. "Now relax and eat."

He picks up some pieces of bread from another box and throws them to us, and I instantly realize how hungry I am from not eating all day. I almost swallow the whole piece of bread in my sudden hunger and immediately feel full even though it wasn't much bread. Sumit takes the hovering pot, pours up some tea in small silver cups and puts them on the table-like platform before he sits down on one of the cushions with his legs crossed.

"Wait for it to cool a bit, please," he says as I reach out for the cup.

"I saw something similar in Kathmandu," William says and points at the pot. "A monk made balls hover in the air."

"Yes, you are right," Sumit says. "We are all free people and can do what we wish to. Some of our people want to explore the world, and they are welcome to do so. They can earn money for their travels with their knowledge, as long as they keep it a secret."

"Why keep it a secret?" I ask. "Do you mean it's like magicians who don't want to tell how they do their tricks?"

Sumit offers me another smile.

"Nothing like that, my friend," he says. "For now, I will let you know that it is for safety reasons."

He takes his cup and gestures for us to do the same.

"Again welcome to our village," he says and puts the cup to his mouth.

I take a sip of the warm tea and immediately feel a

well-known sensation of sunshine warming my body on a happy summer day. I feel free and safe at the same time. I almost wonder if…

"No, there is nothing euphorically in it," Sumit answers to the question that was developing in my head. "We call it *Din Chiya*, which I believe is translated into *day tea*. We drink it during the day-time instead of water. On hot days, we let it cool down before drinking, of course. Healthy, tasty and clean."

"It's good!" I admit and take another sip of the refreshing drink.

"Are you having guests like us a lot?" William asks.

"No," Sumit answers. "Not a lot of people know about this place. We are not connected to any modern society in any way. We have knowledge which helps us create methods that guide people away from our village. Sometimes the universe wants us to receive guests, and when that happens, we gladly welcome them."

I realize that Sumit looks me deeply in my eyes. I almost suspect him for trying to read my mind. After seeing the hovering pot, I almost believe that he actually *can* read my mind, but that would be silly. His eyes flicker from my shoulder to my eyes, and it reminds me of the pain. However, it's not as painful now as it was this morning. Maybe the tea has some kind of pain-killing effect.

The sound of laughing children flies through the house from outside. Through the window, I spot the running children from the temple. It makes me wonder what kind of beliefs they have here with a temple like that.

"I hope it's okay to ask, but are you religious?" I ask Sumit.

"Not in the way that the modern world believes religion to be," he answers. "We only believe in the knowledge we have, but we base our life upon that, so I guess you can call us religious."

His answer confuses me.

"So you don't believe in any gods?" I ask.

He puts down his cup on the round table.

"We believe that God is the souls of our ancestors. They love us as we loved them, protect us as we protected them, and are always amongst us as we are with them. They are us as we are them. God is all of us," Sumit replies. "You might not understand it now, but time will explain. One day you will understand."

He gets up from the cushion and gestures for us to do the same.

"This might be a good time to visit the temple," he says and gestures for us to go through the door.

We exit the house and Sumit begins sauntering away, but leaves the door open. People must surely trust each other here. I must admit that I love the thought of living in a society of trust. It's rare to see that in our part of the world.

William

We enter the huge temple, and the first thing that catches my attention is the silver and golden ornaments everywhere. Warm rays of sunlight enter from the windows in the ceiling and illuminate the temple well, especially the bright shining ornaments, reflecting the light in fine, thin lines. I smell the scent of flowers and notice the incenses that are burning from golden bowls on the floor. Beside the incense, and the cushions on the floor here and there, the temple is pretty much empty. At the back, a group of children sits in a circle with a female monk explaining something.

"The temple has two functions in our village," Sumit says. "We use it as a school and as a place to connect with ourselves and our beloved ones."

He guides us toward the group of children. Some of the children wave at us while the teaching monk gives us a smile and a nod before continuing her lesson. In the middle of the group is a circle of silver and golden sand, just as we have seen it a few times before, but this time there is something inside the circle. I squeeze my eyes to determine what exactly that is. A bunch of ants running around in a thin line formation. They run clockwise in a circle following the sand. The teacher closes her eyes and reaches out with a flat hand towards the circle. Instantly, the moment she touches the circle of sand, the ants reverse and run the opposite direction, now anti-clockwise. The children become just as excited as me, clapping and bumping up and down in their seats. However, the teacher manages to calm them down to focus on the lesson. She points at one of the boys in the group and says something before gesturing at the circle. I guess that he has to try to reverse the loop now.

The boy closes his eyes and takes his time to reach out a flat hand. For some reason, my nerves can not handle this. I am excited and nervous for the boy at the same time. As he finally reaches the circle of sand, nothing happens as he touches it. What a shame. The teacher says something to him, and he keeps the hand on top of the sand. I can almost hear him concentrate. However, still nothing happens. The boy gives up and opens his eyes, looking quite disappointed. As he pulls back his hand, he accidentally pulls some of the metallic sand with him and breaks the circle. Instantly the formation of the ants is broken and the small insects run randomly in all directions. Some of them stay confused inside the broken circle while others escape by simply running over the sand. The teacher keeps the happy and calm expression on her face and talks gently to the children, who stays in their seats observing the ants.

"The circle must not be broken," Sumit says. "I will explain later. One thing at a time."

I hear a bark behind us, coming from the entrance, and I turn around to see Bob lying in the corner of the temple. A cat is pressing itself up against him, and he happily licks the cat while making short happy sounds.

"Ah yes, this is where he lives," Sumit says and gestures at Bob. "He decided to become a guard dog for the temple as a puppy. He and the cat are best friends."

It occurs to me that Bob might have a different name, but I honestly do not want to know about it. For me, he is a *Bob*. A popular dog from an unexplainable village in the mountains. I know how silly it sounds, but I am starting to believe that Bob planned to lead us to this village all along. I guess I am just confused by all these new things happening here in this place. This mysterious and unbelievable village.

"Now you have seen the temple," Sumit says. "It's time for you to see where we grow some of our food."

Then we leave the temple.

Iris

Sumit leads us five minutes out of the village and stops at a ledge with a free-fall drop from which he gestures for us to look down. William and I move to the ledge to check what's down there. There are large fields of green crops, each of them on its own level on the mountain hills.

"These are our rice paddies," Sumit informs us. "The most important place in the village."

I spot a few people working in the fields. They seem happy about their work. One of them stops to take a drink from a wooden flask that was attached to his hip-belt, but as he sees us, he puts it down and greets us with a big arm wave. Sumit returns the greeting with a similar arm-waving, making it look like some kind of traditional gesture.

"He looks happy," I hear myself saying.

Sumit turns around to speak to us.

"People work because they *want* to, not because they are *told* to do so," he says. "This way, we find life to be better, and we *do* enjoy doing work for the village and the community. If one wants to help in the rice paddies one day, one is welcome to do that. If one wants to help teach or perhaps gather materials for the village, one can do that. No pressure means more pleasure."

Sumit giggles of his small saying.

"I made that up myself," he says proudly.

"What else do you grow besides rice?" William asks.

"We grow root vegetables on fields, which are located a few hours on foot from here. There are a few houses there, so people can stay when working in the fields, if they wish to," Sumit replies. "Then we have *gatherers* who collect things like wild fruits, berries and nuts that grow in the mountains."

"That's awesome," I admit all fascinated. I have another question I want to ask, but yet again, Sumit answers my unspoken question.

"We never eat meat," he says and smiles at me. "Corpses of wild animals are collected for skin and meat, but the meat is for the animals of the village, while the skin and fur are for our tools and clothes."

I have heard about monks who don't eat meat and don't exploit animals, but being here and discovering it to be true is something else. These kinds of communities actually do exist. Incredible.

A cool breeze passes by, bringing a beautiful singing with it. I spot a young girl working in the fields next to someone who could easily be her father. Her song sounds magical with the foreign words.

"Everybody can help if they want to. Age does not decide," Sumit says. "You are more than welcome to help us out with the rice if you decide to stay here for some time."

It occurs to me that we're still lost, besides having arrived at this amazing place. Sumit can most likely direct us in the right direction, though he said that there was no official connection between this village and others. However, something in me doesn't want to leave this place just yet.

"Well, you can not leave at this time of day," Sumit continues. "Let me show you to your accommodation. You can decide your plans after a good sleep."

"Sounds good," I reply as I now realize that I'm still exhausted.

With that said, we return to the village.

William

We follow Sumit to a small house, a few buildings away from his own. The house is parted in two, so we enter one of the rooms. It is a small room which is only illuminated by violet colors from the sunset outside. There are two cotton blankets on the floor, spread out like thin madrases. On top of them are two woolen sheets. The thing that I like the best, though, is the food. A wooden bowl with rice, a basket with bread, a jug of water and two silver cups stands next to the beds. I almost can not control my manners and get an urge to run for the food to eat it like a crazy animal. Yet I manage to stay put.

"I will let you be for now," Sumit says. "You deserve to eat and sleep. I will be in my home if you need anything. I will find you in the morning."

"Thank you for everything," Iris says before Sumit gestures a goodbye and leaves, closing the door behind him.

"It is food time!" I say eagerly.

"Definitely!" Iris agrees while we almost run to the food.

Neither the rice or bread taste of much, but it is still the best food I have had for a very long time. We shovel the food down in our stomachs in no time before finding ourselves sitting content on each of our beds. We watch each other for a while, making me unsure if I am dreaming or if I am awake at this moment. The mix of feelings that are in my body right now is surreal. Being all tired, while being confused and surprised by finding this unexplainable village, topped with being completely in love with this, apparently, sick girl, is almost too much to bear. I move myself next to her and put my arm around her. She puts her head on my shoulder.

"What do you think of this place?" she asks, sounding all tired.

"I am not sure," I admit. "But I am curious."

"Me too," she says quietly. "Do you think we should stay here?"

"We can take one day at a time," I reply. "We can stay here tomorrow at least."

Iris lifts her head and kisses me on my cheek.

"I like that idea," she says.

She holds on to me and pulls me down on the bed, making us lie face to face. I put my hand to her hair, and she does the same to my hair, somehow pressing our foreheads together. My heart beats rapidly and slowly at the same time. I feel so close to her at this moment. I feel her breath and every exhale gives me goosebumps. She puts her lips to mine and we kiss. My hand moves from her head to her back, and I press our bodies closer together. The kiss gets more intense for every second. It feels like my body is filled with electricity. Iris tries to whisper something in between the kissing, but I do not register what.

"What?" I manage to whisper in between the kissing.

This time I understand what she is saying.

"I think I love you... Will..."

- Knowledge & magic -

Iris

I wake up to rooster crowing and sunlight in my face. I squeeze my eyes to enable myself to see out the window from my lying position, and I realize that the sky is amazingly blue and free of clouds. I wonder what time it is, and if people even care about time up here. I move my gaze to William, who is lying right next to me. He still sleeps, looking cute as always. Did I seriously tell him that I *love* him yesterday? Yes, I am *in love* with him and all, but *I love him*? Isn't that something you say to people that you have been married to for years? I have only known William for less than two weeks, and I tell him that *I love him*. I have never said that to anyone before, besides my parents, of course. However, William *does* mean a lot to me already. It's strange. I feel like I have known him for years and that life wouldn't be the same without him. Oh man, I do *love him*. Is that even possible so fast? A sudden panic hits me. This can not be true. I get a death sentence and *then* meet William. I am told to leave the world while being given more reasons to want to stay. That is not fair!

William opens his eyes.

"Why are you crying?" he asks and wipes away a tear from my chin.

"Oh… ehm… no reason," I reply and give him a kiss to change his focus.

We lie for a while, just watching each other. If somebody saw us do this, they would most likely roll their eyes and throw up. This much love would be horrible to watch.

"I was thinking about helping out in the rice fields today,"

William whispers.

"That's not a bad idea," I whisper back. "It would be a nice way for us to thank the village people for the hospitality."

Somebody knocks on the door, and we both instantly get to sitting position. The door opens and a pair of eyes glance in from the door chink. As Sumit sees us sitting up, he opens the door entirely and walks in with a golden tray, which he puts down in front of us, and gestures for us to take from it. I see two cups of coffee, a cup of tea and three pieces of bread.

"Good morning, William and Iris," he says and picks up the teacup. "Please, have breakfast."

"Thank you, Sumit," I say and grab one of the cups with coffee.

"How did you sleep?" Sumit asks and breaks off a small piece from one of the breads.

From the corner of my eye, I see William finishing a yawn.

"Like a baby," William says and picks up a cup of coffee as well. "How about you, Sumit?"

"Good as always, thank you," Sumit replies, sounding like a monk version of a gentleman.

It doesn't take us long before the coffee is drunk and the bread has been eaten. I feel the coffee working in no time, though it could have used some sugar. Also, the bread wasn't tasty, but I can't complain. I'm full and energized, as much as I can be these days.

"I have something to show you," Sumit says and picks up the golden tray. "Please, follow me to the temple."

William

As we enter the temple, Bob comes running to greet us before returning to sleep in his corner. It is good to see him again. He is such a charming temple protector dog. I wonder what he decided to protect the temple from though.

Sumit guides us to the middle of the temple and makes us sit on the floor pillows. He puts down the golden tray on the floor and removes the cups before finding a small skin pouch from his pocket.

"I don't expect you to understand," he says while opening the pouch. "But I will try to teach you."

He pours some of the content from the pouch out in a large circle on the ground. It is the silver and golden sand which we have seen quite a few times now.

"Please, first watch and I will explain," he tells us.

He picks up the golden tray and places it in the middle of the circle of sand. Then he closes his eyes and inhales, leaving Iris and me in excitement and wonder. He moves his hand to the circle, and as he touches the sand, the golden tray begins hovering in the air. It does not surprise me as much this time, but I am anxious for an explanation.

"Let me try to explain," Sumit says while letting the plate hover. "This is not magic. This is what modern society might call undiscovered biology, even though this is as ancient as humankind, if not older. It is simply magnetism."

He closes his eyes and puts his hand to the circle again, and the tray hovers even higher.

"Magnetism? But how do you control magnetism like that?" I ask in confusion.

"Same way as the birds who find their way with the help

from magnetic fields," Sumit replies gently. "But our species is somehow able to control magnetism instead of only reading it."

I look at Iris to see if she has ever heard about this, but it seems like a no.

"Our species?" she asks. "Like humans in general, or are you people a different species?"

I can hear her doubt her question as she speaks it up loudly.

"We three are indeed the same species," Sumit says. "However, modern society has forgotten about this ability. They have had so much focus on discovering new things and expanding their brain capacity, that they forgot about what our bodies are capable of without our brains having to actively think about it. People fill their brains with new knowledge, which they will never use. Eventually, some knowledge will get lost."

He clears his throat.

"Think of it as if you're in a big library with empty bookshelves," he continues. "You stack books nicely on the ground as you get more of them, and you decide to sort them on the shelves later. Eventually, the stacks get too tall and collapse, and the books are now lying in a big mess, which is almost impossible to sort. You then realize that there is not enough space on the bookshelves for all books, so you have to decide which books to keep and which to get rid of. With the big messy pile of books, it is almost certain that one of your important books will stay in the pile and be lost forever."

I am speechless from all this information, but I somehow understand what Sumit means.

"But why have the modern world not rediscovered this

ability yet?" I ask like he is some all-knowing professor.

"The same reason that modern people don't know how birds and other animals use their abilities," he answers. "Modern people are aware that these birds have the ability, but they still have not figured out how they use it. When it comes to humans, the modern scientist has no reason to think that humankind has the same ability and even a more advanced one. Maybe one day they will rediscover, but let's hope not."

I nod at him in understanding. If a friend ever told me that humans perceive the ability to magnify objects, and that we have always been able to, but somehow just forgot about it while focusing on discovering new things, I would call it a lie. However, hearing it from Sumit who somehow proved it to be true is something else.

"What would go wrong if the modern world knew about this?" Iris asks.

Sumit shakes his head.

"It just would not be good, trust me," he replies. "This ability can be used for more than making metal hover."

"Like trapping ants?" Iris asks.

For some reason, the question makes Sumit smile.

"You're getting closer, my friend," he replies. "Ants trap themselves in this type of magnetism. They try to follow the magnetic fields of the earth, but the magnetic circle will trick them. Ants are the easiest way for our children to train their abilities."

"So it is some kind of special sand?" I ask in an attempt to understand how scientists and biologists do not know about this ability.

"It is simply silver and gold dust," Sumit replies. "We

have much of it in the mountains. These metals are not magnetic on their own, so they are easier to work with."

I am still trying to figure out why this could be bad to know for modern society. What else can this ability be used for? What else don't we know about? So many questions are developing in my head.

"Please, no more questions for now," Sumit says. "It will only confuse you and you might never learn. It is important to focus on just doing it from within your body, and not only thinking it with your brain."

He touches the circle of sand, and the tray slams down the ground with a loud gong sound. The sound kinda restarts me and my brain. I feel like I just awoke from a dream.

"I want you to try, William," Sumit says. "Close your eyes and start breathing deeply until you're fully relaxed."

Without question, I do as he tells me to. A few deep breaths, and I feel my heart slowing down.

"Now, empty your mind," Sumit continues. "Try to think only of the circle of sand in front of you. Try to visualize a magnetic field around it."

As told, I try to imagine the circle of sand. Around it, I visualize some sort of blue energy, which I might have seen in science fiction movies. Nevertheless, I find it hard to concentrate on the image and not thinking of what I am supposed to do.

"When you are ready, try to move your hand to the circle and visualize that you pass this energy into the sand itself."

As I move my hand to the circle, nervousness arrives. I feel my palms getting sweaty from the idea that I will get this tray to hover. I am doing real magic. I feel my hand touching the sand. It is quite cold against the tips of my fingers. I open one of my eyes to check up on my magic, but unfortunately, nothing happened, and the smile on my face instantly turns into disappointment. Iris giggles and pets me on my chin.

"Oh no, I'm sorry," she says like I am a little baby.

"No one can do this the first time, don't worry," Sumit tells me to cheer me up.

He gestures at Iris to close her eyes and do the same procedure, and I try brainstorming for a sweet way to mock her when she fails her attempt as well. Sumit tells her to do the same as I did: calm down and think of nothing but the sand and the force around it. Then she gets ready to lower her hand to the circle. I prepare myself to do some mocking, but to my surprise, as she touches the circle, the tray flies high up in the air. My surprise is so big that I release a weird sound from my throat. Iris opens her eyes for a moment, looking like she is scared to death. I can not believe she did it!

Sumit burst into loud laughter.

"I am making fun with you," he says and touches the circle so the tray drops.

He catches the tray with his hands this time and puts it gently down on the ground.

"I'm sorry, I could not keep myself from doing it," he continues. "*I* made it happen."

He gets up on his feet and gestures for us to do the same.

"As I said, this is not a thing that you learn overnight. You have to get rid of that modern way of thinking," he says. "But when you are able to clear your mind completely, and feel what your body is capable of, this is how you do. But it requires patience."

"I definitely also need patience if I should ever absorb all of this information," Iris admits.

"What she said," I say, pointing at Iris.

Sumit laughs again.

"You have all the time you need, my friends," he says. "You can stay here as long as you want and practice whenever you want to."

"Speaking of which," Iris says. "William and I were talking about helping out in the rice fields today."

"You shall be very welcome," Sumit says. "Let us go see my mother and ask where you can help."

Iris

Sumit's mother, Heena, greets us in the doorway as we approach her house. Sumit tells her something in their foreign language, and she nods silently before calling for someone in the house.

"It seems that my little sister is home," Sumit tells us.

A young woman in the, apparently, ordinary beige rope appears in the doorway. Her dark shoulder-length hair is hanging loose with a hair clip holding her front hair away from her face. Heena says a few words to her before the young girl moves her dark eyes to us.

"Hello there!" she says and walks over to greet us. "William and Iris, I assume."

We shake her hand, and she nods respectfully to her brother. She must be the other one with English skills, whom Sumit told us about. The English speaking siblings of the village.

"My lovely big brother told me about you," she continues. "I'm Numit."

"Nice to meet you, Numit," I say. "And what a similar name to your brother."

Her eyes fill with joy.

"I know," she says happily. "It is normal here for siblings to have similar names."

"My sister is volunteering in the rice fields today," Sumit says. "She will guide you there and show you how we do. Today, I, myself, will be working with my mother, so I am here if you need me. I will see you later."

He nods at us and enters the house with his mother, leaving us with his sister, Numit.

"Shall we go?" Numit asks and starts moving.

She walks rapidly, almost prancing her way forward. The sun is still shining bright and feels warm in the fresh breeze. This will be a good day. I'm not sure how much work I can do before my pain returns, but I feel optimistic and ready for doing a good job.

"Are you two boyfriend and girlfriend?" Numit suddenly asks from in front of us.

I await to hear if William has an answer for that, but he stays quiet. There is only one easy way to answer this question without getting awkward.

"We are indeed!" I reply.

William turns his head to me, with joy glowing from his eyes. We will have to talk this one out in private, but if he's good with it, I will be more than okay with titling us already.

"That's cool," Numit says.

"Do *you* have a boyfriend?" I ask her nicely.

She shakes her head.

"No, I am only eighteen, so I have a lot of time to find the right one," she replies, still prancing happily.

"That's smart of you," I tell her. "Don't just go for anyone. Find the right one."

"That is sweet of you to say, Iris," she replies. "Thank you."

I see the similarities between Numit and her brother. They are both very polite. Numit, on the other hand, seems to be more open-minded, yet less mature and less mysterious, probably because she is the younger one. Nevertheless, I like both of them already.

"Are there a lot of potential boyfriends around?" William asks her. "How many citizens are you in the village?"

She turns around on her heel and walks backward.

"Not enough," she answers. "We are only about a hundred people in the village, which means that only 25 people are around my age. With half of them being males, and when only half of the males in my age are not married, there is not a lot to choose from."

She turns around and prances again.

"Does it bother you to be so few people here?" William asks her.

"No no, I could not see myself living anywhere else. This is my home, and it is the best place to live. The people in the village are the best!" Numit replies. "I'm happy here, boyfriend or not."

We finally reach the rice fields, and Numit guides us down a steep path to a paddy field with nothing but a foot thick layer of water. On the way, she picks up a small basket with thin green plants in it. We stop at the watery field, and she hands both of us a bunch of the green seedlings from the basket.

"We need to plant as much as we can," she tells us. "Normally we would be more people doing it, but a lot of people are harvesting today because of the upcoming storm."

She then shows us how to do it. It looks simple when she does it, and she is quick. Just put a seedling in the soil under the water, take a small step backward and repeat. Both William and I find it quite intuitive but are nowhere near as quick as Numit. She slows down to our speed though.

"What is that storm you mentioned?" I ask while continuing planting.

"A big storm," Numit replies. "Our weather tellers say it is strong enough to destroy all of our fully grown rice plants, so we have to harvest before it's too late. The seedlings here are too short to be affected by the wind, so it is okay for us to plant them now. The weather tellers expect the storm to arrive within seven days, but they can never tell exactly when. It could even be tomorrow or the day after."

"Weather tellers?" William asks.

"Yes, the people who know how to read the weather," Numit answers. "They measure wind and geomagnetism and compare it to the behavior of the moon. It's the best way to predict mountain storms. I have always dreamed about becoming a weather teller one day, but it is an important job, and I am still too young for that."

She sighs from the thought of not being old enough to make her dream come true.

"You use magnetism for many things," William concludes.

"We do, yes," Numit says. "Elderly people here say that your modern world doesn't know about magnetism as we do. They say that what we can use it for is unimaginable in your eyes. I am actually not supposed to talk about it to visitors."

"That's understandable," I tell her. "We are just too curious, you know."

"It's okay. All living beings are curious," she says.

A couple of small brown birds chase each other in the distance. Their twittering somehow makes me consider if they are in love with each other. I wonder how it must be like to be free as a bird. They can fly wherever they want to with no need of a map. They have their built-in GPS system. They can read geomagnetic fields to find their way around, as Sumit said. He also said that humans are somewhat capable of doing the same.

While continuing planting, I close my eyes and try to see if I can feel some sort of magnetism or direction. I feel nothing. If anything, I feel the pain in my shoulder more now. I also feel exhausted from working already. I open my eyes back up and raise myself from my bend position. Dizziness hits me. I try to ask Numit for some water, but no words escape my mouth. I suddenly feel trouble breathing. I try to focus my gaze on the seedlings in my hand, but I only see black spots. Cold sweat drips from my forehead, and the seedlings drop from my hand. I feel myself collapse before everything turns dark.

William

"Iris!" I yell and run to her to pick her up from the water.

Sitting on my knees in the water, holding her limp body, I turn her around so I can see her face. Her eyes are closed and she appears extremely pale. Numit gets on her knees next to me.

"She is breathing," she says all calm.

How can she be so calm?!

"She is okay," Numit says and puts a hand on Iris' forehead.

"How do you know?" I ask, annoyed by her weird calmness

"As I said," Numit replies. "She is still breathing. Besides, if you look close, you see her eyes move. She is dreaming."

Just as I am about to argue that people are not okay when fainting like that, Iris mumbles something, which I can not clearly understand. She takes my hand and holds it tight. Her eyes open halfway so I can see the edge of her shining, blue pearls.

"What did I say," Numit says proudly.

Iris tries to get to a sitting position, so I position myself as a chair for her. Numit finds a seat in the water in front of us, taking Iris' hands.

"We'll give her a minute to wake up," she says.

I decide to go with what Numit suggests. She must know about what is going on. Iris mumbles something again but is still not awake. I hug her tight. My mind goes back to last night before we went to bed. She told me that she loves me. I still can not believe that. And on top of that, I simply cannot understand that she is sick and that I am losing her. It still sounds surreal in my head. She can not disappear now. She can not disappear *ever*. It can not be true. She makes me feel complete. The frustration of not being able to do anything about it hits me big time. It is *not fair*!

"William, I think you should…" Numit says, but cuts herself off.

I realize that I am hugging Iris a bit too tight. I instantly release my grip and a loud inhale sounds from her.

"What…" she asks, confused.

It seems that choking her awoke her. Who would know?

"Welcome back," Numit says with a big smile on her face.

"Are you okay?" I ask.

She nods.

"I feel a little soaked, though," she says in an attempt to cheer up the mood.

"Can you walk?" Numit asks.

Iris gets up on her feet, but has trouble finding the balance, so she finds support in me. For a short moment, she puts her hand to her shoulder but removes it again when she realizes I am watching. She is in pain, and I can not do anything about it. My frustration peaks. A drop of water runs down my chin, though I am not sure if it is from my eye or the water beneath us.

"We should get you back," Numit says.

"That would be good," Iris replies.

I keep supporting Iris while we walk back to the village. The sun is shining bright and blinds me most of the way. The clear sun that I would usually think of as a pleasant thing is now the most annoying thing on the planet. The walk to the village feels like an eternity. I want to run from this situation. Escape the frustration. But I can not do that. I can not do anything other than wait for the end to come. I can not take it!

We finally reach the village. We enter our room and I sit down next to Iris on our bed.

"I will be right back," Numit says and runs out of the door.

For some reason, the room is dark at this time a day. Not much light gets in from the windows when the sun is high in the sky.

"What happened?" I ask Iris after a while

"I am not sure," she answers. "I just suddenly felt dizzy and lost control."

"Are you in pain now?" I ask

"No, it's okay. Don't think about it," she replies.

I know that she is lying. She is protecting me from more frustration. There is no reason for me to feel pain or frustration whenever *she* does. That does not help her. But I somehow want to feel her pain. I wish that I could take some of it and that we could share this sickness and die together. Nevertheless, it would be selfish of me to demand her to be honest about her pain, if she does not want to at this point.

"Iris, my mother would like to speak with you," Numit says from the door opening.

Iris

Numit leads me to her mother's house and into a room similar to the one in Sumit's home. On the floor, there's the usual circle of silver-golden sand with a cushion inside, but this time the circle is larger. Next to it sits Numit's mother, Heena. Numit finds a seat next to her mother and points at the cushion in the circle of sand.

"Please, sit inside the circle," she says.

Even though I find it strange, I have no reason not to do it, so I find my seat in the middle of the circle. I realize that there's a circle around Heena as well, and a line of sand connecting our two circles.

"Don't worry. You won't feel anything," Numit tells me. "Just relax, and I will explain later."

I do my best to calm myself down to wait for my explanation of what is going on. Heena closes her eyes. Her left hand stretches and touches her circle gently. Instantly I feel a weird sensation through my whole body, but I can't decide exactly how it feels. It's like a combination of feeling stressed and fully relaxed at the same time. I will indeed need that explanation now.

It doesn't take long before Heena opens her eyes and removes her hand from the circle. She looks me deep in my eyes. The powerful look she has had until now shows a hint of sadness. She says something to Numit while keeping her gaze at me.

"I will translate for her," Numit says.

Heena keeps talking to her daughter who translates the unknown words for me.

"As you already know, your body is in a bad state," Numit

translates. "Your condition is getting worse every day. There is no cure, and you are in pain."

I see the expression of Numit becoming more and more concerned with every word.

"You seek a peaceful end, yet, something inside you does not want to leave this world," she continues. "You were ready to leave but a new thing in your life conflicts with this."

Knowing exactly what she is talking about, I nod silently.

"You need to come clean with this conflict and accept your reality to find your peaceful ending," Numit continues, still translating her mother.

They give me a moment to absorb the information. It's clear what Heena wants me to do, and it makes sense to me. I need to accept that I'm not going to grow old with William, and I need to make sure that he understands that as well. I can only find peace within myself if I'm sure that William is okay with what is happening and that he can accept it.

Heena speaks more, but this time Numit stays quiet. After a few minutes of talking, Heena gets up, nods at me and leaves the room.

"My mother thinks that it will be best if you stay in our village," Numit says. "You can find peace here. We have medicine for your pain too."

"I would like that, Numit," I tell her with a sudden clear decision that this is where I need to be.

A timid smile appears on her face.

"Good," she says. "I'm sorry, Iris. I didn't know…"

"No, don't be," I interrupt. "How should you. I'm an expert in hiding these things."

Her smile grows.

"So can I have my explanation now?" I ask to change the

subject.

I have to stop fleeing from talking about my sickness and my feelings. I will never get clear of the conflict of finding peace if I don't. And I *have* to speak to William about it.

"Yes, of course, Iris. It's simple," she says. "Magnetism transforms energy from one body to another. This is how we figure people's conditions."

"Oh, it's like when transforming wind to electricity?" I ask.

She looks confused at me.

"I guess," she replies.

I'm not sure if she knows what I'm talking about. I haven't seen any electrical things here and surely she has never seen a modern windmill. She must be just as confused about my question as I am with her explanation. But I have more important things to think about than trying to figure out how things work up here. I have to go talk with William and find the peace I have been searching for. And I will need to tell him that I'm staying here.

"Can I go to see William?" I ask Numit.

"Yes," she replies while we get up from our pillows. "I will bring you some medicine for your pain by tomorrow."

"Thank you, Numit," I say.

As she walks towards the door, I misinterpret the situation and throw my arms around her for a hug. To my luck, she hugs me back.

"Thank you, Iris. I needed that," she tells me.

"Me too," I say before releasing my grip.

With that done, we exit the house. The sun is not as high on the sky anymore, so I believe it's already afternoon. Just as I am about to go and see William, something catches my attention. I turn my head to see three people marching into the village.

"Oh there's Sumit," Numit says. "With two new guests, I see."

Just then, I spot the two large backpacks. No way…

- Reunion -

William

Iris has been away for a long time now. At least it feels like that when sitting alone here in our room, just waiting for her. I wonder what Heena wanted to talk to her about.

Oh, finally, here she comes.

"William!" a dark male voice shouts from the doorway.

I look up to see Noah standing in the doorway. I do not believe my eyes. He steps inside and behind him comes Tom and Iris.

"Seriously?" I yell and jump up to greet the guys with a hug. "I can not believe you are here? How?"

Noah releases his famous deep laughter.

"Trust me, I want an explanation too," Iris says.

Sumit enters the room with blankets and a tray with food and tea.

"Goodnight and welcome again," he says to Tom and Noah before putting the tray and blankets down and leaving the room.

"Thank you, Sumit," Tom says and turns around to me. "What a nice guy."

Tom and Noah find a seat on Iris' bed while me and Iris sit on mine. I am not sure where to start. I am still not sure if this is real.

"Okay, first thing first. What happened to you in the avalanche?" I ask.

"That we are not sure about," Tom begins. "Everything around us changed from the avalanche, so we were quite disoriented. You guys had both the map and compass, and the trail was destroyed, so we had to make a guess and off-road our way back to the trail, but we got lost. Well, now we are here."

"You guys actually gave us some direction," Noah adds. "We saw your fire in the distance. When we finally got there the day after, we found that you forgot your American batteries there, Will."

"That is awesome," Iris says. "It's so nice to see you guys."

"We were quite worried about you," I add.

I must admit that my mind was more on Iris and her sickness than on Noah and Tom. On the other hand, I was confident that they were okay. I had no idea that they were lost and were following us. It is great to see them again, so I am a little disappointed for myself by not giving them more thoughts. Still, Iris deserves my full attention. I can not even compare her importance to me to anybody or anything else.

"So this place is cool," Tom says. "The young monk, Sumit, welcomed us the minute we stepped into the village. No questions asked."

"There is so much more to this place," I tell them. "It is like everything here is made of magic."

I can see that Noah and Tom have no clue what I am talking about. They will see eventually. If they decide to stay here longer, that is.

"We will see," Noah says. "We wanted to get back home tomorrow, but Sumit said that a storm is coming anytime soon and that it would be dangerous of us to be escorted back."

"It's a little annoying," Tom adds. "There's no phone connection here, and I want to talk to my girl and tell her that I'm okay and that I will be back home to take care of our upcoming baby soon."

"I guess you guys got the same suggestion about waiting to return home, since you're still here?" Tom asks.

I'm about to tell them that we stayed here because we're in no hurry, and that we probably will return home with them when they get an escort after the storm. However, Iris speaks up first.

"About that," she says. "I decided to stay here for a while."

She watches me with questioning eyes, looking like she is asking for forgiveness. Noah and Tom do not know that she is sick and dying, so they most likely do not understand exactly why she wants to stay. For me, it completely makes sense. There is no need for me to think this through.

"Me too," I say.

Iris takes my hand and squeezes it. Noah and Tom get eye contact for a second, clearly making their mental friend-ship communication without words. I expect a childish joke about us being boyfriend and girlfriend but am surprised by a better reaction from the two friends.

"It's good to see you two together finally," Tom says calmly. "If I didn't have a baby to get home to, I would also stay here if the village is as magical as you say."

"Ditto," Noah says. "Tom's kid cannot survive without a cool uncle, so I have to get back too. Besides, a lot of French chicks are waiting for my awesomeness."

A low group-giggling sounds from all of us, and I'm reminded of how different a situation we are in now, com-pared to just a few days ago, when we were in full control of everything and were just having one single goal: to get to the base camp before getting back home and continuing our lives.

"At least we'll have some days together here until the storm is gone," Iris says.

We grab some food and tea from the tray which we eat and drink like children around a candy bowl. It appears that we were all starving. It was not a lot of food, but it seems that you get full from the food here quite easily. Noah yawns. As usual with yawns, it spreads so that we are all yawning alternately.

"Sorry guys. We have been walking for ten hours," Tom says. "I think it is time for us to get some sleep, and we can catch up tomorrow."

"That is perfect," Iris says. "I could use some sleep as well."

I am still curious to know what happened when Iris was with Heena. Iris obviously decided to stay here after their talk. But she looks tired, so I guess it can wait. I just hope that she is not in too much pain. Noah and Tom take the blankets that Sumit brought and unwrap them on the floor, making two new beds. With all of their clothes still on, they get into the beds and get ready for sleep. They must be exhausted. Iris and I find our sleeping position in her bed and pull a blanket over us.

"Goodnight guys, and again welcome," Iris says.

"Goodnight friends."

Iris

I wake up in blinding light. The sun has begun to reach my face from the window. I guess we slept late. I try getting to a sitting position but am put down again by a burning sensation from my shoulder all the way down the left side of my body. It's one of those painful days. They are coming more and more frequently now. I rub my eyes to wake up properly, but they seem to be exhausted and aching too. I turn my head to get ready for waking up William, but he is not in his bed. Actually, no one is in here but me. I slowly manage to get to a sitting position without it hurting too much. Where are the guys? I feel a slight disappointment for them not including me in whatever they're doing, but I get the reason why William would let me sleep. I wonder if he told Noah and Tom about my cancer. I hope not. I don't see any reason why they should know. They will be home when I'm dead, and maybe never know that I died. William could tell them that I just went home to Iceland. There is no need to worry Noah and Tom.

"Good morning, Iris," a sweet girl's voice says from the doorway.

"Oh, good morning, Numit," I reply. "Do you know where the guys are?"

She slides inside and puts a tray with two cups of tea on the floor. She sits in front of me on Williams bed, takes one of the cups and hands it to me.

"This is pain-relieving tea," she says. "I'm having a normal day tea myself."

I take a sip of the tea. It tastes horrible. It's like drinking dirt. Numit laughs from seeing my silly surprised expression.

"Yes, it is not a tea for the taste," she says. "It's only for relieving pain. It's the medicine my mother told you about."

To my amazement, I instantly feel the pain ease. The tea helps with every sip! Incredible!

"To answer your question," Numit continues. "Your friends are out gathering roots for this type of tea. Our gatherers have been busy with the harvesting, so we are short on materials. This tea was an infusion of our last root. Your friends are with my brother and should be back by the evening, don't worry."

"Oh, that's sweet of them," I admit though I feel it strange to not be with William.

Numit reaches her hand out to me. I take her hand and we sit just like I would do with my best friends when telling each other supporting words.

"Only William and my brother know why they are gathering roots," she says. "They didn't tell your friends about your condition. Your friends don't know."

"That's good," I say. "Thank you, Numit."

I have come to like Numit a lot. It's nice to have a girlfriend here already.

"Are you okay, Iris?" she asks.

I find it sad that she is the younger one who has to take care of me, but it seems like she is used to helping out.

"I'm okay. Though I hoped that I could talk to William today about staying here and finding peace," I tell her. "But it's just as good talking to you. What're your plans for today?"

"I'm with you today," she says happily. "My plans are to make sure that you're having a good day while your friends and my brother gather roots."

Knowing this cheers me up. I can't remember when was

the last time I had a day of just hanging out with a friend, with no actual purpose but to hang out and have fun. Now with the pain eased I'm sure this will be a good day. I feel a hint of happiness inside, removing some of my concern of talking to William about the acceptance.

"That's perfect!" I tell her. "We'll have fun!"

William

"What is the queen's husband when on the top of the mountain?" Noah asks while we continue walking.

As usual, Tom and I just wait for the answer to the joke to come by itself. Even Sumit has already gotten to the point where he does not guess or ask for the answer.

"High King," Noah answers to his joke with a loud Noah-laughter. "You know… High King… Hiking."

"Yeah, we get it," Tom says. "How long have you wanted to tell this joke?"

"A few months, but I'm a Noah, so that's cool," he responds.

I realize how much I missed these guys and their telling-a-joke hating-on-the-joke thing. It is so much fun hiking with them again, and a slight relief to get my thoughts removed from Iris, as much as I now can. I miss her every time I think of her, so I better try to enjoy this hike.

It looks like it is going to be perfect weather today. The sky is completely free from clouds, and the sun is getting high. There is no actual trail to follow, so until now it has been a challenging hike. We have passed several steep mountainside ledges where we had to climb or to step our own paths to cross them. And Sumit told us it would only get worse. But even though this is extremely dangerous, I have managed to stay calm. I *have* to get those ingredients for making a pain-relieving medicine for Iris.

"Why is Iris having pain exactly?" Tom asks me.

I can not postpone an answer anymore. Naturally, Tom and Noah wanted to know this when they were asked to join for this gathering trip, but I did not want to tell them the truth. Iris should be the one to do that herself, yet I somehow know that she does not want *them* to know.

"She is just having the flu," I lie. "On top of that, she hurt her arm in the avalanche."

I decide not to put details on my lie in fear that I might expose the truth. Instead, it would be better to move the focus to the actual mission.

"So where exactly are we going to find those roots?" I ask Sumit

He points on a mountain top in the distance.

"At the foot of that mountain, there is a small forest," he answers. "It will take us four hours of hiking from here, so we should be there in the afternoon and ideally be back in the village tonight before it is getting dark."

"And we're sure to find our way back without a map or compass?" Noah asks.

Sumit nods.

"That will be no problem," he replies shortly.

Tom and Noah did not have the chance to see what people in the village are capable of. They still do not know about magnetism and how humans strangely have the ability to take control of it. I imagine that Sumit has trained the ability to be capable of doing what birds do: to get directions based on magnetic fields and the locations of the sun. Perhaps even topped with human memory and logic. If I told Tom and Noah about this, they would think that I was trying to make a weird joke.

"Be careful here," Sumit suggests as we approach another ledge on the mountainside.

As with the previous ledges, my heart begins to beat like crazy. The others pass the ledge with ease, which makes me the last person to step out onto it. With this one, I have to grab whatever I can on the mountain wall to make sure I do not lose balance. I move sideways one step at a time, never looking down into the steep drop beneath me. Luckily it is only a few seconds of dangerous clinging, and we are back on a plane surface that goes *up* the mountain and not on *the side* of it. I see now what Sumit means by it being a difficult hike. We have to climb up and down and cling to the rocks constantly.

A couple of birds chase each other above us. They have so much freedom. If they wanted to complete this assignment, they would simply fly to the forest, pick up the roots and fly back again. Simple and easy. I hear a scream from one of the birds and see feathers falling as I glance up at the scenario. The screaming bird flees, most likely being banished from the hunting area of the other bird. It appears that the fleeing bird is having trouble flying straight. Its left wing flaps quicker than the right, indicating that it is obviously hurt. I wonder how animals deal with pain when they do not have pain-relieving medicine like us.

Anyway, back to reality, Iris needs this medicine, and I am going to get it for her.

Iris

"It's your turn, Iris," Numit says.

I return from my daydreaming to the real world and look down on the wooden board. It's Numit's favorite board game. I compare it to chess, besides that the pieces are animals and not war figures. There is only one of each animal, so I'm still adapting to some of the new movement rules. I decide to pick up my eagle.

"Was it three straight squares in any direction?" I ask to be sure I'm doing it right.

"Yes, the eagle flies freely and over other animals," Numit replies.

With that concluded, I move my eagle to her ox. As in normal chess, the attacker always wins, so my eagle just killed her ox. I imagine how such a fight would look like if it happened for real. I'm not sure that the eagle would actually win. However, I don't see how the ox would win either. To be honest, I don't think such a fight would ever occur, but that is the fun thing about games: everything can happen.

"Good move," Numit says.

"Thanks, Numit," I reply. "Not so sure I'm winning though."

"You never know with this game," she says comfortingly.

I sip from the day tea that Numit served. It tastes like heaven, especially after drinking that horrible pain-relieving tea. The effect from that should wear off in a few hours, but knowing that more tea is coming when the guys return, topped with having a lot of fun with Numit, makes me okay. I just hope that the guys are doing fine.

William

Sumit was right with his schedule. We just arrived in the forest, and according to my amateur guessing from the sun's position, it is indeed afternoon. The forest is smaller than I expected. The trees are short and crooked with only a few green leaves here and there. The ground beneath the trees are of soft moss, and the familiar, amazingly colorful butterflies are present as well.

"These are the trees from where we gather roots," Sumit says.

He moves to one of them and pulls it up from the ground.

"They are easy to pick up," he continues. "That's why they don't have many leaves currently. When a storm comes, they release their leaves to make less friction and not be blown away in the wind."

He drops his skin bag down on the ground, takes his knife from his belt and cuts the roots of the small tree into the bag. Noah instantly walks to one of the trees and pulls it up from the ground. I see on Sumit's face that something is wrong, but he doesn't have time to react before Noah grabs the roots of the tree with his other hand.

"Wait!" Sumit yells. "Drop it!"

Noah instantly drops the small tree and stares at his hand. He pokes it with his other hand before moving his gaze to Sumit for an answer.

"The roots are very numbing," Sumit informs. "It should not be in contact with our skin unless we need local anesthesia."

Noah opens and closes his hand several times, clearly not happy about not feeling anything.

"How long will it last?" he asks.

"Only for a few hours, don't worry," Sumit says. "Because of the strong effect, we mostly drink it as a tea for full pain relief. We eat the roots raw when having to operate people, but doing that will make you sleep for at least half a day, and that is risky, so we treat the roots with respect."

"So no touching," Tom says and finds his knife.

With that concluded, we carefully start filling our bags with roots. They have a strong smell of a mixture of ginger and garlic when cutting them from the trees. In curiosity, I poke one of the roots with the tip of my little finger and feel the numbness right away. Scary stuff. I get why they treat it with respect. I pick up another tree, and to my surprise, I see that this tree has black fruits hanging on it. They remind me of small plums, but much darker.

"*Phala!*" Sumit shouts and runs over to me to gently takes the tree from my hand.

He picks one of the fruits and hands it to me.

"Try one," he says happily.

At first, I am not sure if he is joking around and if I will be paralyzed from the fruit or something like that. However, considering that Sumit is an intelligent and friendly person, I doubt that this will happen, so I take a bite of the fruit.

"Wauw, that is delicious!" I admit in surprise.

"Yes, very delicious," Sumit says smilingly. "But very rare, unfortunately. We dry and save them for special events."

He fills his bag with the fruits and hands me back the tree.

"The village will appreciate your finding, William," he says and closes his bag. "The finders name will be mentioned at the event."

I offer Sumit the rest of my very rare fruit, but he refuses and gestures for me to eat the rest of it. I do not complain about that. These are incredibly tasty. It is typical that such delicious things are scarce. They are even rare enough to have the finder mentioned, like some hero.

"Sumit, I want you to be the finder of the fruits," I say, as I could imagine that it must feel better for him than for me to be appreciated by his village.

However, he shakes his head.

"No, I can not do that," he says. "It is nice of you, though, William. Thank you."

Noah and Tom join us.

"Well, our bags are full of roots now," Tom says and claps his bag.

Sumit turns around.

"That's very good," he says. "We need to get back before it gets dark, so it would be good to start returning now."

Without questioning the direction, Sumit begins marching. Tom, Noah and I stare at each other and realize how lost we would be without Sumit, so we immediately follow our friendly, young monk.

Iris

Lying flat on my bed, I open my eyes to check if Numit is awake, but she is not. I asked for a quick nap, and Numit thought it to be a good idea, so she decided to join in and take a nap in William's bed. Of course, *I'm* the one who can't fall asleep. The pain has begun to return so I find it hard to relax. Considering the position of the sun, it appears to be late afternoon, so the guys must be on their way back with the roots. I just have to lie here waiting like a princess. It's nice to have a lazy day with nothing to do. I honestly start to believe that I will be able to find peace in this place, especially when the pain is gone.

Anyway, I'll give my nap another try.

William

"Are you okay, William?" Tom shouts from behind.

I wipe sand and small stones from the new wound on my hand. A few drops of blood develop on my skin, but nothing terrible. I got lucky with that fall. The embarrassment of tripping over what appears to be my own legs is worse than the pain on my skin.

"I'm okay, thank you," I reply. "Will try not to be that clumsy from now on."

We are only halfway on our way back, and we are all already exhausted. Expect Sumit of course. It might be because we have been eating nuts, bread and dried apples instead of our usual hiking snacks filled with sugar. Somewhere inside of me, I feel like we have been cheating when eating chocolate bars and other sugar-rich snacks. With Sumit's natural snacks, we have to use our own energy and not just be drugged on sugar-power, so to say. Anyway, we are halfway now, and the sun is setting on the horisont, resulting in a unique, purple scenery. According to Sumit, we are late, so we have to move fast if we should make it back before dark.

"Be careful here," Sumit shouts from in front of me.

I glance back at Noah and Tom to check if they heard it. They both give me a thumbs-up. I turn my head back to see Sumit clinging to the mountain wall, stepping on an extremely narrow ledge. I do not remember passing this on the way to the forest. It seems impossible, yet Sumit somehow makes it look easy. My heartbeat raises yet again. My palms sweat waterfalls. I take in a deep breath. I can do this!

"Don't be clumsy, William," Tom says from behind.

He does not sound nervous at all, which is sort of motivating. I take a step out on the ledge and find a crack in the mountain-wall to grab on to. Even though I know that I am not supposed to, I can not resist peeking down. *Holy sh…!* A direct drop which seems to have no end at all. I pull myself closer to the rocky wall, trying to find calm breathing. My legs shake. I move sideways another step and find another crack in the wall where I can find a hold. A quick vision of me falling off the ledge flies before my eyes. *Holy cow!* The increasing amount of sweat in my palms make my hands slippery. This is bad! This is so bad! I take another step. A few small rocks break off from the mountain where my hands cling to, but I react immediately and grab another crack. *Fu…!* Quickly, I take yet another step. Then another. Finally, the ledge widens, but my shakiness remains. Sumit grabs me as I reach him at a spot where the ledge is wide enough to be safe.

"Well done, William," he says.

Before I can open my mouth to reply, his eyes turn to what I imagine to be pure terrifying fear. A loud, echoing cry makes me freeze. I turn around in the direction of the scream, only to see Tom desperately trying to pull himself up from the ledge. Noah clings to the wall next to him, trying to reach a hand down, but he is too far away. Sumit drops his bag and runs toward them to help. Tom hangs loose from the ledge, now even more desperately trying to climb up, but the ledge keeps breaking. I can not move. My body is frozen from fear. The cries for help from Tom penetrates me like needles. My hands go to my head in panic. This is not real! Noah takes a small step closer to Tom and bends down his knees to reach out a hand for Tom. I see their fingertips touching, but the ledge breaks again and Tom fights to cling to the mountain. Sumit approaches them, but Noah is in the way, so Sumit can not reach Tom, who now found what seems to be a more stable part of the ledge, also with a bit of foothold. I see the panic in Noah's wide flickering eyes and my body is totally refrozen. This *is* real! Sumit takes off his shirt and ties the end to his wrist. He grabs onto the wall and throws the other end of the shirt to Tom, like a rope, but the rocks under Tom's feet break loose and he lets out a scream as he clings to the ledge with his arms, desperately trying to find foothold again. Noah gets all the way down to his knees and is finally close enough to reach Tom. He reaches out his hand to grab Tom, but the ledge that Tom clings to breaks loose.

NO!

Dizziness hits me as I see this. I feel like fainting. Everything is happening in slow-motion. *Tom falls.* No screams. No sounds. Everything turns mute. I close my eyes. I am *not* seeing this... This is not happening...

Silence...

Iris

It's getting darker outside. Time is passing slowly now when being alone in our room. Shouldn't they be here by now? Where are they?

William

We sit in silence. It has been like this for who knows how long. The occasional crying from Noah is the only thing breaking the silence. The sun set a long time ago, but none of us care. None of us know what to do. None of us want to realize the fact that Tom is dead.

Tom is dead!

I still can not believe it. I continually expect him to walk up to us from behind and joke about why we didn't go meet him at the foot of the mountain, and how we were lazy when just waiting for him to climb up by himself. But he could *not* have survived that fall. We concluded that. Multiple times. I pinch the wound in my hand to move my thoughts from Tom's family to some physical pain. My thoughts are a mess. I can not imagine how Noah must feel. This is awful. I can not stay here any longer!

"We should return," I say silently.

Iris

Finally! Somebody is coming. I sit up in my bed, and the door to the room slowly opens. William and Noah walk in but stay completely mute. It must have been a tough hike, considering the zombie-like expressions on their faces.

"Hello there," I greet them. "Where did you leave Tom and Sumit?"

They simultaneously turn around to look at me but remain silent. I get a nervous feeling from this.

"Guys, seriously. Where are they?" I ask again.

This time William opens his mouth.

"Sumit is at his mother's home," he says, but closes his mouth shut and becomes mute again.

I see tears running down from Noah's zombie-face-cheeks. For some reason that makes me stand up. Something is wrong.

"Tom?" I ask, taking a step towards the guys.

Noah breaks into loud crying.

"He fell," he manages to say in between the crying breaths.

Fell? What?!

William falls into tears too. I'm out of words. What happened to Tom? Is he...?

"It should have been me," Noah says. "He's about to become a father..."

Tears fall from my eyes as I hug Noah tight and William gets in on the hug.

"His life was just beginning," Noah continues. "People need him. It should have been me..."

I shush at him gently to stop him from talking this nonsense.

"Don't say that," I tell him. "You're confused."

The truth is that I'm the confused one. I still haven't understood what exactly is going on. It doesn't seem real. Is Tom *dead*?

"I tried to save him," Noah continues with a completely broken voice. "He couldn't... I couldn't reach him... I..."

"Stop it, Noah," William interrupts and releases himself from the hug. "It's not your fault. There was nothing we could do."

Noah lets go of me and finds a seat on his bed. I wipe the remaining tears from my eyes. The room turns painfully quiet again. Noah cries in silence, clearly lost in his own thoughts, and it's obvious to see on William that he is holding back tears. I sit down on my bed, and the idea of never seeing Tom alive again hits me. I hear myself cry out loud for a split-second. William finds a seat next to me and puts his arm around me. It makes me think of Tom's pregnant girlfriend who is sitting at home and awaiting Tom to return and hold her and their to-come child. He should have been a great father. Now he will not be there. Never. I can't handle the thought that she will have to get that information. The reaction. The sorrow. And Noah's sorrow. His best friend is gone. He will probably be the one who delivers the message. She will hate him. It's awful!

William kisses me on the cheek and removes some of my tears, which helps me to escape my sad thoughts for a moment. A few knocks sound from the door and Sumit walks in with a silver tray with three cups.

"I'm sorry," he says. "I have made this for you."

He puts down a cup on the floor in front of each of us.

"Strong root tea. It will help you sleep," he continues.

"Progress can be made when the mind is stable."

He avoids eye contact and leaves the room again immediately. I get the point of his message. We need sleep and a fresh mind to understand what exactly has happened. I take my cup and sip from it. It tastes exactly like the pain-relief tea I had earlier, but a lot stronger. I look at Noah to see that he has already emptied his cup, even though it's still burning hot. It doesn't take long before he yawns and lie down in his bed and falls asleep. It indeed is a strong tea. I blow my tea cold and empty my cup as well. Time for sleeping this one out.

- Goodbye -

William

We all wake to noise and talking outside our room. To my confusion, the sun seems to be setting yet again. I rub my eyes and try to make sense of what is going on. Did we sleep all day? For a moment, I forget about the strong tea that we had yesterday night. It might have been stronger than we first assumed. Then the memory of yesterday returns.

Tom!

I am still too tired to figure out if all of that was real or just a bad dream. Tom is not here, though. The sleep has given me more control of my feelings, just like Sumit said, but I still find everything surreal.

A few knocks come from the door, and Sumit silently enters our room.

"I'm sorry to interrupt," he says, almost whispering. "We collected your friend."

Noah's eyes open wide, and I can almost see them sparkle with joy. However, Sumit notices that as well and makes sure that no misunderstandings are made.

"His body, that is," he continues, making Noah realize that Tom is still not alive. "However, I request a decision from you."

He gestures for Noah, Iris and I to get up from our beds, and we do so, standing in front of him like tired school children. He continues speaking.

"France is a long way from here. It will take a very long

time to transport Tom there," he explains. "We offer to do a ritual to release his spirit peacefully, which will remove his psychical body from our world."

He gives us a moment to reflect and understand.

"I know it's a hard decision, but I'm afraid you will have to decide for him and his family," he says.

Instantly I see the dilemma. Will it be any good for the family to have a decaying body home to say goodbye to, or will it be better to remove their opportunity and save them from seeing their loved one in such a bad condition. I can not believe that these thoughts are actually running through my mind. It is *Tom,* not just a *body.* How can I think of him like this?

"How long will it take for transportation?" Noah asks.

"About two weeks, I'm afraid," Sumit answers, clearly ready for the question.

Noah closes his eyes and inhales deeply. Naturally, he should be the one making the final decision. It is a lot of pressure on his shoulders, but that is for the best.

"That's too long," he says with his eyes still closed. "He wouldn't like his family to see him like that."

Sumit nods.

"You wish to fulfill the ritual?" he asks.

"Yes," Noah concludes.

Iris puts her arm behind his back for approving support on the decision.

"Very well," Sumit says. "When you're ready, meet me outside."

He leaves the room and silence appears. A few minutes pass while none of us feel like saying anything. We are all processing what is happening and what is to come. Noah is the one breaking the silence.

"We should go," he says quietly.

It is strangely painful to hear the always happy and joking Noah sounding this sad. At the same time, it is hard to accept the fact that there is no easy way out of this.

Noah opens the door and walks outside. Iris and I follow, and we meet with Sumit outside. It is indeed dark already, though the full moon shines bright, allowing us to see where to step while Sumit leads us towards the temple. I spot smoke and fire in the distance, which makes it clear to me that they will burn Tom's body. The fire appears bigger for every step we take, until we finally reach the huge bonfire. To our surprise, we discover that everybody in the village has gathered around it. The fire releases crackling sounds while yellow burning sparks hovers around the red and orange flames. I am touched by the thought of everybody showing up, even though most of them did not know Tom. He lies right there in front of the fire, covered in wool. Motionless. Dead. Sumit asks us if we want to see him, but we all decline. There is no need to get that image of him printed into our heads. It is better to remember him the way he was when he was alive.

I see Sumit's mother and sister in the crowd. They nod at us with the most respectful nod. Everybody in the crowd takes each other's hands. Sumit takes mine and I figure that I should take Iris' hand as well, while she takes Noah's hand. A young girl starts singing beautifully with a fine, bright girl's voice. I do not know the words, but the singing goes right to my heart. A few more children begin singing with her, forming a perfect children's choir. I feel tears escaping my eyes. The faces of the singing children are illuminated by the burning fire, which makes them look like small angles. The unknown words sound magical with their innocent voices. Iris squeezes my hand, but I can not stop focusing on the beautiful song. The rest of the crowd gradually join in on the gentle singing, making a huge, yet silent, choir. I get chills all over my body. I have never heard anything so beautiful and sad at the same time. Three men from the crowd move to Tom's body. They stop and send us a respectful nod as well, before reaching their arms out and releasing some metallic sand over Tom's body. The sand sticks to the wool and shimmers in the light from the fire. The men pick up Tom's body and move majestically toward the fire. They stop right before the fire, closing their eyes and whispering what seems to be some sort of prayer, which I can not completely hear from the choir surrounding them. Then they carefully move Tom's body into the fire. Flames of all colors of the rainbow burst out from his body. The village people stop their singing, leaving everything quiet, except the crackling sounds from the fire. I hear the heavy, but silent, crying from Noah. It is surreal.

Iris lets go of my hand and finds a paper from her pocket and unfolds it. It is the drawing she drew on her way up here. She kept it all this time. She stands completely still, just staring at it for a moment. It is a drawing of Tom and his child. The realism of Tom's face gives me goosebumps.

"I would have given it to him when he reached his goal," she whispers.

She takes a few steps towards the fire and puts in the drawing, which ignites and curls up immediately. She watches it burn for a moment before returning with tears running down her cheeks. Silently she throws her arms around Noah and me for a comforting group hug. The longest hug in history.

Iris

Goodbye, Tom.

- Secrets -

William

It has been three days since we lost Tom. Everything has begun to feel unreal now. Sometimes I am not sure if I am awake or dreaming. I have only seen Noah a few times since the accident. He seems different. Sad and lonely. I have tried to talk to him, but he seems to be avoiding contact. I am not sure where he is hiding in the daytime when he leaves our room early in the morning and returns late, only to sleep a few hours. I am not sure that it is a healthy way to deal with sorrow like that, but everybody deals with such things differently. I miss Tom too, but of course, Noah feels worse than I do.

To be honest, my concern is aimed at Iris at the moment. She is becoming sicker every day. The pain-relieving tea makes her tired, she says, but I doubt that the tea alone causes her exhaustion. She looks sick now. She stays in bed most of the time, sleeping. She has trouble walking without losing her breath and getting dizzy. Even in her sleep, she gasps for air. On top of that, her lack of appetite is worrying me. It might all be in my head, but I can see her getting thinner for every hour. I fear that I will go crazy from all this concern. Also, my colored sparkles have begun to reappear sometimes when I sit and watch Iris. I was almost certain that they were gone for good. If I did not have this strange magnetic ability training to focus on, I would definitely have gone insane or somehow depressed at this point.

I look around. The temple is still empty, except for Bob who lies in the corner sleeping. I turn my gaze to the ring of metallic sand in front of me. I watch the ants inside running around in a circle. I learned to magnetize the sand, but for some reason, find it harder to demagnetize and to change the magnetism. It just seems impossible to make those ants reverse their running. I close my eyes and focus on what Sumit taught me. Carefully, I move two fingers to the sand, trying not to get distracted by thoughts. Be patient, William. Do it slowly.

Just as I touch the sand, a voice calls out from the temple entrance, making me pull my fingers back and break the circle. The ants flee in every direction, and I have to jump to my feet to avoid them crawling up on me. Sumit enters the temple and continues speaking.

"How is the training going?" he asks.

"I am progressing," I reply, not sure if I truly am or not.

He gives me an acknowledging smile.

"That is good to hear," he says, giving himself a moment to find the right words. "Iris is not feeling well. She wants to speak with you."

Instantly, without thinking, I begin finding my way back to Iris.

"She is in our room still, right?" I ask Sumit as I pass him.

"Yes," he replies shortly.

Just before exiting the temple, I stop and turn around. I just realized something.

"Thank you, Sumit," I tell him. "You are a very good friend."

He smiles.

Iris

William enters our room and closes the door behind him before finding a seat next to me. I try to sit up, but I don't find the strength and decide to stay in a lying position. Black dots appear everywhere where I look, and I'm exhausted, but I have to have this conversation with William now. I need him to understand that I am okay with the situation.

"How are you feeling?" William asks.

I can hear in his voice that he's not entirely sure what to say and how to act. It's cute.

"I have to talk with you about something," I begin. "I don't expect you to understand now, but I hope that you will one day."

He looks concerned at me, but takes my hand and nods for me to continue.

"You know that my condition is getting rapidly worse for each day," I tell him. "I know that you are scared and that you wish you could do something to change the situation."

I take a moment to remember the speech I have rehearsed in my head all morning, but it's gone. I will just have to tell him what I feel. Luckily he stays mute and gives me the time to find the right words.

"The thing is…" I continue. "…that I'm… okay… with the situation…"

A scared and surprised expression appears on William's face. He opens his mouth to speak, so I continue so that no misunderstandings are made.

"Well, I would like it to be different, of course," I continue. "But now that I can't change the facts, I have to accept the situation and enjoy what is left. I'm not afraid of death,

William. I have had a great life and had the opportunity to see and experience so many things. Not a lot of people in the world are that lucky."

William is desperately trying to figure out where this is going.

"Well, what I'm trying to say is that I have accepted my situation and where it ends," I continue. "I have found the perfect place to find peace, and I have found the perfect people to help me find it. But there is one thing that prevents me from enjoying the peace fully."

I squeeze his hand. I have to be careful about these words. If I tell him that he is the only thing that makes me desperate for staying, I will break him, which will only end in making myself sad and more desperate.

"I need you to accept reality, Will," I tell him. "That's the only way I can find peace. I need you not to be sad and to be able to enjoy the rest of our time together. I need to know that you are as okay as I am. I'm not scared. All I want is to have a peaceful time with you."

I give him a smile.

"You are going to die yourself, you know? Nomather what," I weirdly inform. "Noah is going to die one day. Bob will also die. Everyone else in the world will die. I just have to try it out before you."

I see him holding back tears. Seeing that would normally make myself cry, but I'm just too exhausted. And I need to stay strong to convince him that I'm okay. He opens his mouth, but no words escape. He nods his acceptance instead, so I pull him down to me for a big hug. The hug lasts for a while. This is the *only* thing I simply can not accept: I will have to leave William. I squeeze him harder but find it too painful, and I hear myself putting sound to the pain. William releases me.

"Are you okay?" he asks. "You're in pain?"

He glances at my empty silver cup.

"Can I get you some more tea?" he asks.

"Actually that would be good," I say, suddenly feeling a lot of pain after the effect of my last cup wore off. "Thank you, Will."

He picks up my cup and moves to the door.

"I will be back in a few minutes," he says before leaving the room.

What a gentleman.

William

The sky has turned dark and gray. That happened fast. The air feels moisty and cold. It looks like the predictions about the storm arriving tonight are correct. A blow from the wind makes me drop Iris' cup from my hand. I bend down to pick it up, but another hand is already at the cup. Noah! I did not see him coming. He hands me the cup and is about to walk away again.

"Noah?" I say, hoping that it will make him stop.

It actually does. Noah stops and turns around to stare at me. He looks broken. I wonder if he has slept at all since the loss of Tom.

"How are you?" I ask, not sure where to begin.

He shrugs his shoulders.

"I'm okay," he says emotionless.

Of course, he is not. I wish that there was any way to make him talk about his feelings, but I would be acting the same way if I was in his shoes.

"Is there anything I can do?" I ask.

He shakes his head. It is strange to see him like that. The always happy, joking and laughing Noah has changed to the complete opposite. I could never imagine him like this. It occurs to me that I have only tried to talk with him about Tom and how he feels about the loss. Maybe he needs conversations about something else. A break from his depressing thoughts.

"Are you ready for the storm?" I ask.

Iris

I see William and Noah talking through the window. I wonder what they talk about. Or what William talks about, apparently. Noah looks so sad. I wish that there was anything I could do to cheer him up. He might just need more time to reflect by himself, but I'm afraid that it's not enough. On the other hand, I'm not sure that I have enough energy at the moment for such support. A rush of exhaustion runs through me. The light from the window hurts my eyes, even though the dark clouds block a lot of the sunlight. Feeling a bit dizzy, I close my eyes and lie down. I will have a quick nap before William returns.

William

Noah turns around and walks away. These five minutes are the most I have seen him in days.

"Is he alright?" a female voice asks.

Numit stands in the doorway to her mother's house.

"I am afraid not," I admit.

"He might just need time," Numit says. "Well, I suppose you're getting more tea for Iris?"

I nod and enter her mother's house with her. I am not actually surprised anymore when she and her brother seem to read my mind, but I am still amazed. It appears that Numit is alone in the house. Her mother is probably preparing for the storm with the rest of the village. Numit pours some water in a small silver bowl and makes it hover above the burning fireplace before she turns around to me.

"Are you okay, William?" she asks. "I know that Iris' situation is not easy for you."

A lump builds up in my throat. I have not been able to speak with anybody about my part concerning Iris' sickness. I find it difficult to pick the right words for how I feel. Where to begin?

"You're not able to accept that you will lose her," Numit continues while starting to peel and chop a large root. "You don't want to return to your old life. You want to begin a new one with this new girl in your life. She was everything you searched for in this adventure, and now you're going to lose her."

I stay mute.

"You believe that it's not fair," Numit continues. "It's not fair that she has to die. It's not fair that you will have to lose her."

My hands shake. What is she doing? How does she know?

"It annoys you that you can not control the situation," she continues and throws the chopped root in the pot. "You're desperate to find a solution to this problem, but there is none. You can not do anything."

She looks at me.

"It's okay, William," she says. "I know exactly how you feel. I had a father once."

She suddenly becomes quiet, and I realize that I am not the only one losing someone I love. I definitely *feel* alone in the world at the moment, but in reality, I am not alone at all. Right now, *Iris* is my world. I feel alone without her. Even though she is still with us, I am more or less living in the future, feeling like she is already dead. I should be present at the moment and enjoy our time together until the day comes when she has to leave. This short conversation, or monolog, helped more than I could ever imagine.

"How did you lose your father?" I ask in the hope that more relieving words will come.

She stirs the pot for a moment before answering.

"He had suffered from moon fever," she says. "No cure for that."

"Moon fever?" I ask

"It's hard to explain," she replies. "My father's brother tried to make a sacrification ritual to save my father's life, but he failed and both of them left us that night."

She stops stirring the pot.

"I miss both of them every day," she admits quietly.

I walk closer to her and put a hand on her shoulder.

"I am sorry to hear that, Numit," I say.

"It's okay, William," she says. "You learn to deal with the sorrow in time. Missing them has become a good thing for me now. You might not understand now, but one day you will."

She takes the silver cup from my hand and fills it with tea.

"What is that ritual your father's brother tried to do?" I ask as she hands me the cup.

"It's nothing. I overspoke. Sorry, William," she says.

"No, please, you can tell me," I say in all curiosity.

She thinks for a moment.

"Well, magnetism can do more than you currently know," she says. "But I'm not supposed to talk about it. It's dangerous."

For a second, I consider pushing more information out of her but figure it would be rude. I have to respect that there are things that I'm not allowed to know. I'm still just a guest here.

"Thank you for everything, Numit," I say.

She hugs me tight before walking me to the door.

"Thank you too, Will," she says. "Now, Iris needs her tea."

Iris

William

"Iris! Wake up!" I desperately yell into her face.

Why does she not wake up? I slap her face for the third time, this time harder than I wanted to, but she does not react. What is happening?! I put my finger to her neck. Her heartbeat is slow. Her breaths are short and shallow.

"IRIS!" I yell again. "Please!…"

In my panic, I run out of the room and back to Numit. She glances scared at me as I slam the door open.

"Numit! What was that ritual your uncle tried to do?" I ask loudly. "Please tell me!"

She stays quiet. I know that she is not supposed to tell me about it, but I am too desperate.

"Please, Numit," I continue. "Iris will not wake up!"

I realize that Numit's mother, Heena, is back and are watching me from the corner of the room. She walks in front of me and looks me deep in the eyes before gesturing for Numit to get by her side. She starts speaking to Numit in their own language. It seems that the speech is for me, as Numit begins to translate.

"We do not decide people's decisions," she translates. "You wish to know about our rituals, and you shall have that knowledge."

I nod in appreciation to both Numit and her mother.

"Most things in this world are made of different types of energy," she continues. "It is widely known, in your modern world, that magnetism is one of the most efficient ways of converting energies. However, there is one thing that your modern world has become blind of: the energy of life."

I stare confused at Numit, but she removes her eyes from

me. This is not her words.

"When our life energy fail to maintain our bodies, there is no place to contain our energies, and it simply converts to heat and disappears into the wind," she continues. "All life energies are different but can be converted and transferred to other containers. With enough fresh life energy, our bodies are able to repair themselves, which again makes us able to store the energies within ourselves. Some people even gained the ability to see this life energy escape bodies when control is lost, but that is a whole other story."

I slowly get where this is going, even though some of the information might be mistranslated.

"What that means is that one human can transfer their energy to another," she continues. "But it will lead to an instant breakdown of the body which now doesn't contain energy."

Her mother stops speaking and looks seriously at me. She allows Numit to express some of her own words now.

"William, it's not safe," she says. "There is no guarantee that it will work. It's risky. I lost both my uncle and father that way."

I understand what she means, but I am in no doubt about what to do. Iris deserves to live. I want to take that risk. She means everything to me. This Icelandic hippie girl that I have only known for a few weeks. I simply can not imagine my life back in New York without her. She enjoys life so much more than I do. I went on this trip to find joy in life, and I found it: I found *Iris*. If she dared me on this one, my odds would be one in one, even if the odds of her surviving could be one in a million. I might be crazy, but this is how I feel.

"I want her to live," I say, confident in my decision.

Numit looks down the floor.

"Very well," she says. "As my mother said, we can not control your decisions."

"Are you sure about this, William?" a familiar voice behind me asks.

I turn around to see Noah and Sumit in the doorway.

"I have never been more sure of anything in my life," I inform them shortly.

Heena speaks to her son for a moment before he nods and turns his gaze to me.

"I will get the ritual ready," he says and walks out the door with Noah silently following him.

Just as they close the door, a loud thunder catches my attention. I suddenly become aware of the heavy rain on the roof and the howling wind from the windows. The storm is here. The seriousness of the situation hits me. I am sacrificing my own life. I am dying tonight, and maybe for nothing. I doubt my decision for a brief moment, but in the end find that I can not bear to see Iris die. To burn her dead body. To never look into her astonishing, blue eyes and never hear her laugh again. Never hold her hands and become incredibly nervous about that. No, my decision is made! Iris will live!

- The Ritual -

William

The walk to the temple feels like an eternity. I am blinded by the darkness and heavy rain, but the flashes from the lightning on the horizon offer me quick notifications of where Sumit walks in front of me. I am soaking wet and freezing cold. Everything seems more surreal than ever, like a horror movie, although I am not truly scared. A bright flash from a nearby lightning strike reveals that the temple is right in front of us. Sumit is already inside, so I enter immediately as well.

There is a strange calmness in the temple as I shut the door close behind me. The loud rain turns to a low, calm ambiance, and the thunder suddenly seems to be deep and calming. The temple is illuminated by burning touches, which are set up all over the place. A few monks silently idle near some of the touches, and I see Iris lying lifeless on the floor in the middle of the temple. She is surrounded by two circles of golden and silver sand. The outer circle is connected, with a line of sand, to other circles of sand, in which monks are sitting. I realize that there is an empty circle, which is connected to both the inner and outer circle surrounding Iris. This is obviously *my* circle, so I find my way there and sit down inside. One of the monks next to me nods respectfully as we make short eye contact. My eyes then move to Iris. I focus my sight for a moment to make sure that she is still breathing, and I manage to panic for a second before seeing that her chest is moving slowly. I inspect the two circles around her, as well as the connecting lines to the monks' circles, and I somehow do not question how this works. I do not care to be honest.

I just want it to work. I want Iris to live, even though I will not live myself to know if this will turn out good. Maybe that is for the best.

I examine the circle around me to make sure that there are no gaps in it, remembering all that I have learned. Broken circles mean loss of magnetic control and will result in no energy transferring, and with that no life energy transferred. The circle seems to be complete. Perfect. This can not go wrong.

Sumit steps up behind me and puts a hand on my shoulder.

"Are you ready, my friend?" he asks.

I nod.

"I am ready, Sumit. Thank you," I reply.

I decided earlier not to say long goodbyes to everyone. That could end up in me breaking down and not going through with this. I am sure that Sumit and Numit know how much I appreciate having gotten to know them. I would have liked to say goodbye to Noah, though, but I have not seen him since he left the house with Sumit earlier. Nevertheless, this is happening now. What difference does it make to me anyway? All that matters is Iris.

"Best wishes to you, William," Sumit says and takes a few steps back.

He gestures to one of the elderly monks who initiates the ritual with a low humming. The other monks join him one by one, gradually turning the humming into a singing similar to the one they sang when Tom was cremated, yet more hymn-like. This singing seems to have no real words in it, making it sound beautiful and scary at the same time. Goosebumps appear on my skin, and I wonder if it is from the singing or some effect from the ritual that has already started to transfer energy. I take one last look at Iris and then close my eyes. Everything turns black. I wonder if this is what it is like to be dead. Pure darkness. Emptiness. Nothingness. Perhaps there is more in the afterlife. Curiousness hits me and I suddenly become somewhat eager to see what death is like. However, the curiosity turns to fear as dizziness hits me. All of a sudden, I fear the moment between life and death. How will that feel? Does it hurt? Does it feel good? Will I feel the exact moment of dying? Is it instant or do I just slowly fade away?

I hear birds screaming behind me, and something flies by my head. As a reflect, I open my eyes to see what is happening. The crow-looking bird flying by me lands at the outer circle around Iris. A few more birds fly by my head to join up with the first one. They are joined by several more birds flying in from the windows of the temple. The birds begin pecking from the circle of golden and silver sand. Iris' breathing becomes heavy. In concern of the birds breaking the circle, I glance around to check the reactions from the monks, but they do not seem to mind the birds.

Just as I almost manage to calm myself down, Iris releases a loud moaning sound, freaking me out completely. It sounds nothing like her! It almost does not sound human! The monks' singing becomes louder and more intense. Bright sparkles ignite before my eyes, though without color. Why are they returning? Why are they black and white? An explosive thunder echoes through the temple. Iris releases another moan. The birds start screaming around her. Is this right? Lightning flashes from the window and makes me delusional. I lose a sense of reality. It is happening! As the singing tenses even more, Iris releases another loud moan. Her body shakes. The birds around her flaps their wings like they have gone insane. The entrance door behind me slams aggressively from the wind, and I feel that something entered. I turn my head to check and see that Bob is standing scared at the door. Tale between his legs, shaking from the cold rain.

As I turn my head back to the monks, I see something from the corner of my eye. Something wrong. I look down to inspect what I saw.

No! My circle is broken!

I feel my spine freeze from the top of my head to my lower back, all the way down my feet. I feel like fainting. The white and black sparkles are intensifying and destroying my vision. Someone broke my circle! This can not be true! I try to repair the circle, knowing that it is too late already. The circle must never be broken. My hands shake from panic. Iris releases the loudest moan I have ever heard in my entire life. I turn my head to see what the hell is happening, and instantly everything turns silent. The sparkles stop glowing and become static in the air. Dead sparkles everywhere. Iris lies completely still. I lose a sense of time. Everything gets blurry.

The monks stopped their singing, and some of them are getting up from their seats. I try to inform them about my circle. To order them to sit down again. But no words escape my mouth. *No! I did not just lose Iris! She can not be dead!* I feel the idling, dead sparkles fall to the ground all around me, and I feel them dissolve and disappear. I get on my shaking knees and crawl my way over to her, from where the birds flee in all directions. She is so pale, almost like a ghost. Her eyes are closed. I can not breathe from realizing that I will never look into those amazing, blue eyes ever again. I will never see her beautiful smile. Never watch her nervously rubbing her nail roots. Never hug her, kiss her or feel her warm skin against mine. I will never wake up in a huge, green sweater with this perfect girl again. Never again listen to her cute laughing from my weird fright of everything. She was all I could ever dream of. I miss her so much already. My heart tightens up like never before, and I get a sense of choking. I can not handle this!

I take her hand and squeeze it hard. The coldness of her fingers breaks me. I put her hand to my lips and kiss them before putting it down, releasing it.

"Iris…" I whisper with tears running from my eyes.

I feel like saying something to her, but I can not find the words. A tear drops down my cheek and lands on her chin. With a gentle hand, I wipe it away, but as I do, I realize that she is still breathing. I feel her breath on my hand!

"Iris!" I hear myself yelling and almost jump onto her to wake her up.

Before I manage to do anything, she opens her eyes and smiles at me. Confusion and happiness hit me. I do not understand…

"Hey Will," she whispers, still smiling.

A weird combination of crying and laughing escapes me.

"Hi, Iris," I mumble silently. "How are you feeling?"

She continues her beautiful smile on her face while keeping her sparkling blue eyes locked on mine.

"I feel perfect, Will," she replies

How can this be? My circle was broken. The ritual went

wrong. But yet Iris lives. What?

Just then, I spot the second line of sand from the inner circle. My link to the inner circle was not the only one. I keep inspecting, with my eyes following the line to a circle in a darker part of the temple, which is not illuminated by torches. A few monks have gathered around the circle, watching someone lying lifeless inside. A body shape that looks very familiar. *No!* I run to the circle and throw myself on the ground next to the body.

NOAH! NO!

I find myself shaking his shoulders in a desperate attempt to wake him up, but it does not work. He does not move. I feel Sumit's hand on my own shoulder.

"I'm sorry, William," he says calmly. "He insisted..."

I stop my silly shaking attempt and lower my head to calm down and try to understand what is happening.

"How could you let him do it?" I ask from the corner of my mouth, not sure if I am angry or sad.

"We do not control people's decisions," Sumit replies. "Noah lost his focus point in his life and couldn't bear to watch Iris lose you if you went through this ritual."

I shake my head in denial.

"How could you not let me know?" I ask, still unsure about my current mood.

"I promised Noah not to," Sumit replies. "He knew that you would not let him do this, and he would not put you in a position where you had to consider agreeing or disagreeing. This was what he wanted."

I finally understand what Sumit is telling me. Noah was

broken and sacrificed himself for Iris and me, and I can not even thank him for it. A burning sensation appears in my stomach. I feel responsible for Noah's death. I feel both angry and thankful for him not telling me and making this decision on his own.

A hand is put on my back, and the owner sits down next to me. Iris has been assisted over here. She glances at Noah before turning her gaze to me. Her wet, blue eyes sparkle from the torches in the temple. She smiles at me

"Everything is going to be okay," she whispers.

I turn my head to take one last look at Noah.

"Thank you," I whisper.

Everything turns quiet.

- A new Beginning -

Iris

Three days have passed since the ritual. It feels absurd to be sitting here with William, enjoying the warm sun on this incredible mounting cliff, when we just had our ceremony for Noah yesterday evening. The view here is just astonishing, as the mountain tops stand tall with clouds hovering lightly around them.

It feels strange that both Noah and Tom are gone, but if there is an after-life, after all, they are probably having the time of their lives right now. I wish that there was some way that I could thank Noah for sacrificing his life to save mine. Just a few days ago, I was dying. Now I'm cancer-free. My secret is gone. I came here to find a peaceful end to everything, but instead, I got a fresh start. I will definitely take full use of this new chance in life. Noah's life will not be wasted. I will be happy and enjoy every second on Earth. I will live! With William! I will do whatever I can to help out Tom's coming child and his widow. I will tell Noah's adoptive parents how he saved my life and that they did a great job raising him. I will make sure that William knows how much I love him. Not because he wanted to sacrifice his life for mine, but because he's the person that he is. I will love him for the rest of my life, wherever we decide to settle down. I might just go ahead and ask him about that now actually.

"Will, do you think we should stay here?" I ask.

William

I have been thinking about asking Iris the same question. Should we stay here, return home to one of us, or maybe continue adventuring? To be honest, I do not care where we will go right now, as long as we are together. This Icelandic girl clearly means everything to me. I mean, I almost died for her. Love can be dangerous when it makes you want to trade your life for someone you have known for such a short time. But I love her, and there is no doubt that she is the one. Maybe destiny is a thing after all. Perhaps destiny has already decided where we should settle.

I pick up a small rock from the ground and toss it out from the cliff in hope for some sign that would make up my mind, but as I flick the rock away from my finger, something falls out of my pocket. I look down and see the silver compass that Noah and Tom gave me in Kathmandu. I put it in my pocket yesterday to burn it with Noah as a gesture, but then forgot about it. I pick up the compass and examine it. First now I notice the small ornaments that are carved into the silver. I never took the time to examine their generous gift properly. I run my finger down the side of the compass and realize that it has a small button. As I press it, the compass pops open, dropping a little paper note on the ground. The note almost gets caught by the wind, but I manage to grab it before flying off of the cliff. Carefully, I open up the note:

—

Hi William.
Congrats on finding this note.
(we probably told you to find it)
We hope that you found
what you were seeking.
Until our next adventure.
-Noah and Tom

—

I read the note to myself a few times before putting it back into the compass. It is strange to get a message from them like this. There is no way that I can message them back. A message from the past, when nobody had any clue that they would not be with us anymore. Well, I *did* find what I was seeking: a new beginning. A new way to see things. A new way of living. I found all of this in Iris. With her, I could not wish for more at this point. I am with the perfect girl, at the perfect place, in the perfect time of my life.

It hits me how amazing this place is. Returning to modern society with expectations, stress and carriers would be going back to what I was fleeing from. There is nothing for me back there. Here, people are who they are, and not what their jobs are. People help each other. They helped me and Iris without asking for anything in return. That is it! We are staying here, helping out in the village! We are free to leave if we should want to someday. Also, I am just getting the hang of controlling my magnetic abilities. Yep, I have made up my mind.

"I think we should stay here for now," I finally reply to Iris' question. "If you want to?"

Iris

"I think that's a good decision," I tell William and kiss him on the chin.

He blushes. It's cute. I take his hand, just like when we first met on the airplane. I can not believe that we sit here like that. Me and the cute hiker guy from the flight. Who would think that it should end up this way, that we would end up together, now choosing to live far away from what we know, and settle down together in a small, magic village in the mountains. I imagine what would have happened if we didn't get those flight seats next to each other. If I didn't dare to take his hand. If I didn't see him in the bar in Kathmandu. So many things could have made this turn out differently, and I might not be alive now. I feel so lucky.

"Hello, lovebirds," a familiar female voice says from behind.

Sumit and Numit have joined us, taking a seat next to us. Bob is with them and finds his place as well.

"Hey, friends," I say happily. "We just decided that we're going to stay here for a while."

I see the light ignite in Sumit's eyes as he figures what I just told him.

"That's great!" he shouts, seeming to be less serious than he used to be.

"Yeah, we hoped you would," Numit adds cheerfully.

Her gaze randomly moves to the compass in William's hand. She appears suspicious for a moment, opens her mouth, but shuts it again without a word. She repeats this a few times before finally deciding that she will say whatever is on her mind.

"We should contact Tom and Noah," she says, immediately closing her eyes in regret.

Her brother sends her a serious look.

"What?" William asks, sounding just as confused as I am.

"No, sorry. I over-spoke again," Numit whispers sadly, but with a smirk on her face.

Numit and Sumit get eye-contact for a couple of seconds, and Sumit's serious look transforms into a grin. He nods at his sister and her sad face turns into an enormous grin as well.

"Oh, there's so much you guys need to learn about our abilities," she says in excitement. "You will speak to your friends again soon, just wait and see. I promise."

I look at William who looks back at me. He squeezes my hand and smiles.

Everything will be alright.

Acknowledgment

This book was under development for nearly three years, in which I was fortunate to travel and find inspiration in a lot of different people. The story is mainly fiction, yet many aspects are inspired by real people and scenarios, like my own experiences with the Annapurna Base Camp trail. Thanks to everybody along the way, including my sister who was with me in Nepal. I had the best time and already planned a new visit to this incredible place.

I want to thank every single one who read this book. Publishing books isn't the same without you. A huge acknowledgment to my family for being the best people in the world, and to my partner who took the time to help me out refining this book.

I always love to get feedback, whether it's positive or negative. Please feel free to review or contact me with your thoughts.

Best Regards
Mill Woods

More by Mill Woods

If you liked this book, here is something for you.

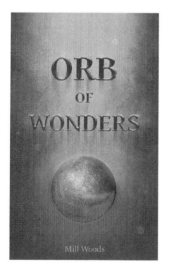

Orb of Wonders is an emotional thriller, filled with mystery and eye-opening philosophy.

Follow Christian on his journey through time, encountering wondrous creatures and hidden secrets destroying the world as we speak.

Printed in Great Britain
by Amazon